Kola
(Friend)
Debra) !

MW01488356

Mitakuye oyasin (Star Woman)
(We all are related)

Bernie J. Hunt

Lawrence J. Hunt

10-05-23

Wonderful
to meet you!

This work is dedicated to all who have supported and labored with us in preserving our American Indian heritage and instilling pride and hope in the hearts of our children.

Wicahpi Win (Star Woman)
Bonnie Jo Hunt

RAVEN WING

A TALE OF LOVE AND SPIRITUAL SEEKING EMBROILED IN A CLASH OF CULTURES

by

Bonnie Jo Hunt

and

Lawrence J. Hunt

*. . . Do not forget every dawn as it comes is sacred,
and every day is holy, for the light comes from
your Father. . . And also you must always remember
that the two-leggeds and all the other people
who stand on this earth are sacred and
should be treated as such.*

White Buffalo Woman, Lakota

A Lone Wolf Clan Book, Vol. II
Revised Edition, 2003

RAVEN WING

Copyright 1997 by Bonnie Jo Hunt and Lawrence J. Hunt

All Rights Reserved

First Printing, 1997

First Revised Edition, 1999

Second Revised Edition, 2003

Fourth Printing, 2007

Library of Congress Catalog Number: 99-93134

International Standard Book Number: 978-1-928800-01-9 (Vol. II)

A special thanks to Harriet Braden for her unstinting loyalty
and tireless work with Artists of Indian America, Inc.

Published by Mad Bear Press
6636 Mossman Place, NE
Albuquerque, NM 87110
Telephone and FAX 505-881-4093

The publication of RAVEN WING is the effort of many people.
To these kind people the authors express their deepest appreciation. Proceeds received by ARTISTS OF INDIAN AMERICA,
INC. (A.I.A.) go to support its work with Indian youth. For information concerning A.I.A., contact Mad Bear Press. Contributions to A.I.A. are tax deductible and most gratefully received.

Cover designed by CYBERDESK Solutions
Ricardo Chavez-Mendez & Michelle Marin-Chavez
Back cover photograph courtesy of Jerry Jacka
Printed in the United States of America

ABOUT THE AUTHORS

Bonnie Jo Hunt (*Wicahpi Win* - Star Woman) is Lakota (Standing Rock Sioux) and the great-great granddaughter of both Chief Francis Mad Bear, prominent Teton Lakota leader, and Major James McLaughlin, Indian agent and Chief Inspector for the Bureau of Indian Affairs. Early in life Bonnie Jo set her heart on helping others. In 1980 she founded Artists of Indian America, Inc. (AIA), a nonprofit organization established to stimulate cultural and social improvement among American Indian youth. To record and preserve her native heritage, in 1997 Bonnie Jo launched Mad Bear Press which publishes American history dealing with life on the western frontier. These publications include the Lone Wolf Clan series: *The Lone Wolf Clan, Raven Wing, The Last Rendezvous, Cayuse Country, Land Without A Country, Death On The Umatilla, A Difficult Passage, The Cry Of The Coyote* and *The Great Powwow.*

#

Lawrence J. Hunt, a former university professor, works actively with Artists of Indian America, Inc. In addition to coauthoring the Lone Wolf Clan historical series he has coauthored an international textbook (Harrap: London) and published four mystery novels (Funk and Wagnalls), one of which, *Secret Of The Haunted Crags*, received the Edgar Allan Poe Award from Mystery Writers of America.

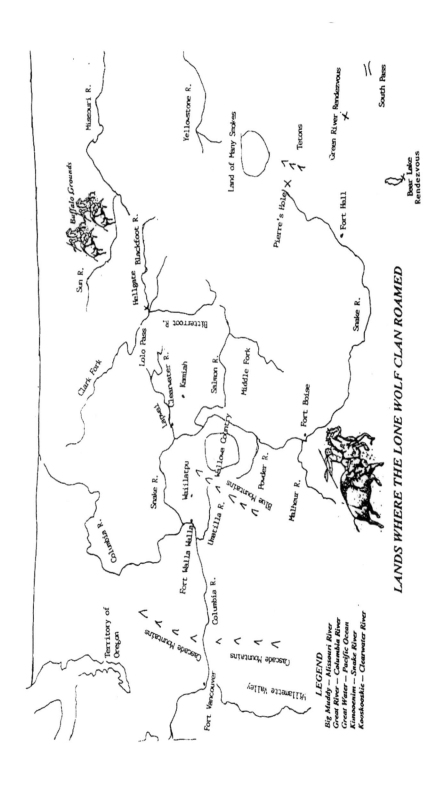

LANDS WHERE THE LONE WOLF CLAN ROAMED

LEGEND

Big Muddy — Missouri River
Great River — Columbia River
Great Water — Pacific Ocean
Kimooenim — Snake River
Kooskooskie — Clearwater River

RAVEN WING

All things on Mother Earth are two - male and female.
This is true whether of men, animals, trees or flowers.

Proverb of the Pawnee

The morning after the marriage had been consummated Raven Wing walked in a daze, thoughts buzzing in her head like a hive of swarming bees. The night's events were unlike any she ever had experienced. Except for what she had observed among Mother Earth's four-legged creatures, she knew little about such things. Matters like these never were mentioned among family members and she never had taken time to sit and gossip with the village girls. Sometimes Granny, whose man passed to the other side in the war with the Snake, would chuckle and wink when the subject emerged. Yet, if questioned the old woman would cluck and sidle around the topic like a skittish colt. "When the time comes, you will know," she always answered.

"Ah!" Raven Wing raised her face to receive the warm rays of Father Sun. This bright morning Raven Wing's walk took her beneath stately pines and into a thicket of aspens. A freshet of wind made the pine needles whistle and the aspen leaves ripple. She stopped to listen. As a child she had learned trees have a special language of their own. Today the pines spoke and the aspens answered in whispers, but what did they say? She wished she had listened to the teachings of her brother, Vision Seeker. He knew the language of trees, grasses, birds, . . . even that of the four-leggeds.

Now that the night was over Raven Wing asked herself, what actually had happened? To relive the night was as difficult as recalling a dream, everything blended together like a field of wild flowers in the Season of First Grass. No single blossom stood above the others. A soft breeze caressed her. The pine scented air refreshed her. She gazed at the beauty that surrounded her. The warmth she felt when her man had gathered her in his strong arms returned. Those moments of love she never would forget.

When she opened her eyes to make certain the experience had been real, the space on the pallet beside her was empty. The big man with the shock of black hair and white skin was gone. Then she remembered. Before daybreak, while still drugged with sleep, his noisy friends had come and drug him away. Why had they been so rude? Surely, they knew it was their wedding night. An ominous thought suddenly popped into Raven Wing's mind. This never would have happened if she had chosen a mate of her own kind. She now realized she knew very little about these people who came from beyond the River of Many Canoes (Mississippi) and called themselves mountain men. A short distance away, the raspy voices of two of these people cut short Raven Wing's reverie.

"So long, ol' hoss. If'n yer headin' Yellerstone way, watch yer topknot. The blinkin' Blackfeet're mighty techy these days." The battered buckskin clad figure, beard resting on a protruding belly, raised a three fingered hand in farewell.

"Yuh ol' coot. Don'tcha be concerned 'bout me health. Yuh'd best be worrin' 'bout yerself. If'n yuh don't stop usin' fingers fer bait, yuh'll wind up No Finger Jake." Shag, another bearded, potbellied fellow, had aroused himself just in time to bid his friend good-bye. Shortly, when he felt up to it, he also would be gone.

These two rapscallions were typical of hundreds of mountain men who gathered at the south end of Bear Lake in the summer of 1828. In their youth they came from the east to seek their fortunes in the wilds of the western wilderness. They brought guns called "Hawkens" and traps with steel jaws. They donned clothes made of canvas and rawhide. They acquired pack mules on which they loaded their belongings and supplies of beans, flour, salt, bacon, tobacco and headed into the mountains. There they built themselves shelters and set up trap lines. They took the pelts of beaver, otter and an occasional fox or muskrat to bring them riches. They never realized these riches but they became obsessed by the life of freedom they led in the mountains and thus became labeled "mountain men". To survive, these men were forced to deal with unbelieveable challenges.

Three Fingered Jake had his finger bitten to the bone by a trapped beaver. There was little left but bone and gristle. With a hand axe he hacked off what was left of the damaged digit. Then continued on down the trap line, ignoring the pain. It was all in the day's work.

Like bear coming out of hibernation, each summer these men emerged from the mountains to sell their pelts and renew supplies. Traders from the east soon realized they could turn handsome profits by meeting these trappers halfway. These meeting places they called "rendezvous". Others called these meetings "summer fur fairs", for after selling their fur pelts the men let themselves go, playing and carousing as hard as they had worked all winter. For some this aspect of the rendezvous was a death trap. Gambling and drinking drained away the hard earned profits, leaving them dissolute, penniless. The rendezvous also attracted Indian contingents: Utes, Bannocks, Flatheads, Nez Perce and other tribes came to view the white man's trade goods and join in the fun.

As usual at these summer fur fairs liquor, brought in great casks and made palatable by dilutions of creek water, flowed freely. The power of the firewater produced different effects. It made the Indian stagger about and fall asleep. It had the opposite effect on mountain man and trader. They came alive. They challenged and jousted each other in various feats of physical skill. Black eyes, bandaged heads and arms wrapped in slings were in evidence aplenty from these athletic endeavors. These were proud souvenirs. The way they were earned would be remembered and discussed on trap lines and around lodge fires for years.

It was mid-July. Two weeks of the rendezvous had passed.

Most traders and trappers by now had bargained away their wares and played themselves out. The gathering was breaking up. The traders, with their coveted pelts, would trek back to the great commercial centers on the frontier: St. Louis, St. Joe, Independence, Santa Fe, Taos. The trappers, their pack animals buried beneath loads of flour, beans, bacon, tobacco and other supplies deemed essential, would return to set up trap lines on the Yellowstone, Upper Snake and Missouri rivers or lose themselves in the Bighorn, Teton and Bitterroot mountains.

A vague sense of abandonment hung over the rendezvous site. A lone coyote slid out of the shadows to sniff at a pile of debris. The Bannocks and Utes had broken camp. The meadows where they had set up the picturesque tipi lodges lay bare. The high grass where sleeping pallets had been placed was flattened and broken. Blackened stones marked the location where campfires had blazed.

The square where native celebrants held their dances lay vacant. Only a tattered moccasin, too worn to repair, remained. The pasture grounds where the horse herds had grazed were cropped clean. Only the Nez Perce, the tribe who called themselves "Nimpau" (The People), and their Flathead friends, still were encamped. Many Horses, eldest son of the Nimpau leader had fallen during a battle with Blackfeet raiders. It took the skills of a bald-headed mountain man named Deacon Walton to bring him back from the brink of death.

Another reason the Nimpau and Flatheads were still encamped was that Lone Wolf, leader of the Nimpau, had accepted a mate for his only daughter. Coming so soon after the near death of his eldest son, the event took the entire rendezvous encampment by surprise. Raven Wing was going on 18, but had the maturity of one much older. She possessed the eye-catching beauty of a prize appaloosa pony and the striking temperament of a mountain cat. She could purr with contentment one moment and lash out in fury the next. Over many seasons her father arduously attempted to find her a mate. Raven Wing always managed to break up the match. It took a stranger, a big black-haired mountain man, to capture her heart.

#

This morning, still pondering the strange events of her wedding night, Raven Wing continued to walk. Members of the Nimpau band were amazed to see the lissome bride strolling by herself. Where was her mate, the big *soyappo* (man with wide brimmed hat); had he tired of her so quickly? Raven Wing knew the curious were watching and whispering. She did not care. So much had happened she wanted to be by herself . . . to catch her breath and sort out things. Her path took her to the edge of the lake where she paused to gaze across the shimmering blue/green water. A silver-sided trout broke the surface, snapping at a fly. A woodpecker began a rhythmic rat-a-tat against a dead tree trunk.

Normally these acts of nature would have delighted Raven Wing, but worrisome thoughts had started worming their way into her mind. She knew so little about this man who now was her mate. As hard as she tried to suppress it, secret fears began to emerge. Had she chosen wisely, or had she made a mistake? What would it be like to live with a man, especially a *soyappo* with hairy body and skin the color of milk, for the rest of her life?

"Ah!" she uttered. Their joining was a mystery. How could it have happened? It was like a fable from the village storyteller's stock of tales. It started when the three mountain men had appeared. They came from the east, crossing the lands of the Blackfeet, Sioux and Crow. They brought with them many items of trade. She never had seen such finery. Shiny cut beads, necklaces made of colorful stones, wonderfully decorated belts, arm bands and hair pieces of bone and onyx, carvings of buffalo horn and red pipestone, bright cloth and buckskin garments adorned with beads, ivory and porcupine quill. . . .

There were so many things to admire. She wanted them all. Yet it was the elk skin dress possessed by the big black-haired man that caused her downfall. Once she saw it . . . it never left her thoughts. She had been taught that love of material possessions was a weakness, if it was not overcome it would disturb one's spiritual balance, lead one away from the Great Mystery. Happiness came from giving, not from receiving. She believed and observed these teachings, until she met the mountain men and saw the beautiful elk skin dress.

The arrival of the mountain men had been magical. Like lost spirits wandering the buffalo plains, they suddenly had appeared with the first snow and spent the Season of Falling Snow taking beaver pelts. When the snow had melted they invited Lone Wolf to accompany them to the summer fur fair called "rendezvous". "Many items of trade will be there," Buck Stone, the leader of the trappers, promised.

Lone Wolf and his band then had endured the long, dusty ride to the Bear Lake rendezvous site. Although her mother, Quiet Woman, had scolded her, Raven Wing often rode by the side of the big black-haired man.

"It is not proper. The big *soyappo* is not of your kind. He will take it wrong, think you a wanton woman. People will whisper and could say you soil yourself. No man will want you as a mate. You bring shame to your father. Weasel Face sees all and stores in that narrow mind of his everything you do. Someday he will use these things and hurt your father! You know he wants Lone Wolf's place as leader of the Lapwai band."

This was the start of another family quarrel. Granny, who listened in the background, uttered clucks of disapproval. "I warned you," she said to Quiet Woman. "You brought up this daughter badly. She does not know her place. She should stay in the column and walk alongside the pack mares. Who knows what dangers lie out there. Blackfeet could be waiting to raid and steal. How they would like to capture Lone Wolf's daughter! It would be a great coup."

Raven Wing paid no attention to either Quiet Woman or Granny. She continued to ride with the big man with black hair. She liked his gentle manner. She admired his big hands, bold face and strong arms. His bigness and easy way he handled horses and weapons made her feel safe and secure.

As they approached the rendezvous site, Lone Wolf's band and the trapper trio had parted. Following tradition, the Indian people prepared themselves for the meeting. They painted and decorated their horses. The men donned ceremonial garments and trappings. Only then did they ride on to the rendezvous site. The trappers and traders welcomed them with great ceremony. They were viewing the wealth of trade goods when the Blackfeet war party struck. Shouting war cries, the enemy had surrounded a column of late arrivals. Shooting, spearing and knifing, they cut down the men and made off with loaded pack animals. In the melee a *soyappo* mistakenly shot Raven Wing's brother, Many Horses, who was scalped and left for dead. The Lone Wolf camp was grief stricken. Quiet Woman wailed. Granny tore her hair. Lone Wolf, with a face as dark as a rain cloud, sat in a corner blaming himself for his son's tragic death. The family could not have been more devastated if Mother Earth had turned her face away from the sun.

Raven Wing found herself transported back to that terrible day. The outpouring of grief had driven her nearly mad. At first she wept, then attempted to console her mother. Quiet Woman pushed her away. She refused to be comforted. To escape the tortured tipi lodge, Raven Wing had stumbled outside, tears blinding her. She paid no attention where she went. Suddenly she found herself in a street where traders had spread out their wares. Her grief was forgotten as she remembered all of the good things the big black-haired man had in his pack, especially the elk skin dress. Would she find him here? Had he traded away the precious elk skin dress? Did someone else possess it now? These thoughts pressed her on.

Belatedly, Raven Wing realized she was in danger. Traders and trappers smelling of firewater called to her. She did not have to understand the words to recognize what they said. They thought her a loose woman that anyone could have. Her face burned with shame. Abruptly she turned to leave. She wanted to run, instead she controlled herself. She put one moccasined foot in front of another as if taking a stroll. Someone uttered a cheer. Another clapped his hands. Raven Wing took heart. The end of the street was near. She would escape. Then a tall dark man with a mustache no larger than an eyebrow, blocked her path. He doffed his hat and smiled, coming so close she felt his hot breath. An arm encircled her waist. His touch stopped the beat of her heart. He laughed and held her tightly. As she attempted to pull away her legs lost their strength. The man leaned forward until his lips touched hers. The bristles of the mustache tickled her nose. Like a hare cornered by a snake she was paralyzed, helpless in his grasp.

Suddenly out of the shadows stepped a large figure. It was Black Hair who owned the elk skin dress. The light was so dim and the movements so fast, the memory of what happened never was quite clear. The tall dark man disappeared, tossed aside as easily as if he had been a sack of straw. Raven Wing did not wait to see more. She turned and ran toward Lone Wolf's lodge as fast as her legs would move.

She arrived at the lodge to learn Many Horses had been found, but so wounded there was little chance he would live. Then the medicine man came, attempting to drive the spirits of sickness away. His exorcism had little effect. Many Horses remained still as death. Second son, Vision Seeker, had sought out Black Hair's friend, No Hair On Head. Applying a remedy learned from an old Paiute woman and a sip of firewater, the baldheaded *soyappo* miraculously brought wounded Many Horses out of the deep sleep.

The gloom in the Lone Wolf lodge had lifted. Now that his son was on the road to recovery, Lone Wolf made plans to return to his Lapwai home. The thought of leaving left Raven Wing depressed. She did not want to go until she possessed Black Hair's tantalizing elk skin dress. She asked Lone Wolf to bargain for it. He refused. Then one day Black Hair appeared carrying the dress under his arm. He held it out to her.

Hardly knowing what she did, Raven Wing had seized the dress and dashed into the lodge, inadvertently pulling Black Hair after her. When her father saw the dress and the couple standing together, his eyes grew large. He clapped the big *soyappo* on the back and prepared his special pipe. At last a suitor had come to bargain for Lone Wolf's daughter. Before she knew what happened, Raven Wing had the coveted elk skin dress and a handsome blue-eyed, pale-skinned mate.

#

Now, at the lake side, in the midst of her musings, Raven Wing paused to dip her hand into the blue/green water. Just as she did this, two of Mother Earth's creatures reenacted an age old drama. A hawk swooped down to snatch a fish. As the claws struck home, the fish twisted and squirmed. The hawk struggled to keep airborne but the prey pulled it down. The deadly talons let go. The fish dropped back into the lake. The hawk soared away, its wings barely clearing the water. The fish disappeared beneath the circling ripples that marked the place of the deadly encounter.

The tableau of life and near death gripped Raven Wing. Somehow it was a sign of foreboding. Finding her legs trembling, she sat down on a sun-warmed boulder to compose herself. She watched the hawk to see if it would return but it climbed above the trees on the far lake shore, flying higher and higher until it was only a black dot against a distant cloud.

Raven Wing would have lingered longer but from the rendezvous site came the sound of gunfire, then resounding shouts. "Hai! Hai! Ya-ee!" Startled magpies fluttered out of the trees and flew away. Darts of cold fear made her shiver. Blackfeet raiders! Had they returned?

Raven Wing's elder brother, Vision Seeker, galloped in from the pasture. A group of armed men came running from the Indian camp. Her younger brother, Running Turtle, snatched up a fallen limb that lay beside the path for a club. He spotted Raven Wing and shouted.

"Take cover! Bad trouble!"

More shots and shouts rang out. "War party! Blackfeet!"
The warning cries came from the running warriors.

Raven Wing ran to follow the warriors. She wished for a
weapon. Was her white-skinned mate in danger? That black
shock of hair would be a prize a Blackfeet warrior would love to
possess. The thought of her man with a denuded head made her
feet move faster. The running Nimpau and Flatheads came
to the top of a rise that overlooked the rendezvous grounds and
stopped dead in their tracks. Fearfully, Raven Wing approached.
What terrible sight did they see?

"Agh!" someone uttered in disgust. "No Blackfeet. No
war party. Only *soyappos* making fun."

"Aiiee!" a painful cry came from Raven Wing's throat.
There was her new mate still in his under garments drinking and
carousing with his rough trapper friends.

II

Like blood, like good, and like age make the happiest marriage.
J. J. Clarke, PARAEMIOLOGIA

The shots and shouts that caused the Indian camp so much concern came from a few trappers and traders who, ignoring heavy hangovers, continued with the rough-and-tumble play that had gone on since the start of the rendezvous. A horseshoe pitching contest, a barrel rolling race and a rifle shoot were in progress. Wagers were made and drinks taken but there was little enthusiasm on the part of either contestants or spectators. Most of the celebrants had empty purses and little stomach for more firewater.

There was one exception, the nuptial party. Four *soyappos*, three dressed in buckskin and one in long johns, romped and played like children released from a hard day at school. A tall man with broad shoulders, a shock of black hair, wearing baggy, rump-sprung underwear, was the center of attention. A black wide-brimmed hat sat on top of his head making him appear even more absurd. His name was Little Ned, the *soyappo* who had taken Lone Wolf's only daughter for a wife.

Raven Wing, looking down from the top of the ridge, uttered a horrified gasp. It was her first good look at long handle underwear with its drop seat and row of buttons from neck to crotch. She noticed the strange garment the night before but then other things had occupied her thoughts. In the bright light of day it made her man look the camp fool. What was he doing acting like he had lost his brains. What if her father should see his *soyappo* son in this shocking state? He would give up the leadership of the band and hide his head in shame.

Unaware of his watching mate, Little Ned continued to frolic with his friends. His trapping partners had employed every means possible to keep him separated from his new bride. Before the light of day they had aroused him from the marriage bed with a bedlam of shouts and banging of cans. The European custom of celebrating wedding nights with noisy celebrations had awakened the entire Indian camp. Clapping a hat on Little Ned's head, but otherwise refusing to let him get dressed, his trapper friends had taken him on a rigorous bareback mule ride along the fringe of the lake, then unceremoniously had dumped him into its cold waters. After that, still in his dripping long johns, they had baited him into competing in every skill they could think up. Little Ned entered into the horseplay with good grace. He was an easygoing person. He did not want to be a spoiler for his friends. It might be their last carefree time together.

The celebrants had worked their way through horseshoe pitching, foot racing, arm wrestling, knife and hatchet throwing and walking a straight line while balancing a pine cone on the nose. Until they came to the rifle shoot, Little Ned had bested them all. Hawk Beak, a gangling *soyappo* renown as a sharpshooter, won the shoot with three bull's-eyes in a row. The "yippee!" and ribald utterances were victory shouts at finally putting Little Ned down.

While his trapper friends decided what feat of skill to take up next, Little Ned glanced at the slant of the sun. He should quit this tomfoolery and return to his new lodge. His bride surely was bewildered by what had happened. An old fashioned shivaree was not the way Nimpau marriages were launched. The first night already had been a disappointment. It was his fault. A feeling of guilt had made him awkward. He acted like a boy who never had been with a woman before. He kept wondering if he had done right by taking this lovely maiden for a wife. His family and friends back east certainly would say he had gone mad. He could hear Mrs. Abernathy, the gossipy next door neighbor.

"Lord have mercy! The man is daft. A pagan wife! She probably eats with her fingers!" She would not be able to rest, Little Ned thought ruefully, until she poured out her disgust to

Pastor Barclay. The sanctimonious preacher would utter a loud disapproving "harrumph!" like a swamp bull frog clearing its throat, then wrinkle up his long nose and sniff as if a family of skunks had made themselves at home in the sanctuary of the church.

"Shocking behavior for a man who was reared by God fearing Christian folk!" Pastor Barclay would declare. He had no use for anyone who knowingly broke the rules of upper-class New England society. The pious, paunchy preacher would sink his teeth in the matter like a terrier. He would worry with the shocking news until he wore it out. It would be the subject of Wednesday night Bible study and a lengthy sermon on the Sabbath.

Thoughts of the stir his marriage would cause the smug church community made Little Ned smile. He didn't care what people back east thought. He did not intend to take his Nimpau wife home. It would be cruel to expose her to New England's bigotry. He would have trouble enough making the marriage work without the interference of a bunch of busybody gossips smothering him with attention, yet all the while regarding him as a social outcast.

Actually, only just now was he beginning to realize what marrying into an aborigine family meant. Hardly had the marriage settlement been completed before Lone Wolf began to issue orders as though Little Ned was a backward child. Quiet Woman and Granny bothered him even more. They hovered around as if they feared any moment he would take off with or without his bride. He had to find subtle ways to put these niggling irritations right if he was to get along with his new Indian relatives.

"Haven't we had enough of this nonsense?" Little Ned asked his trapping partners. "It's been fun but I have responsibilities. What are my bride and in-laws going to think?"

"Yuh cain't quit now," the potbellied, bald-headed man named Deacon Walton chided. "We're jest gittin' warmed up.

Trick shootin's next. Ol' Hawk Beak's first." He handed a rifle to his thin partner. Standing side by side, the two trappers were caricatures of Jack Sprat who could eat no fat and his wife who could eat no lean. Deacon had a squat and wide figure, topped by a fur cap that came down to rest on his ears. It was an item of apparel he wore day and night. It covered a head as hairless as a skinned muskrat.

Hawk Beak Tom Nelson looked the opposite, thin as a rake handle and tall as a beanpole. On top of his lean frame unruly hair fanned in all directions as thick and spiky as porcupine quills. The rifle barrel appeared to be an extension of his long, spider-like arms. Deacon threw a half dollar into the air. Hawk Beak's rifle muzzle spit fire. Bull's-eye! The coin ricocheted across the open space and into the trees. He reloaded and, at 50 yards, dotted the letter I on a can of Richmond Red snuff, then plugged a darter that ran up a tree stump. He put his rifle down expecting applause. Instead, Deacon scoffed.

"Anybody kin do those fancy tricks. It's when yuh havta risk life an' limb, thet's when real shooters come ta the front. Now, yuh take the legend of William Tell. When thet rascal king, who had it in fer poor old Will, put an apple on his son's head, ol' William shot it dead center. Thet's what I call real shootin'. The kid's life was on the line."

"Well, I ain't got no sons an' we ain't got no apples but how about pretendin' yer my son? The apple kin be thet there thimble yuh use fer darnin' yer socks. Get off 20 paces an' put it on yer head. I'll shoot it off quicker'n a flea hoppin' off a wet dog." Hawk Beak rubbed spit on his sights and took aim at a distant tree leaf and blew it to bits. "Yuh see, I hit 'most anythin' I aim at. It's steady hands an' a sharp eye thet does it. Git yer thimble. We ain't got all day. Little Ned's rarin' to git with his wife."

"Not on yer life. Thet word 'most' leaves me gun-shy. It'd be jest me luck ta hev yuh git a bug in yer eye. I ain't ready ta greet ol' St. Pete up yonder. He mightn't let me in."

"Come on, yer jest skeered, thet's all."

"Yep, I am an' I ain't too proud ta admit it. Now, yuh take some brave uns like Buck here, or Little Ned, they ain't got yeller streaks like me. I'll betcha they'd stand out thar with a mosquito on their nose an' let yuh snip the bill off it without flinchin' a whit. What 'bout it?" He turned to Little Ned and the fourth trapper, a man with hair the color of ripe yellow corn.

"Not me. I admire Hawk Beak's shooting but I'd just as soon it not be near my noggin," the man with yellow hair said. He spoke with a soft New England accent. Some said he had the voice and manner of a choirmaster. Others, who witnessed him in tight spots, claimed his voice and manners were more befitting a ferocious lion. His name was Buck Stone, the acknowledged leader of the four roistering mountain men.

"Well, to get things moving, I'll oblige," Little Ned said. "Where's that thimble?" He stretched to his full height of six-feet-four inches, took a dozen strides to the east and turned to face Hawk Beak's long-barreled Hawken.

"Sidle a piece to the north," Hawk Beak instructed. "Don't want the sun gittin' inta me eyes."

Raven Wing, who watched from the ridge, sucked in her breath. She never had seen this side of her man before. He was worse than an impetuous child. How silly, offering himself as a target to the man who looked like an overgrown fish crane. She knew nothing about him except his name was Hawk Beak. He had joined the three other trappers here at the rendezvous. He was named properly as he had a nose like a buzzard's bill that curved to a peak and hung over a pair of narrow lips. From the very first, she had not liked him. There was a wariness in his eyes that filled her with distrust. Someday he would come to an evil end.

"All right, all right, let's not stand around," the big mountain man said impatiently. "I haven't got all day. My missus is probably throwing a fit."

"Yuh ain't serious, are yuh?" potbellied Deacon protested.

"Of course I'm serious. I'm a newly married man. I can't expect my bride to stay by herself."

"I mean shootin', yuh dummy. Ol' Beak don't always hit the mark."

"I have every confidence in Hawk Beak. Get the thimble and let's get on with it whilst I still have my nerve."

The thimble was brought out and perched on the thick mane of hair. In the bright sunlight it looked like a diamond set in a background of black velvet. Now it was Hawk Beak's turn to question the wisdom of the target shoot.

"Hell, man, I might git a speck a dust in me eye an' then where would yuh be? Yuh cain't go trappin' with a' extra hole in yer head."

"You'll do fine," Little Ned assured. "If you can shoot the warts off a toad like you said, this'll be duck soup. Now, don't let me down. I don't want you messing up my hair."

Hawk Beak shuffled his feet and glanced at Buck Stone. Buck nodded. "Might as well get it over with. You better aim straight. I can't stand the sight of blood."

Hawk Beak rubbed spit on the rifle's sights. He threw the gun to his shoulder and fired. There was a flash of silver as the thimble went flying. Hawk Beak threw down the rifle and reached for the whiskey jug. "Dammit, Little Ned, yer a fool. Jest 'cause yuh married a good lookin' filly ain't no reason to show off. Thet's the last time I'm goin' to be a party to anythin' like this. It makes me nervy. Buck, it's yer turn to shoot."

Waves of murmurs ran through the Indians watching. The *soyappos'* reckless behavior shocked them. Some uttered clucks of astonishment at the thin one's expert marksmanship. All were impressed by the *soyappo* with black hair, who was one of them now. Everyone agreed he was a warrior of merit but why was he not properly dressed? He looked like a stork that had been attacked by an otter and lost its feathers.

Running Turtle and Raven Wing were unimpressed by the shooting exhibition. "Sister! This is foolish. Why do these *soyappos* shoot at each other?" Running Turtle asked, shaken by the performance.

"They are crazy, that is why. Like children, they play silly games," Raven Wing answered furiously. She was surprised at her feelings. The icy fear that gripped her heart must mean she cared deeply for her new mate. She should take him by his big ears and shake some sense into him. All the way from buffalo country he had appeared so competent and trustworthy. Yet, here he was, looking and acting like a callow youth. Raven Wing's brother, Vision Seeker, two years senior to his sister and already a person viewed with respect by tribal elders for his sound judgment, added to her fury.

"What a display of courage," he said admiringly. "You have a prize mate. He is the envy of every warrior in camp."

"Ah, you men, all you think about is acting brave and collecting coups. It is stupid and silly. My man could have been killed."

Vision Seeker gave his sister a glance of surprise. During childhood they had been constant companions. Never before had she shown the least amount of feeling toward members of the opposite sex. In the past she had accepted the homage of young swains as though she deserved their ardor for being the most attractive female in the tribe. Had this big trapper truly captured her heart? He hoped so. The Lone Wolf clan had suffered enough pain and grief without dealing with trouble between Raven Wing and her mate. There were people around who would enjoy that. One of them came up to join the onlookers.

"Is that not the *soyappo* who has taken Lone Wolf's daughter for a mate?" asked the voice of Weasel Face. "What is he wearing? I have never seen such strange clothing."

"Those are undergarments," Running Turtle guessed.

"Undergarments?" Weasel Face exclaimed. "Why wear them? He looks like a snake shedding its skin. What is happening to our people, women having to accept strange mates like this? Look at him, playing foolish shooting games when he should be home with his new woman. That is no way to start a marriage. I want you to remember, my sons," he said to his four boys who silently stood watching. Their eyes, like their father's, were set so near each other their noses seemed to disappear. "Foolish beginnings lead to foolish endings. One of these days you will see your father speaks wisely. The mating of this strange *soyappo* and the Nimpau maiden will end badly."

Weasel Face herded his boys away but the thoughts he expressed remained with Vision Seeker who feared for Raven Wing. Would the man with the black mane and white skin make a good addition to the Lone Wolf clan or would he soon tire of his Indian relations and go back to his trapper friends? That was the question Vision Seeker kept asking himself. The stories he heard of how mountain men took women and tossed them aside or traded them away like an unwanted horse or camp dog, filled him with anxiety.

The words of Weasel Face also affected Raven Wing. She did not believe a word he said but the uneasy feeling in the pit of her stomach grew into a sharp pain. Her marriage had not begun well, that was certain. She could not restrain herself any longer. She strode down the hill determined to get her mate and take him to their new lodge. There she knew how to take his mind off these silly games and his trapper friends.

Vision Seeker watched her go, aghast at his sister's boldness. Nimpau women did not go alone into a white man's camp unless it was for disgraceful purposes. To interfere in a mate's affairs was not proper. It would bring shame to their lodge.

"What are you doing?" Vision Seeker asked, hurrying after her.

"I'm taking my man away before he gets himself killed."

"It is not right to enter the camp of the hairy faces. You will shame your mate in the eyes of his friends."

"Shame is better than death. There is enough sorrow in the Lone Wolf camp. We do not need more."

Vision Seeker fell back. When Raven Wing was in this

mood there was no point in arguing. His headstrong sister did what she wished without regard to the consequences. He had learned that long ago. Still, he felt a surge of pride as he watched his sister's determined stride. She would bring her man back no matter what anyone thought.

"A-Ho!" Vision Seeker uttered as a tall dark man riding by swung down from his horse to block Raven Wing's path. Vision Seeker hurried forward. He feared something like this would happen. He should not have let her go alone into the rough-and-tumble trappers' camp.

For a moment Raven Wing's footsteps faltered. The tall man who blocked her way was the same one who had accosted her in the trading street. This time he did not appear under the frightening influence of firewater. He doffed his hat politely and took her by the arm as if to escort her into the rendezvous site. She darted a glance at his face. Dark, almost black eyes, looked back. The man smiled, revealing a row of brilliant white teeth. She quickly looked away. The touch of his hand sent shivers racing through every limb. Goose bumps came out on her skin. Although the weather was warm, she shivered and pulled away. At that moment Black Hair appeared. Although dressed in the baggy, silly looking clothes, his presence overwhelmed her with relief. His big hands seized the dark man by the shirt. The voice that spoke such quiet, loving words, had the hardness of steel.

"You damned Canuck, keep away from my woman. Don't you ever come near her again." Black Hair gave the man a vicious shake and shoved him sprawling into the dirt. Agile as a cat, the fallen man sprang up with a knife, the bare blade glittering menacingly in the bright morning light.

Vision Seeker, who had followed Raven Wing, came up from behind. Deftly, he seized the uplifted arm. The slender youth gave the wrist a sharp twist. The knife dropped to the ground. Vision Seeker applied more pressure. The squirming horseman uttered a painful howl and fell to his knees. Vision Seeker jerked the fallen man to his feet, drawing him close until they were face to face.   He memorized the features: dark, hard eyes, thin lips topped by a narrow mustache; a small mole marred one side of the nose. The uncompromising light in the cold eyes had the glint of a venomous snake. He released him, gave him a push and motioned for him to mount up and leave.

Raven Wing stood by, shamelessly watching. Vision Seeker gave her a glance of rebuke. "Wagh!" he uttered to himself. Why didn't she act properly? Taking a mate had not changed her a bit. She was as willful and irresponsible as ever. Her big mountain man mate should put his foot down, give her a good scolding and order her to stay in her place. Instead, he put his arms around her making light of the whole affair.

Vision Seeker turned his attention to the dark stranger. The arrogant man brushed himself off, his eyes as cold and hard as black agates. He glanced disdainfully at the newly weds and mounted up. As the stranger reined away Vision Seeker was seized by a terrible and shameful urge. He wanted to pull the man from his horse and carve those dark agate eyes out. He forcibly got a grip on himself. It was not the way of his people to mutilate, not even a hated enemy. But something told him the next time he met this man, blood would be let.

III

A maiden with many wooers often chooses the worst.

Scottish Proverb

The encounter with the tall dark man troubled Little Ned more than Vision Seeker realized. Francois was a French Canadian and former member of a Hudson's Bay trapping brigade. He was an expert trapper and knew the mountains and rivers of the northern regions well. He had an unsavory reputation. He was the type of man who never forgot a grudge. It was said more than one man who gained his ill-will paid for it with his life, but his expertise made him welcome in most trapping companies. These powerful entities were interested in the number of prime pelts a man produced. The character a person possessed mattered little. Leaders of trapping brigades respected rough-and-ready men and the fur trade was a dangerous business. Only men with courage and knowledge of the wilderness prospered and survived.

The incident also brought to mind another problem that troubled the man with the black mane. How was he to protect and keep his wife happy while working the trap lines? She was accustomed to leading a rugged existence but family and friends always were around to visit and lend support. The trapping life was more austere. For hours he and his trapping partners would have to leave her alone while they tended the traps. Then there was the messy business of skinning and fleshing the pelts. For months they would live every day and night with the omnipresent musty musk odor of the rodents they trapped. Could his young, lovely woman endure the life of a mountain man's wife?

As they walked up the hill toward their new lodge Little Ned looked down on the glossy black wing of hair, the rose petal cheeks and the soft but determined set of lips. His heart lurched. She was one in a million; there was no doubt about that. How could he have been so fortunate? It was up to him to guard and protect her. This he vowed to do with all his might.

Little Ned did not blame Raven Wing for interfering with the rifle shoot. He attempted to explain the custom of shivareeing. He did it badly. Over the winter months he had learned Sahaptin, the language of the Nimpau (The People), the tribe French explorers falsely had named the Nez Perce (Pierced Noses). The big mountain man cudgeled his brain. He could think of no custom Indian people observed that was the least bit similar to the white man's shivaree. The harder he tried to explain, the more tangled he became. He switched to sign language, but that made matters worse.

"Talk and wave your big arms all you wish," Raven Wing stormed. "You run away the first day in our lodge without proper clothes. You place your life in the hands of the thin man with face of a turkey buzzard. Only people without brains do such foolish things. You bring shame down on the heads of the Lone Wolf clan."

"But-but it was only a game," Black Hair stammered. "We meant no harm. It is just the thing us white folks do when a marriage takes place."

Raven Wing strode along, keeping her face averted. She knew one glance of the big man's soft blue eyes would make her heart melt. But her mate's actions could not be overlooked.

"What would you think if I left the marriage bed half dressed and went to play silly games that placed my life at risk," Raven Wing retorted. "Would you not be hurt? What if that ugly man called Hawk Beak had missed, taking the life of my mate? I would be left to live a lonely life. No Indian man would take me into his lodge . . . a woman soiled by a pale face."

The big man hung his head. He had not been reprimanded like this since childhood. The trouble was, he deserved it. Not once had he thought of how it, especially the shooting incident, might affect Raven Wing. After the ducking in the lake he should have put a stop to the shenanigans. His trapping partners would have fussed but would have let him go. He had kept right on,

mainly because he wanted to prove marriage had not chained
him. His part in the trick rifle shoot was sheer bravado, to show
he had not lost his nerve. It was something insecure school boys
or youngsters green to the west might do. After nearly a decade
in the mountains he was one of the best trappers in the business.
He had no need to prove himself.

"Ah!" he inwardly groaned. He had given Raven Wing
the opposite impression of what he intended. He wanted her to
believe he was a person of responsibility, committed to make this
marriage work. It was not going to be a case of a mountain man
taking an Indian woman just for a lark. He had seen many of his
trapping partners pick up women at rendezvous and trek happily
away into the wilderness. The next summer they returned either
without them or their Indian mates looked old before their time.
He did not intend to let this happen to beautiful Raven Wing.

It had been a crazy, unbelievable courtship. He'd had no
intention of taking any woman for a wife. In fact it was against
his principles to allow his emotions to rule him, especially in
making such an important and long lasting commitment. It was
that elk skin dress that got him trapped. Now he knew how foolish a beaver must feel when the steel jaws snapped shut. If he
had been alert he would have discovered the danger. The subject
of marriage had come up as unexpectedly as a lightening flash
that precedes a summer storm.

The whole business had started when Vision Seeker asked
how many beaver pelts it would take to purchase the elk skin
dress. It was obvious he wanted it for Raven Wing. He was on
the verge of giving it to the young man as gesture of good will as
the Lone Wolf camp had gone through a bad patch. If the dress
would bring a breath of cheer to the family, he gladly would have
let it go.

That interfering bald-headed Deacon was to blame for
what happened next. Old No Hair On Head always was gabbing
about something. He started yapping about the elk skin dress,
how it would be a useful bargaining chip to buy a wife. He had

the tenacity of a bulldog. When he latched onto an idea he would not let loose. He still could hear old baldhead's cackling voice.

"Raven Wing takes ta thet elk skin garment like a duck ta water. Little Ned, loosen up, start thinkin' right smart on taken a wife. Thet dark-eyed beauty'd be a good catch. Sit down with Vision Seeker an' drive a bargain. No time like the present ta make a deal. Vision Seeker kin speak fer his sister. Yuh'd better let me speak on yer behalf."

That was the way that pesky bald-headed popinjay riled up the water. Vision Seeker had sat there, his face as blank as the side of a house but not missing a single word. He should have crowned the baldheaded idiot with the barrel of his Hawken. Instead, they yapped back and forth like a couple of camp dogs slavering over a scrap of meat. He ordered Deacon to shut up. If there was any dealings to be made, he would do it himself. But old No Hair On Head kept blathering.

"Don't growl at me like thet. Of course yuh wanta make a deal. Yuh busted up thet half-breed Francois when he put a hand on the lass an' yuh been castin' sheep's eyes at thet gal since yuh first met. Now it's time fer yuh ta suck up yer gut an' quit bein' so hard ta get. Think of them good things thet little woman kin do fer yuh on the trail; think of her settin' up camp, cookin' yer grub, keepin' yer bed warm at night . . . ."

"Wagh!" Little Ned kicked at a stone with a moccasined toe and grimaced. That's what he should have done to the prattling old bustard, kicked him right where it hurt, shut him up. Deacon then did the unforgivable. The sly fox, instead of bargaining on Little Ned's behalf, he began to dicker with Vision Seeker for Raven Wing's hand on his own behalf.

"I'm thinkin' a second wife would be right nice! Yuh bet yer life. Let's see, what do I hev thet'd make her happy?"

That was the last straw. He would rather see Raven Wing dead than pawed by that potbellied polecat. That was when he dug out the elk skin dress. At the moment it appeared the right thing to do. If Raven Wing possessed the elk skin dress No Hair

On Head would not stand a chance.

Without realizing the drastic events his actions would take, he lumbered up to Lone Wolf's lodge trailed by Vision Seeker and his trapping partners. Raven Wing, herself, came out to greet him. He held the dress out to her. With a squeal of astonishment, she seized it and dashed back inside. Like a fool he had held onto the dress. She pulled him inside along with the dress. Lone Wolf, seeing them holding the dress together, thought he had come courting. The Nimpau leader's face lit up like a candle. He had clasped the big trapper by his two arms and sat him down by the fire. He clapped him on the back, did a little jig and uttered a string of unintelligible words.

"Hey! Hey!" Lone Wolf thrust his head through the tipi flaps to report the happy news to those who waited outside. "Raven Wing has chosen a mate," Vision Seeker translated the announcement.

He had attempted to protest that it was all a mistake, but no one listened. The men crowded inside the lodge to offer congratulations. Wounded Many Horses raised himself up to smile. The men sat in a circle to celebrate the event with a smoke. Everyone was so pleased he did not have the heart to protest. He glanced at Raven Wing. She fondled the dress and looked so happy and beautiful he could not spoil her happiness. Like a fool, he had entered into the spirit of the occasion, smoked, joked and laughed with the rest of them. Then came the first hint that all was not well. Lone Wolf ordered Quiet Woman to prepare food. She refused. She uttered a few sharp words, turned her back and sat facing the far side of the lodge.

That was when he turned to Vision Seeker. "This is all a big mistake," he had attempted to explain. "I came to give the dress to your sister, no strings attached." He got to his feet and ducked his head to go outside. Lone Wolf clucked angrily at Quiet Woman and pulled him back.

"You cannot leave. You have been accepted," Vision Seeker said in alarm. "Lone Wolf approves. Pay no attention to

Quiet Woman. She is not herself. She is still deeply troubled by her firstborn's wounds."

"Yuh mean she said, 'Marriage in haste is sure to bring disgrace', or some such similar Injun sayin'," No Hair On Head blurted. "It's only natural. A mother always hates ta lose an only daughter. Sit down, Little Ned. Pull out now an' yuh'll insult these people. Yuh cain't do thet. It ain't right. Yuh gotta start actin' like a member of the family. It won't take Quiet Woman long ta git accustomed ta the idea of havin' a bullheaded brute fer a son-in-law. Wait an' see, afore long she'll be all over yuh like a coat of honey."

Little Ned kicked another rock out of the pathway. If they had been alone he would have throttled that cursed No Hair On Head. The galoot always was gabbing about things that were none of his business. He did not blame Quiet Woman for being upset. He had rushed into the lodge after her daughter like a randy bull. Any mother in her right senses would have been vexed.

A normal Nimpau marriage was sedately carried out over a considerable length of time. The suitor made it known he was interested in a particular maiden. The parents of suitor and maiden watched to see if their offspring were agreeable to one another. When both sets of parents approved an intermediary was asked to arrange the match. For a short trial period the couple would live together. If this proved satisfactory gifts were given on both sides, the groom's first, then the bride's. At the completion of the gift giving the couple was considered married.

Raven Wing's marriage was upside down, Little Ned thought. Gift giving, offering of the elk skin dress, had come first. Upon its acceptance the pact was sealed. There was no thought of a trial marriage. Lone Wolf had disdained the idea. It would only get in the way. At last the Lone Wolf clan leader had found a satisfactory husband for this troublesome daughter. Little Ned had the feeling that Lone Wolf feared if the wedding was delayed the potential groom might discover Raven Wing's many faults and call the whole matter off. Although she was the apple of her father's eye and he loved her dearly, once rid of her, Lone Wolf did not want Raven Wing back on his hands. Obviously, she was spoiled, unruly and threw tantrums at the drop of a hat. As leader of the band Lone Wolf could not afford to have a woman tell him, as Raven Wing often did, what he should and should not do.

The way Lone Wolf had kept things moving should have been a warning, Little Ned ruefully reminisced. Even Quiet Woman had fallen in line. After the first display of concern the bride's mother did everything expected of her. She even gave a cluck of joy when presented with a bright red shawl. "Ah!" He had been so generous. Before the ceremonial gift giving had ceased, most of his winter catch rested in Lone Wolf's lodge.

He had to admit, Lone Wolf had done his bit by seeing the newly weds were properly housed. He had ordered a tipi built. Of course he did it for a purpose. He did not want the two moving into his already crowded lodge, nor did he like to see his daughter and new son live in a trapper's lean-to. It would not look good to his people. To make the tipi tripod he ordered his young son, Running Turtle, to cut heavy poles from the fringe of trees that surrounded the Bear Lake encampment. He had Quiet Woman go through the camp bundles for tipi coverings and robes and mats for the bedding and floor.

When everything was in place, Lone Wolf, himself, came to inspect the neat, new lodge set in the grove of trees. "Hmm!" he had grunted his approval. "It is good. One thing is missing. Make the clay paint," he said to Running Turtle. After the consistency of the clay pleased him, on one side of the tipi Lone Wolf had drawn the outline of a wolf's head and colored it in various shades of gray and black, the muzzle, above open jaws, pointed artistically skyward.

"It is good," he said when finished. "Everyone who passes will know it is a lodge of the Lone Wolf Clan."

The gift lodge was now ready for the newly weds to occupy. Of course, Lone Wolf reminded his *soyappo* son, these only were temporary quarters. When they arrived at their home village in Lapwai Valley, he expected the newly weds to have the fire next to his in the permanent long lodge.

   Little Ned suddenly was jerked out of his reverie as a shadow fell across the path. He glanced up in surprise to see the newly married couple's tipi lodge. His father-in-law's painted wolf with its muzzle in the air, stared back. The eye almost looked alive. It seemed to send a message. "Whether you like it or not, you are now a member of the Lone Wolf clan. Be prepared for a new way of life."

IV

Marriage is like two people traveling in a canoe.
The man paddles, the woman steers.
Anonymous

Except for worry over injured First Son, Lone Wolf never had felt happier. Black Hair's gifts of pelts gained him wealth beyond his wildest expectations. It had been so easy to take advantage of the big man with the black mane, he almost felt sorry for him. However, ownership of the pelts was not completely assured. He noticed the dour looks on the newly weds' faces as they silently marched to their lodge. They did not appear happy. A feeling of apprehension made Lone Wolf shiver. Had Raven Wing already quarreled with Black Hair? Couldn't that daughter of his be good for one day? "Wagh!" he muttered. When the big man discovered Raven Wing's true nature he would be within his rights to return her and demand his bridal gifts back.

The thought of losing all his riches jabbed at Lone Wolf like a patch of thorny brambles. He snapped at Third Son. "Bring the pack mares."

When Running Turtle returned with the mares Lone Wolf ordered him to load up the recently acquired bundles of furs. Immediately afterward he set off for the trading street. Lone Wolf reasoned if he traded away the pelts it would be impossible for his son-in-law to ask for their return.

Once in the trading street Lone Wolf's fears faded away. Barter excited him as much as buffalo hunting or horse racing. He hunkered down in front of the first trader's lean-to and began to inspect the wares. "I come to bargain for many things," he informed the bearded trader, waving his hand at the three pack loads of pelts.

Before the day was done Lone Wolf haggled with every trader left in camp. He outfitted Many Horses, Vision Seeker and himself with new rifles, powder and lead. He laid in stocks of tobacco, sugar and molasses. He purchased colorful blankets, several lengths of calico, and two iron kettles for Granny and Quiet Woman. He bartered the last of the pelts for trade goods: hand axes, knives, beads, tiny mirrors, ribbons and froofraw always sought by customers on his trading trips. Then he ordered pack saddles to transport his purchases home.

Worried over his father's long absence, Vision Seeker went in search of him. Lone Wolf saw his son coming and waved. "Come! Help load up all these things." He proudly pointed to the piles of goods he had acquired.

Vision Seeker looked at the display of possessions with distaste. It was not good for the leader of the band to possess so many things: shiny pots, fancy guns, sharp knives, hand axes, blankets and clothing. . . . He wished he could make them disappear. People would see Lone Wolf's array of new possessions and say he was getting too big for himself. He watched silently as his father continued to haggle. Almost overnight Lone Wolf had been transformed from a desolate father grieving over a son near death, to a man who acted like all things on Mother Earth lay at his feet. He was not sure he liked the new Lone Wolf as well as the old. The delight his father took in the pile of goods made him appear avaricious, a leader who thought more of acquiring possessions than caring for the welfare of his people.

Vision Seeker loaded the pack mares and led them back

to the lodge, but left them tethered some distance away. He did not want to upset his mother. With Raven Wing gone, all the care for the wounded Many Horses fell on Granny and Quiet Woman. Every waking moment, they watched over him, prepared his meals, bathed him, fanned away insects and carried out his every wish. Some nights they sat up until the wee hours holding his hand crooning lullabies as they had when he was a child.

Gradually, the outside wounds healed but those inside festered and worsened. It was these hidden wounds the two women feared most. How did one treat a broken spirit? An enemy who took away a warrior's scalp, also took away his will to live. As long as he lived Many Horses would be an oddity. Wherever he went people would stare at him and, when he was not looking, whisper behind their hands. Never again would he receive respect. He had let the enemy get the best of him. What was far worse -- never again would he respect himself.

Quiet Woman also was worried sick over her daughter. She, too, had seen the couple's silent walk and the strange dress of the big *soyappo*. From what she had gleaned from listening to other women, mountain men who took Indian mates often did with them what they wanted, then sent them away to fend for themselves. After a few winters the women had no lodges nor friends. Mountain men also were known to trade Indian wives in the same manner they would a horse or a camp dog.

The big man, Black Hair, appeared to speak straight and have a generous heart. He made much over Lone Wolf's gift tipi lodge. He clothed Raven Wing in the best skins and cloth, some of which he himself had sewn into clothes. But this also was troubling. The man of the lodge sewing for his woman caused talk. Even his friend, No Hair On Head, thought it not good.

More than once she had heard him scold the big man, telling him he was starting married life "off on the wrong foot." It was the woman's task to do all the work inside the lodge.

Quiet Woman, like Vision Seeker, was dismayed by the change in Lone Wolf. Ever since he had given away his daughter, he barely entered the lodge. From early morning until after dark he was gone, either in the trading street haggling over anything that took his fancy, or in the pasture working with his prized spotted horses. It was time he should have spent talking to Many Horses, helping heal First Son's hidden wounds.

Family members were not the only ones disturbed by Lone Wolf's actions. Everyone in the Lapwai band had waited patiently for the wounded Many Horses to heal. Now that he was on the road to recovery they wanted to hit the trail. They had been away from their Lapwai Valley homes nearly a year. Soon the camas bulbs would be ready to harvest. Bands from every corner of the Nimpau homeland would gather in the meadows where camas grew. If Lone Wolf's people did not hurry and cross the mountains they would miss out on this most festive time of the year: visiting old friends, playing games, trading, gambling, hunting and feasting until one could eat no more.

Weasel Face, who had watched Lone Wolf's good fortune with envious eyes, was the first to approach the Lapwai band leader. "Old friend, your son is recovered, your daughter has a mate, you have made many trades. You have many good things. Why is it we linger in this rendezvous place? Our people are restless. Why then is it we stay? Everyone wishes to return home."

Lone Wolf glanced at close set eyes, narrow pinched nose and ears that were as pointed as those of a jack rabbit. Weasel Face always had been a pain in his side. He hankered to be leader

of the Lapwai band and did everything he could to make Lone
Wolf look bad. Yet, he felt sorry for the man. On the way to the
rendezvous Weasel Face's oldest son, Toohool, had been killed.
He felt partly to blame. Blackfeet raiders had stolen a dozen
horses. Lone Wolf sent a war party after the thieves. Many Horses
and Vision Seeker had led the men. The war party accomplished
nothing but grief. Some said the leadership was bad; Lone Wolf's
two sons could have prevented Toohool's death. Lone Wolf had
no desire to cause the grieving father more pain. After his own
son's narrow escape he knew full well what sorrow the loss of a
son could bring.

"Your words are good," Lone Wolf said. "We should return to Lapwai Valley. Have your family ready. We will take the
trail at dawn."

Upon returning to his lodge Lone Wolf sent youngest son,
Running Turtle, for Vision Seeker. When Vision Seeker appeared
he told him the news. "We break camp at first light. Tell our
Flathead friends. Prepare the horses. First of all go to Raven
Wing's lodge. Speak to her mate. I expect him to ride by my
side."

Vision Seeker knew it would look bad if the band leader's
new son delayed the column or remained behind. Realizing the
importance of his errand, Vision Seeker clothed himself in his
best buckskins. He combed his hair and fastened it with rawhide
ties decorated with feathers and beads. He did not want to bring
shame to his father or to Black Hair's new lodge. Although it
was a short distance, Vision Seeker rode his favorite mount with
its spotted sides and rump. Before he arrived he memorized a
short speech. He made a circle around camp to give himself time
to repeat the words to get them right. Beside the tipi with the

freshly painted wolf on its side, he dismounted and carefully tethered his horse. He brushed himself free of dust and set his face to express proper respect. Once again, he rehearsed his speech. Before he had time to say a word Black Hair bounded out to greet him. The *soyappo's* exuberance made Vision Seeker flinch. Why were these white-skinned people so jovial and loud? As a child he was taught to be still, to listen to Mother Earth when all was seemingly quiet. As he grew up he learned the spiritual meaning of silence. It was during periods of silence the Great Mystery spoke. Also, silence was self-control, dignity and reverence. It was the cornerstone of one's character. Did not white skinned parents teach these good things?

Unaware of Vision Seeker's discomfort, the big mountain man took him by the arm and pulled him into the tipi. "Welcome, Brother! We were hoping you would call. When is that father of yours going to finish trading his skins so we can hit the road back to the mountains and start trapping again? My purse is as flat as a batch of No Hair On Head's flapjacks."

The boisterous greeting and Raven Wing, usually so boyish, lounging on buffalo robes like a woman of idleness, made Vision Seeker forget his mission. The thought of what he might have interrupted made him uncomfortable. He attempted to imagine Raven Wing swollen with child. Would she be a good mother? What would her offspring look like? Would they be big and hairy like their father? Would they have milky white skin and eyes the color of the sky? Would tribal members accept them as equals or shun them? The worst thought of all, would this big man tire of his Nimpau woman and leave a batch of children behind? "Aiiee!" He did not want to think about the terrible grief that would cause.

"Do you not know how to speak?" Raven Wing chided.

"Lone Wolf breaks camp at first light," Vision Seeker blurted. "It is his wish you travel with him."

"Ah! That's good news," Black Hair said after Raven Wing helped translate her brother's strained words. "You visit Raven Wing. I must tell Buck Stone we are leaving." He gave Raven Wing a quick hug and left.

The show of affection embarrassed Vision Seeker. This was not the proper way to act in front of visitors. Finding himself alone with Raven Wing made him all the more uncomfortable. The spirited, temperamental sister he knew appeared so knowing and mature. What had suddenly caused this change? Did bedding a hairy faced one give her some special knowledge?

Raven Wing invited him to sit. He squatted on the buffalo robe beside her. She began to display her possessions: a beaded bracelet, a necklace made of bone, a silver comb, trinkets and gewgaws unlike he ever had seen.

"It is a fine thing to have one's own lodge" she said proudly. "No more can Lone Wolf say, 'do this, do that!' I have my own man and my own lodge. It is good. When you take a mate you will know what I mean."

Vision Seeker listened to his sister in silence. He doubted if he ever would take a woman into his lodge. There were one or two maidens he found attractive, but each time he appeared at their lodges the parents put him off. It was easy to read their minds. They examined him like a questionable horse brought in for trade. He was a serious-minded youth and the band leader's son but what else did he have to offer?

At the break of day Vision Seeker led in the pack animals. Quiet Woman and Running Turtle dismantled the lodge and began to load the family's possessions. While the dew was

still wet on the grass Lone Wolf led his band away from the rendezvous encampment and up the trail that eventually would lead
to their homeland. Bringing up the rear, Little Ned rode alongside Raven Wing. His pack horse, unaccustomed to pulling drag
poles, bucked and reared well into the morning.

Most of the trappers and traders, bleary from a night of
revelry still slept, but Buck Stone, No Hair and Hawk Beak aroused
themselves to see their friends leave. Buck promised they would
follow. The trappers invited their partner, Little Ned, and his
new bride to accompany them to the winter beaver grounds near
the land of the Big Smokes.

Vision Seeker, who overheard, stared at the distant horizon. It did not take a sign in the stars or clouds to know that
trouble lay ahead. Lone Wolf would want to take his family home,
that meant his daughter and her new mate. Already Lone Wolf
was in a stew. Instead of riding up front with him, his new son
with the black mane chose to ride in the rear with Raven Wing.
What would Lone Wolf do when the new son refused to return to
Lapwai and went trapping with his friends instead?

The first day's travel went well. Lone Wolf sent scouts
ahead to watch for hostile signs. Roving bands of Blackfeet could
be waiting in ambush. They would love to raid for horses and
plunder the rich baggage the pack animals carried. The scouts
reported back the path ahead was clear. The column stopped
that evening on the banks of a slow moving stream. While women
and children made camp, Lone Wolf strolled around snapping a
quirt against a pant leg. Vision Seeker could tell he was out of
sorts. His *soyappo* son had disappointed him.

Lone Wolf came to where the newly wedded couple prepared a place for the night. Black Hair had cut boughs. He laid

them out and over the top spread the sleeping robes. The sight of his new son doing women's work angered Lone Wolf. He slashed his quirt at a camp dog, sending it yapping with its tail between its legs. He glared at his daughter.

"Lazy, selfish woman! What kind of mate are you, letting your man do your work? He is not a pet to be tied on a leash. All day you kept him from riding out front where he belongs. Did you not learn anything from your mother about what is right and what is wrong? Do I, myself, have to teach you how to be a proper mate?"

Lone Wolf spoke so fast and with such vehemence Little Ned barely understood a word that was said. "What is the matter?" he asked. He saw Vision Seeker and waved him over. "What does your father want? He should not shout at his daughter like this. She is my woman now. If anyone is to give her orders, I am the one who should do it."

Before Vision Seeker could answer, Raven Wing, her eyes flashing fire, turned on her father. "You were happy to have me leave your lodge. But you don't let me alone. You watch over me and order me about like I was still a child. Why do you not leave us in peace?"

Vision Seeker attempted to smooth things over. He spoke to his father and then to Raven Wing. He only made matters worse. Lone Wolf glowered. Raven Wing sulked. Big Black Hair stalked around in circles with his hands on his hips. He was more shocked by the behavior of his beautiful mate than he was by that of Lone Wolf. She had turned on her father like a harpy fish wife. "What in the world have I gotten myself into?" he glumly asked himself.

Raven Wing also was upset. She banged the cooking pots

around in a fit of pique. She had thought marriage would bring freedom from her parents. Instead, they hovered over her like circling hawks on the hunt. What difference did it make who did the chores? Somehow they always got done. She ladled out salt-less mush and set it before her man. The big man with the black mane bravely ate it, wishing for a steak and a plate of bald-headed Deacon's overcooked fried beans.

V

Even a good marriage is a time of trial.
Russian Proverb

The journey to the hunting grounds was torture for Many Horses. Still weak from his wounds, he found riding a terrible strain. The loss of his scalp affected him in strange ways. Sometimes his head felt light as a feather. He wanted to reach up and hold it in place for fear it would fly away on the wind. At other times he became so dizzy he hardly could stay in the saddle. He always had been good with horses but now he was unsure of himself. He felt much as he did as a child when Lone Wolf put him on his big gray stallion and told him to ride to the pasture by himself.

What bothered him even more were the pitying glances he received from fellow travelers. Although he wore the fur cap that the *soyappo*, No Hair On Head, had given him, people still stared at this warrior who had lost his scalp. What did a man's head, whose hair was sliced away like the skin of an onion, look like? Would it be shiny as that of the bald-headed *soyappo* or would it be rough and dull like a badly skinned carcass?

Many Horses suffered most during the long afternoons when the sun beat down full force and dust billowed up in suffocating clouds. Perspiration made the freshly scarred tissue sting, itch and prickle. He kept wanting to remove the cap and let breezes cool his tortured head. A glance in a trade mirror let him know what a frightening sight his bare scarred skull presented.

One morning as he came out of the lodge he stood up too quickly. Stars flashed in front of his eyes when the tipi flap struck his tender head, causing his cap to fall on the ground. A woman and child were passing. The mother pulled the child away, but not before it screamed at the sight of his disfigured skull.

An even more heart-searing experience came when he first went to inspect the herd. Lone Wolf's special mounts always had lifted their heads in recognition, whinnied and trotted forward. He trained several to come at his call. He would greet them with a scratch under the chin, a pat on the muzzle and scraps of camas cake or other tasty tidbits they enjoyed taking from his hand. After the scalping they treated him like a stranger. Instead of answering his call, they snorted and shied away. When he walked toward them, their eyes grew wide with fear. They would not let him come near. The hurt was like a dagger thrust into the heart. He had tended these old friends with such care. Now they had forsaken him.

It was wise old Granny who understood his problem. "Have patience, son," she said. "You have had a bad turn but all things happen for a purpose. Stars which have shone forever fall from the sky. Mountains capped with everlasting snow spew smoke and fire. Winds that blow so gentle become violent, pulling trees, rocks and creatures high into the air and then dash them to the ground. Why do these things happen? Ah! Only the Great Mystery knows."

Many Horses took Granny's advice to heart. To his surprise he began to see Mother Earth with new eyes. To breathe the air, see the sunlight on the hills, hear the wind whistling through the trees and smell the fragrance of pungent evergreens, made him glad to be alive. Every night after making camp he strode into the grasslands or climbed a hilltop and sat silently listening to the rustle of Mother Earth's little people and the whisper of breezes. He was feeling like his old self until a quickly formed mountain storm descended. Black clouds hovered overhead. Heavy, slanting rain sluiced down. A lightening bolt struck so close the flash left bright yellow and white spots before his eyes. The crack that followed made him jump and cry out. He imagined the rifle bullet had struck again, knocking him from the saddle. The happiness of being alive suddenly turned to dread. Would this nightmare haunt him the rest of his life? Would ever he get used to a head without hair? Would ever he live down the ignominy of losing his scalp to that ugly bearded white man?

It made him sick to think of it. Everything had happened so quickly, the memory of it was a blur. Lone Wolf had sent him to accompany the column of Flatheads and Nimpau to the rendezvous site. He had galloped away astride his special mount. That very morning he had daubed it with ceremonial paint to celebrate the occasion of his first ever rendezvous. He wanted to display the fine horse he so patiently had trained. It was a proud moment. Then the hated Blackfeet had attacked. A frightened *soyappo* saw the painted horse and took him for an enemy warrior. Without warning, the bearded man threw up his rifle and shot. Then those terrible moments descended: the searing blow of the bullet, the tumbling fall, the knife cutting at his scalp, the lying in the swamp, the calling for help. Finally came the blessed relief of unconsciousness.

The irony of what came next made him grimace. He awakened from the deep sleep of death to find pale face No Hair On Head bending over him. For a moment he thought he had gone to the white man's hell. A *soyappo* killed him. Another waited to torture him. A huge *soyappo* with black hair pushed his way into the lodge making Quiet Woman distraught. Three more *soyappos* crowded in to chatter and smoke. Then Black Hair took Raven Wing away . . . The terrible things that happened at the place called "rendezvous" had turned the lives of the Lone Wolf family upside down. For a long time he wouldn't leave the lodge for fear an army of *soyappos* waited outside.

Many Horses wanted to pour out his troubles to his father but once Lone Wolf learned First Son had turned the corner and would live, he was caught up in the wedding match, the scramble to barter away his pelts before traders left the rendezvous and then he was busy placating his followers. His position as leader of the Lapwai band was under attack. Weasel Face, unhappy with the long stay at the rendezvous site, began to harangue the people. There was no need to wait for Lone Wolf, he announced. He knew the way. He would lead them home.

During this frantic period Lone Wolf barely spoke to Many Horses. Always the dutiful son, Many Horses did not bring attention to himself. Instead, he nursed his invisible wounds in silence. Without any healing balm, they festered. Ironically, Lone Wolf thought his son happy and well on the road to recovery. Even though he would have done anything to protect his firstborn from harm, he allowed Many Horses to slowly wither away.

Another problem that absorbed Lone Wolf's attention was the continuing strange behavior of his new *soyappo* son. The big man with the black mane was not acting as he should. It was the fault of his daughter. The scolding Lone Wolf gave Raven Wing had done little good. If anything, she was more willful than ever. Lone Wolf tried to pretend all was well, but he was annoyed. His fellow tribesmen were watching and talking. Their leader had no

more control over his family than if they were a band of mountain goats. It was obvious the clash of wills between Lone Wolf
and his new son would lead to a showdown. Gamblers among
the travelers made wagers on when it would happen.

Yet, the big *soyappo* caused no trouble. He was an excellent hunter and generous, readily sharing the game he killed and
butchered. His skills as scout and hunter earned him respect, but
the fact he helped his woman raise the lodge at night, take it down
in the morning and often did the cooking, made the travelers shake
their heads in dismay.

Every move the newlyweds made was noted and discussed
around evening campfires. Rather than join other family heads
in council, gambling, racing or playing games, every evening Black
Hair remained in his lodge, patiently teaching his new wife the
language of the *soyappo*. In turn he had her teach him the language of the Nimpau. Some evenings they sat and sewed or
fleshed fresh hides like two camp women. Vision Seeker, who
watched over the couple like a setting hen guarding newborn
chicks, overheard elders grumble that Lone Wolf's *soyappo* son
made trouble for the entire camp. Soon all women would be
worse than balky pack mares. They would not work unless their
mates helped or coaxed them with gewgaws and fancy clothes.

The camp gossip annoyed Vision Seeker, but did not worry
him. He envied Raven Wing. She was learning to speak the
language of the hairy faced ones. This accomplishment gave a
person a feeling of power. Vision Seeker knew this first hand.
Shortly after the first meeting with the trappers he had guided
them to beaver grounds on the Bitterroot. Before he could leave
a heavy snow had blocked trails forcing him to spend the Season
of Deep Snow in the *soyappo* camp. During that time he learned

many of their words. He knew enough to make himself understood but yearned to learn the secrets of the hairy faces' talking
paper. He wanted to "write", to put thoughts down on talking
paper so when he was old and mind weak these important thoughts
would be with him always. He would record important sayings
of *soyappos* and of others who spoke wise words. This knowledge would be passed on to the people that followed, knowledge
that would help them deal with the many things they would encounter during their lifetimes.

This yearning to learn drew Vision Seeker to Black Hair's
campsite. Every night, just after the evening meal, Vision Seeker
made it a practice to pass near the newly wed's lodge. The big
man always greeted him with a smile and invited him in. After
the two men had a social smoke Raven Wing sat beside them and
the language lessons began.

Trained to observe and memorize the smallest details,
Vision Seeker carefully watched and listened. He learned many
new words but his progress did not please him. The more he
learned the more he desired to have talking paper speak to him.
Night after night he lay awake thinking of the many things he
could learn from "books". He wanted to unlock the secrets they
held, even the mysteries of the Great Spirit Book. Did it have the
power to guide people to the Great Spirit Land as No Hair On
Head claimed? If he could "read" he would know.

One evening Vision Seeker summoned up enough cour-
age to ask Black Hair if he would teach him The Book's secrets.
The big man shook his head. He was not a teacher of the Great
Spirit Book, he said. There were special men like *tewats* (sha-
mans) who studied and taught the meaning of this book's words.
They were called "ministers" or "preachers". If they came to

teach among Indian people they would be called "missionaries".

"How do we get these people called 'missionaries' to come and teach us?" Vision Seeker asked.

"I don't know. I suppose if you ask for them they will come." If only Little Ned knew what these spoken words eventually would lead to, he certainly never would have uttered them.

#

As the days passed the pace of the column quickened. The travelers were coming into country that felt more like home. They arrived at the junction where the Bitterroot Trail intersected with the Lolo Trail. The Bitterroot Trail continued north through Hellgate Pass and on to the buffalo grasslands that bordered along the banks of Sun River. Lolo Trail headed west over the mountains and down the Kooskooskie (Clearwater) River to Lapwai. Beyond the trail junction, and at the base of the Bitterroot Range, the travelers set up camp in a grove of pine. While the women and children did evening chores, the men gathered to council and smoke. They were near the boundary of the Nimpau tribal lands. Soon they would enjoy the comforts of home.

"Shall we pause awhile here to rest, fish and hunt?" Lone Wolf posed the question to the men.

"Who needs rest?" Weasel Face demanded, his small, close-set eyes glanced around the circle of faces. "It is time we returned to our Lapwai lodges. Who knows what harm may have happened?"

Lone Wolf frowned. If anyone but Weasel Face had made the suggestion he probably would have approved. Depleted from the long trek and the worries of leadership, he was as anxious as anyone to cross the mountains and settle into the permanent home lodge. His keen sense told him Raven Wing already was with child. He wanted the grandchild to take its first breath in their homeland. But to bow to Weasel Face's wishes went against his principles. He glanced at the others. No one spoke. They waited for him to make the decision. They knew bad feeling existed between narrow-eyed Weasel Face and the leader of the band. They did not want to take sides. "We will camp here for awhile. The horses need rest," Lone Wolf finally said. When the meeting broke up Lone Wolf turned to Vision Seeker. "Where's the big man with the black mane? Why is he not here?"

"He and Raven Wing scout for beaver," Vision Seeker reluctantly answered knowing the news would upset his father.

"Find them," Lone Wolf tersely ordered. "Tell Raven Wing and her mate -- before the full moon fades we leave for Lapwai."

Two days later Vision Seeker returned. Impatiently, Lone Wolf waited while Second Son tethered his mount. "Why did you not bring Raven Wing and her mate?" he demanded. A gathering of people listened and watched. Lone Wolf had promised that upon Vision Seeker's return the band would break camp and take the Lolo Trail home.

"Black Hair and Raven Wing have no desire to travel to Lapwai," Vision Seeker answered. "They wish to stay this side of the mountains and trap the beaver."

Lone Wolf scowled. He started to voice his disgust, then, noticing the inquisitive crowd that had gathered, turned on his heel and strode into the tipi lodge closing the flap. He glared at Quiet Woman who, sensing his displeasure, turned away. Lone Wolf flopped down on the buffalo robe covered pallet and stared at the blank tipi wall. Why didn't his daughter and her mate act like normal people? How could he continue to be leader of the band if he couldn't control his own family?

RAVEN WING

VI

*Every fall thousands of buffalo went through this pass to spend
the winter in the hills. Gate of the Buffalo it was called.*

Luther Standing Bear, Lakota

Impatiently, Lone Wolf and the party of Nimpau waited
for Raven Wing and her *soyappo* mate to return. One day passed,
a second day passed and still they did not appear. On the third
day the Weasel Face family took down their lodge and packed up
their belongings. Weasel Face made the rounds of the tipi lodges
telling everyone he was leaving for Lapwai and invited them to
come along. Lone Wolf watched with misgivings. Would the
people leave with Weasel Face or would they remain with him?
It was a test of his leadership powers. His confidence had worn
thin. Even his family was against him. Granny did not say a
word but her little sharp eyes had a worried look as if she disap-
proved. Quiet Woman was outspoken. She urged him to take the
trail home. She had enough traveling about like a homeless creature, she said.

"You have everything one needs: goods, horses, robes. It
is time we go to the long lodge and rest our weary bones. You are
not the young man you were 20 years ago."

Those last words struck at Lone Wolf's heart like the sharp
pierce of a war lance. It was the last thing he needed to hear.
Old! He was not old. He felt as full of vim and vigor as he had in
his youth. To prove it he would lead his people to the Sun River
buffalo grounds. He and his sons had new rifles. It would be

good to try them out. Besides, he did not want to return to Lapwai until his daughter, her mate and their future offspring accompanied him. He summoned his third son, Running Turtle. "Go around to all the lodges. Tell everyone we break camp at first light. We ride on to Sun River for the buffalo hunt."

"Aiiee!" Quiet Woman tore at her graying hair. "Foolish man! You wanted to rid the lodge of your daughter. Now you cannot live without her."

"Silence! Do you want people to think we quarrel? " Lone Wolf glared. What had got into the woman? She had the best of everything: new pots, new cloth, trinkets of every kind . . . Why was it, the more he gave her the less enjoyment she seemed to have?

Unaware his parents were at loggerheads, Vision Seeker hurried in from the pasture grounds. The mare he had been watching finally had dropped a fine male colt. He thought the news would delight his father. Instead, Lone Wolf scowled.

"It could not have happened at a worse time. At first daylight we take the trail to buffalo country. A new foal will slow us down."

The unexpected news astonished Vision Seeker. "We are to stay this side of the mountains and hunt the buffalo?" He glanced at his mother. She turned her back on him. Many Horses, who sat motionless in the semidarkness, would not look up. It did not take a mind reader to see Lone Wolf's decision to journey on to buffalo country was not well received.

"What about Weasel Face? He is packed and ready to leave for Lapwai. Is he going one way, we another?"

Lone Wolf gave his second son a surly glance and stomped out of the lodge without answering. What was the matter with his family, anyhow? Many Horses had become an old woman. Raven Wing and her mate had taken off without notice. His mate had turned into a quarrelsome shrew and now Vision Seeker questioned the wisdom of his father's decisions.

Vision Seeker glanced at Many Horses. As the eldest son it was his place to reason with their father. He started to speak but the vacant look in his brother's eyes made him change his mind. Granny uttered clucks like a disturbed setting hen. Quiet Woman angrily threw things into a pile for the next day's travel. The threatening atmosphere was like that which preceded a mountain thunder storm. Vision Seeker quickly withdrew. What had happened to this family? Ever since they met up with the hairy faced trappers, quarrels and unhappiness had filled the lodge.

Vision Seeker returned to the pasture to keep watch over the new colt. This was a task Many Horses always took upon himself. Lately he hardly ever came to the pasture grounds. He acted almost as if he had an aversion to horses. It was so unlike his brother. Working with the animals had been his first love. The terrible head wound must have damaged his brother more than anyone realized. Many Horses acted like a stranger. He sat and stared into space, taking no notice of what was going on. It was uncanny, almost as if he viewed everything from another world.

Breaking camp caused the usual confusion: excited barking of dogs, children gleefully skipping about, women scolding and men shouting orders. The rested pack animals shied and crow hopped. A screaming child slid down the bank into the cold waters of the creek. In rescuing her the mother lost her balance, wetting herself to the waist.

Weasel Face and family sheepishly appeared. They had

spent the night on a hill above camp waiting for others to join them. No one came.

"It is best to hunt buffalo before going home," Weasel Face said when questioned. "It will be good to return to the home lodge with meat and hides." He took his place in the column as if, all along, he had planned to make the trip to Sun River.

Except for the discord between his parents and Many Horses' strange behavior, Vision Seeker found the trek to buffalo country quite pleasant. He kept watch over the herd, especially the new colt and her mother. The spindly-legged newborn managed with only occasional rides on hastily rigged drag poles.

Hardly did the travelers set up lodges on the banks of Sun River when Raven Wing and her big mate arrived. Accompanying them were Black Hair's three friends: Buck Stone with the corn colored hair; No Hair On Head, wearing his ever present cap; and Hawk Beak Nelson, his thin face with the prominent predatory nose looking so terrifying he sent children scurrying for the safety of their lodges. To Lone Wolf's pleasure the trappers asked if they might set up their tent alongside his tipi lodge. Quiet Woman welcomed her daughter with an unusual cry of joy. She held her daughter at arm's length, admiring her rounding stomach.

"A son by the Season of New Grass," she confidently predicted. "It will be good to have babies in the lodge again."

Before the trappers settled in they came to smoke with Lone Wolf. The leader of the Lapwai band was so pleased with the respect the trappers tendered him, he invited Weasel Face and others to join in the smoke. The men sat in a circle in front of the tipi lodge enjoying the balmy, early fall sunshine. Vision Seeker, who was included, was delighted to find he understood almost every word the hairy faces said. He spoke to them at length in their own language. They politely listened and answered without hesitation. He talked so long Lone Wolf frowned. Second Son had gotten above his position. When the smoke was almost over Many Horses walked up to the circle of men. Scowling, he ignored the trappers. When Lone Wolf motioned for him to join them, he moved away.

"It is not good to set up lodges with these *soyappos*," he said. "They are the cause of this." He referred to his hideously scarred head.

Many Horses spoke in the language of the Nimpau but the trappers understood. Silence fell over the group. They glanced at one another. Since his wounding the first son of the Lapwai band leader made them uneasy. They did not know how to deal with him. Weasel Face, who enjoyed any discomfort that descended on the Lone Wolf lodge, grinned, his close set eyes had the satisfied glint of a well fed fox.

Lone Wolf knocked the ashes from the pipe and put it in its case. One by one the trappers got to their feet, nodded to Lone Wolf and drifted away. Weasel Face went with them, toadying up to the man with the corn colored hair. Many Horses gripped the knife at his belt. For a moment Vision Seeker feared he would take after the departing trappers. Instead, he turned to face Vision Seeker, his eyes cold with hate.

"Wrong to smoke and talk with these *soyappos*," Many Horses said with loathing. "Bad medicine. They cause our people much harm." He stalked into the lodge and sat in the darkness. His eyes resuming the wild, vacant look the family had come to dread. For the first time ever, Vision Seeker felt afraid of his brother.

Many members of the hunting party approved of the trappers' presence. They enjoyed mingling with these strangers who came from lands beyond the River of Many Canoes. Each hairy face was carefully observed and evaluated. The men spoke in respectful tones of Buck Stone, the trappers' leader. They remembered his worth at the battle with the Blackfeet. The womenfolk liked him for his open face and gentle manner. No Hair On Head, who used many words from the Great Spirit Book, was eyed with uncertainty. They feared, yet envied this man who knew much about the mysteries of the book called "Bible". His appearance made them ponder. If he was so close to the white man's god why did he not comb his beard and bathe. He looked and smelled like the stink sack of a skunk.

The man called Hawk Beak they found downright comical. His long, thin figure topped by a tall hat with a single magpie feather sticking out of the band and his narrow face with crooked, hooked nose, gave him a countenance unlike any human they ever had seen. Someone named him "Tomahawk Head". The name fit him perfectly. It was repeated in one lodge after another, sending the occupants into hilarious fits of laughter.

The trappers barely had settled in when buffalo were sighted. In a thin line they drifted from the north. Running Turtle, who was guarding the herd, saw the shaggy beasts first. Switching his horse into a gallop, he pounded over the hill, shouting at the top of his voice.

"Buffalo! Buffalo! The buffalo have come!"

The hunters seized their weapons, mounted up and looked to Lone Wolf for instructions. Taken by surprise, Lone Wolf was at a loss. He had been so occupied with family and community matters he had not tried out his new rifle. Seeing his host hesitate, Buck Stone took charge. He drew a map of the area on a bare square of dirt. "Show us exactly where the buffalo are," he said to Running Turtle.

"Here." Running Turtle pointed to a spot on the crude map.

Buck wet a finger and held it into the air. "Ugh huh! Just as I thought. We're in luck. The wind is out of the west. So far they have not got our scent. We will approach from the east, drive them against that bank of hills." He nodded to the ridge that sloped up to the escarpment.

"The run up the hill will tire them out, slow them to a trot. When they hit that line of rocks they'll be puffing and confused, wondering which way to go. If parties of hunters close in on each side the critters will be trapped. Unless I miss my guess, they'll turn and attempt to escape back the way they came. More hunters need to be stationed here." Buck pointed to the river that ran along the base of the slope.

Buck Stone's plan worked to perfection. Buffalo after buffalo fell to the hunters' guns, lances and arrows. After the first pass, Lone Wolf counted the fallen animals. The buffalo were sacred creatures put on Mother Earth to supply the people with meat. To slaughter them needlessly was a crime against the Great Mystery who, if offended, might withhold bountiful gifts. When the men had reloaded Lone Wolf waved his rifle. "One more firing and finish."

Because they were used to handling guns, the trappers outshone the Nimpau. The most accurate shooter was the tall, thin trapper, Tomahawk Head. He had the uncanny ability to reload on the run. The deep boom of his long barreled Hawken was heard from one end of the hunting grounds to the other. From that day on those who called him Tomahawk Head did so quietly and with respect.

Many Horses did not join in the hunt. He remained sitting in the lodge. Every time Hawk Beak's big gun thundered he flinched. His mouth grew slack and a wild look replaced the vacant stare. Quiet Woman watched in horror, thinking any moment he would be seized by a fit. The ache in her heart was so intense she hardly could breathe. Tears filled her eyes and rolled down her cheeks. This was her precious firstborn. She remembered so clearly the day he took his first breath. He howled as if he had not wanted to emerge from the womb. Perhaps he sensed life would be cruel.

Quiet Woman began to croon the lullaby she sang when Many Horses was a child. Granny joined in. Together they sang songs first heard when they were babies in their mothers' arms. Quiet Woman reached for Many Horses' hand and drew his poor head down and cradled him close to her breast. Gradually, her firstborn relaxed. The shooting stopped. All that could be heard were voices of women softly singing and mournful sighs of the wind.

The plentiful buffalo harvest was cause for celebration. The medicine man said a long prayer asking forgiveness for taking the sacred buffaloes' lives. The people chanted the song of thanksgiving and then the drumming and dancing began. All night drumming, singing and dancing continued. The next day sleepy-eyed women and children went to making pemmican and cutting strips of meat for drying. If they took care the harvest of meat would take them through the Season of Falling Snow. The only dark cloud to mar the event for the Lone Wolf clan was that the band of hunters was beholden to the hairy faced trappers for the huge success. Lone Wolf, who should have organized the hunt, had let them down. To make matters worse, on the first run Lone Wolf lined up a young cow that would make perfect meat only to have his new rifle misfire. He switched back to his bow and arrow, but in doing so he lost sight of the young cow. Weasel Face seized the opportunity to gleefully inform everyone of their leader's misfortunes.

The man with the black mane also received his share of critical comment. Every day he worked alongside Quiet Woman and Raven Wing. With his heavy skinning knife, he sliced the meat into strips for drying and chopped it into chunks for pemmican, then did the unspeakable. He argued with Quiet Woman over the ingredients that went into the making of pemmican. To flavor it Quiet Woman normally used wild berries. Since this was not berry country, into the melted fat she mixed a paste made from dried camas bulbs. Little Ned, who disliked the flavor of camas flour, objected. He dug into his pack and came up with a bag of sugar. He suggested Quiet Woman use it instead of camas paste. She was incensed. Who was this man to instruct her in the making of pemmican, something she had done since she was a child? Yet, to keep peace in the family, she reluctantly agreed. She put a finger into the mixture and tasted it. She smiled.

"It is good. The sweetness is pleasing."

Neighbors, who closely watched the goings-on in Lone Wolf's lodge, were shocked. To change the time-proven recipe for making pemmican was foolish. They would avoid eating food prepared in the Lone Wolf lodge. Pemmican was tricky, if it did not contain the proper ingredients it made people deathly ill.

At first, criticism of her man did not bother Raven Wing. Those who spoke against him were jealous of her new status and many possessions, she told herself. Now, with her belly starting to swell, her thoughts dwelled on bringing up her child. He (for Raven Wing, like her mother, decided the newborn had to be a son) must grow hardy and brave and know the ways of the Nimpau. He must not become a *soyappo*. Her man was large and strong but he had the soft spirit and heart of a woman. He thought he pleased her by doing lodge work. She appreciated his help, yet felt a sense of shame.

Upon learning he had brought her with child, he immediately said he would assist at the birth. She was too shocked to reply. No man spoke of such things. Since girlhood she had been taught childbirth was intimate and sacred. Only the mother herself should be present at this, the holiest of acts. By bringing a new life to Mother Earth she was the instrument of The Creator. Mothers were vital to The Great Mystery's plan. Without mothers all living things would cease to exist.

Raven Wing felt of the small mound that was beginning to make her belly swell and smiled with satisfaction. The faults of her *soyappo* mate faded into nothing. Almost for the first time ever, she truly felt at peace.

VII

*The ordeal is best met alone, where no curious or pitying eyes
embarrass her; where all nature says to her spirit,
"'Tis love! 'Tis love! The fulfilling of life."*

Ohiyesa, Dakota

Shortly after the buffalo hunt Buck Stone and his companions broke camp, prepared to leave. They wanted to set up their trap lines before the first snow. Black Hair and Raven Wing dismantled their lodge and joined them. Quiet Woman and Lone Wolf watched their daughter depart with worried eyes. Quiet Woman knew the travail of childbearing only too well. Carrying the newborn and bringing it into the world amid strangers, all of them men, was an experience she could not imagine. Something about the way Raven Wing slowly mounted her horse and rode away without looking back made her realize her daughter also dreaded the painful days ahead.

Quiet Woman uttered a low moan and turned to go back into the lodge. Tears suddenly sprang to her eyes, blinding her. Raven Wing was the only daughter she had. She bumped into Many Horses who had come out to watch the trapping party depart. Distress had replaced the vacant look on his face.

"It is not good for our sister to live amongst those hairy faces," he said. "You can see she does not want to go. She is afraid. Will you do nothing to help her?"

Lone Wolf, who still stared after the departing trappers, glanced at his first son and grimaced. He, too, could see Raven

Wing was not happy but what was he to do? That was the way of
Mother Earth's creatures. When the time came to leave the nest
they had to fly by themselves. No one could do it for them. Above
all, he did not want Raven Wing back on his hands. She had to
stay with the big *soyappo*. Carrying a hairy faced one's child
made her soiled. Now, no man in the tribe would accept her as a
mate. If the hairy faces ill-treated her, that was too bad.

All day and well into the night Quiet Woman went mo-
rosely about her work. Granny's attempts to comfort her did little
good. Lone Wolf watched in dismay. He could not stand to live
through the winter with his mate whimpering like a whipped dog.

The next morning Lone Wolf caught Vision Seeker before he went to tend to the herd. "Many Horses and Running
Turtle can take care of the animals. I want you to ride after the
hairy faces and spend the Season of Falling Snow in their camp.
You speak their tongue. You find their ways good. Watch over
Raven Wing. When her time comes, bring your sister back. A
first grandson should be born amongst his own."

For the first time since her daughter left, Quiet Woman
became her old self. She bustled about preparing food and clothes
for Vision Seeker to take along. She slipped an amulet made of
an eagle claw and a strip of ermine into a rawhide pouch for the
mother and newborn's safety and good health. She handed the
pack to Vision Seeker. No words were exchanged but they both
knew what they did was good.

On the third day Vision Seeker caught up with the trappers. They were surprised, but readily accepted his presence. "It
is good to have you here," Little Ned said, relieved that one of
Raven Wing's own kin would be around to keep her company.

All fall and winter Vision Seeker lived with the trappers

and Raven Wing. He never liked trapping the beaver. The little animals were too much like humans to kill and skin. The industrious beaver colonies worked together, built lodges, lived together and protected each other like humans did. To do his part Vision Seeker hunted for meat and took care of the horses and pack mules, but time still hung heavy on his hands.

Every morning he watched the trappers set out on their trap lines, returning later with their catches. They looked upon each day as a new adventure, not knowing what their trapping skills might produce. Late into the evenings they worked on the pelts, proudly telling how this one or that one was taken and the price it would bring. They were so content and pleased with their work it made Vision Seeker envious. Yet the thought they killed Mother Earth's harmless creatures just for their skins seemed evil. An even more dreadful thought was that soon all the beaver would be destroyed.

One day Little Ned noticed his brother-in-law enviously watching the trappers depart, he beckoned to him. "Why not come along?" he invited. Vision Seeker glanced at Raven Wing. "Go!" she said. " I will be alright."

Vision Seeker soon found himself doing what he vowed not to do, trapping beaver. The *soyappos* were kind. They taught him how to set traps and how to work the skins into pelts. In the evenings, after the pelts were cleaned and stretched, he sat with Buck Stone and No Hair On Head who taught him words of the talking paper, stories that told of ancient times and of the white man's God. Before long he was able to read words by himself, always keeping an eye on his sister to see to her every need.

At first Raven Wing was dismayed by her brother's presence. She knew it was Lone Wolf's doing. It angered her that he should think she was incapable of taking care of herself. As time passed her feelings changed. It was comforting to have Vision Seeker nearby, especially when the weather turned bad and the men were forced to remain in camp.

The Season of Falling Snow came in with a howling blizzard. For days the men ventured out only to see to the horses and mules. The remainder of the time they sat in the lodge, smoking, talking, quarreling, scratching and smelling up the space like unclean animals. They did relieve Raven Wing of the chores of cooking and cleaning up. Raven Wing did little but watch her belly grow. Black Hair stayed by her side, taking care of her every need. His quiet, patient attention angered her. Why didn't he act like a normal man? The other trappers, who also kept watch over her, made her want to scream. Every night she wished the Great Spirit would whisk her away. Every morning she vowed to crawl from the lodge and lose herself in the snow.

#

At Lone Wolf's hunting camp on the banks of Sun River the storm struck with a viciousness that caught everyone by surprise. Children ran screaming into the lodges. Dogs put their tails between their legs and tried to find protection in the trees. A tipi lodge not staked properly, ballooned up and flew away on the high wind. Bedding and floor mats went skidding into the river, clothing flapped up to disappear into the white mist, cooking utensils spilled their contents and babies cried in terror.

Lone Wolf and other heads of families ran out to shout instructions, "Secure the lodges! See to the children! Count family members! Make certain everyone is safe!" Their next thought was for the herd. Without horses they never would get back to Lapwai. Lone Wolf sent Running Turtle and Many Horses staggering to the pasture fields. In the open, the force of the wind struck like the blow of a war club. Running Turtle was knocked off his feet. He pulled himself into a crawling position, inching forward until he came to a group of horses bunched together with their backsides to the wind. He got a tether line around two of them; tugging and urging, he got them back to camp.

Coming onto a group of animals, Many Horses yelled and flapped his arms, attempting to drive the animals into the protection of the cottonwood groves. Before he could save it, the cap that covered his naked skull blew off. The icy wind sent darts of pain searing into his brain. The flying cap sent the horses skittering. Instead of heading for the cottonwoods, they made for the hills. Many Horses floundered after them. When Running Turtle returned, his brother and the horses had disappeared.

Time after time Running Turtle staggered out to put lines around the necks of more horses, leading them back to camp. Each trip he searched and shouted for Many Horses but his brother did not answer. Crawling into the tipi, Running Turtle broke the heartbreaking news. Granny began to wail. Quiet Woman's face turned nearly as white as the snow outside. She glanced sharply at her mate. "You never should have sent him into this terrible storm. We will never see our firstborn alive again."

Quiet Woman turned her face to the wall and began to weep. Lone Wolf threw a robe around himself and staggered outside into the teeth of the storm. The wind whipped away the lone feather in his hair. In trying to save it, he slipped and fell, wrenching a knee so badly he could not get to his feet. Ignominiously, he crawled for the protection of a clump of willow trees where he sat amongst a cluster of dogs. Lone Wolf was so sick at heart he did not even care when Weasel Face and his sons stumbled on to him looking as pitiful as his canine companions. Finally, Running Turtle came to help him hobble back to the lodge. The sun went down. Darkness fell almost at once. Quiet Woman would not allow Running Turtle to search for more horses. She was afraid he also would get lost. The dark night and driving snow kept visibility to a few feet. Terror filled the lodge. The wind made it impossible to make a fire. Cold penetrated the thickest robes. Quiet Woman took no notice. Her thoughts were on her first son. He was out there, lost and afraid. She seized one of Granny's big shawls and bound it around herself. She forced her way through the tipi flaps and into the driving wind. She staggered a few steps and fell to her knees. She crawled several feet, then gave up and returned to the lodge. It was impossible to find anyone or anything until the storm ceased.

For a long while the family sat stunned, shivering so hard their teeth chattered. Finally, Quiet Woman aroused herself. She ordered Granny to sit alongside Lone Wolf and Running Turtle. She piled robes and blankets on them and then slid in beside them. Somehow, they had to get through this terrible night.

The storm continued until drifts built half way up on tipi lodge sides. In open spaces where the wind was strongest, except for a glaze of ice, the ground was swept bare. When the wind and snow did stop the sun came out with a brightness that turned the landscape into a dazzling brilliance that blinded the eyes. The sky was azure blue. The rest of the world was white and clean. The hunting families crawled from their lodges to blink and wander about like bears emerging from winter caves. Soon the smoke of campfires spiraled into the cold clean air. Children began to run and shout. Dogs shook, stretched themselves and sniffed for food. The riding mounts that had been saved, were bridled and saddled. Riders mounted and galloped away in a desperate search for men and animals lost in the storm.

Lone Wolf and Quiet Woman crawled out of their tipi lodge to scan the horizon like watchful prairie dogs. They were both sick with fear. There was no sign of Many Horses. Yet, they still had hope he had survived. Lone Wolf's knee was too swollen for him to walk or ride. Running Turtle had been out already. He had saddled a horse and was waiting for his father's instructions. Lone Wolf glanced around helplessly. He had not the slightest idea where to start searching for his missing son.

"I will ride to where I last saw him," Running Turtle said. "He can't have traveled far."

The cold fingers that clutched at his heart told Lone Wolf First Son was dead. No one remaining in the open could have lived through the icy storm. He limped up the slope where he could follow Running Turtle's search of the snow covered plain. Quiet Woman followed closely behind, tightly gripping Granny's old shawl that still covered her shoulders, head and back.

Running Turtle, who since childhood had been looked on by his parents as the dim-witted, slow-moving member of the family, suddenly found himself important. With Vision Seeker away and Lone Wolf laid up, it was up to him to find his missing brother. The responsibility that suddenly fell on his shoulders frightened him. He glanced across the expanse of snow and felt small and insignificant. Who possibly could find anything in this vast sheet of white?

Running Turtle rode a ways and stopped. A bulge in the snow caught his eye. His heart was in his throat. He barely could force himself to dismount. Dread made his arms heavy. It was all he could do to brush away the snow. He breathed easier. It was an outcropping of rock. He mounted and rode forward, toward the point he last remembered seeing his brother. He got off to look at another lump in the snow. Nothing. The search went on for hours. Then he came upon a small rise in the snow that had the unmistakable shape of a body. For a moment he could not move. He sat in the saddle and shivered uncontrollably. A large eye stared out of the blanket of white. It was all he could do to keep from spurring his mount and galloping for camp. Then he steadied himself. The staring, unblinking orb was much too large to be human. He dismounted and brushed the snow aside. A furry hide, a pointed ear and then the muzzle of the recently born colt appeared.

"Ah!" Running Turtle's heart dropped back into place. He started to get up and continue the search when he noticed a human hand. It lay on the colt's neck, the fingers buried in the mane. Running Turtle brushed more snow away. Gradually, the scarred skull of Many Horses emerged; a pair of brown vacant eyes stared him in the face. Running Turtle quickly patted the snow back to cover the scalped skull. His brother's expression was so real and lifelike for a moment Running Turtle expected him to speak. The calm, peaceful look gave the impression Many Horses merely had awakened from a restful sleep.

For several moments Running Turtle sat in wonderment at the mystery of death. His brother was so alive yesterday and today he was gone. Where did his spirit go? He glanced up at the sky. Was Many Horses' spirit up there where Vision Seeker claimed people who left Mother Earth went when they died? Or had he traveled to the world below where animal spirits were supposed to go when life was finished on Mother Earth?

Surprisingly, Running Turtle did not feel sad. Many Horses

just had gone from one world into another. He had not gone
alone. The spirit of the young colt had kept him company. Running Turtle's thoughts were interrupted by shouts from a nearby
hilltop. It was Lone Wolf asking if he had found his brother.
Running Turtle shouted and waved back. He didn't want to leave
his brother alone and he looked so peaceful he did not want to
disturb him. He sat and waited while Lone Wolf with the help of
Quiet Woman hobbled across the field.

#

Gradually warm breezes from the south brought a thaw.
The trappers went back to their trap lines. Except for the kicking
baby inside the womb, Raven Wing found herself alone. One
morning, just as the men left for the trap lines, the pain started.
She bit her lip and motioned for Vision Seeker to stay. When the
hairy faces had gone she told Vision Seeker the child was near.
Vision Seeker brought the horses around. He handed Raven Wing
up and they rode toward Sun River and Lone Wolf's lodge.

Before midday twinges of pain became so frequent and
sharp Raven Wing could not stifle a moan. Vision Seeker pulled
the horses to a stop and carefully helped his sister dismount. With
a robe and the saddle blankets, he made a place for Raven Wing
to lie down. Hurriedly he built a fire which cast off more smoke
than heat, and then helplessly looked around. This was Raven
Wing's most sacred moment, a time when she wanted to be alone.
It was not the place for a male, but where could he go? As far as
the eye could see, there was only the grassy plain blotched by
pockets of snow.

Raven Wing gave a distressful cry. Instinctively, Vision
Seeker reached out and took her hand. She held it so tightly he
could feel every surge of pain. From helping foal the mares he

had learned the process of birth at an early age, but never had seen a human being make an entrance on Mother Earth. He had no idea mothers suffered like this. The agony made her squeeze her eyes shut and bare her teeth. When her eyes opened they had the same beseeching look of beavers before trappers bludgeoned them to death. Vision Seeker turned his back. Why was it this holiest of times was filled with such great pain?

Just as it seemed the grueling experience never would end, Raven Wing gave a long painful groan. Vision Seeker turned back to see a pink head appear. Awed by the sight, Vision Seeker watched the tadpole-like creature emerge. He reached for his skinning knife and carefully severed the umbilical cord that connected mother and child. He set the cord aside. When dried it would serve as an amulet to protect the newborn from harm. Eyes still closed, the baby's mouth opened to utter a protesting cry. Vision Seeker held the newborn boy up for his sister to see.

Raven Wing's pain-dulled eyes brightened. She sat up and looked around. Trickles of water gurgled in the nearby creek. A fluffy robin plopped down on the bank to dip its bill in to take a drink. Somewhere on the rolling plain a meadowlark broke into song. The sky above was clear without a sign of a cloud. All things of Mother Earth seemed peaceful and pleased. "It is a good omen," Raven Wing murmured. "My son is born on a beautiful day and is part of this wonderful country, homeland of the sacred buffalo. He shall be called Buffalo Boy."

Raven Wing lay back on the sleeping robe and uttered a satisfied sigh. The weeks of waiting were gone. The pain was forgotten. She was proud and content. She had participated in one of Mother Earth's great miracles. She had created new life, a beautiful man child!

VIII

*Men may slay one another, but they can never overcome the
woman, for in the quietude of her lap lies the child!*

Ohiyesa, Dakota

For the hunters camped on Sun River, the Season of Deep
Snow was a catastrophe never to be forgotten. Men who counted
their wealth in horses were left poor. Family heads with few
horses were left with none. As the thick blanket of white melted
away one equine carcass after another began to emerge. In one
gully alone seven animals were piled up, one upon the other. All
were from Weasel Face's herd. He blamed his misfortune on
Lone Wolf who had made the decision to remain in buffalo country rather than return home. Weasel Face's vitriolic complaints
were voiced to anyone who would listen. After most people were
asleep, he still could be heard grumbling in his lodge.

The deaths of three members of the hunting party were an
even more painful pill to swallow. In time herds could be replaced; loved ones were lost forever. All three bodies were recovered, but the ground was so frozen they could not be buried.
Instead, they were wrapped in buckskin and then wrapped again
in buffalo robes that were tightly secured by leather thongs. After much ceremony and mourning the bodies were placed in nearby
tree tops, above the reach of wolves and coyotes, to await the
Season of Melting Snow when graves could be dug.

Every day the presence of the dark bundles reminded the
hunting families of the calamity that had befallen them. Lone
Wolf, with his crippled knee, remained in his lodge, his countenance as dark and foreboding as the gloom that hung over camp.
He was to blame. If he had not let his pride rule him, this never
would have happened. Many Horses and the others still would
be alive.

The day came when shallow graves could be scooped out

of Mother Earth. The bodies of the dead were taken from the trees, rewrapped and laid to rest, the heads pointing west so when The Great Spirit called they would rise up to face the morning sun. To protect the bodies from marauders great mounds of rock were placed on each grave. At Many Horses' grave site, Running Turtle did most of the work. Quiet Woman and Granny were too overcome with grief to help. Lone Wolf was too crippled to bend down. After the last stone was in place the mourners stood over the grave and wept. Lone Wolf was the last to leave. In spite of his bad knee, he knelt down. He spoke to Many Horses as if he still was alive.

"Forgive me, my son, I brought you here to your death. I would give my life to take your place."

#

Buffalo Boy's unexpected appearance at the Sun River camp created a flurry of excitement. The hunting families streamed out of the tipi lodges. Women and children, seeing the bundled baby, began to shout and talk at once. Lone Wolf had added a new member to his lodge. They surrounded Raven Wing to get a peek at her son, marveling that he was born in the camp of the *soyappo*. Raven Wing did not enlighten them. She clutched the baby to her and glanced around proudly. Lone Wolf shoved his way through the crowd to take the bundle. He carefully uncovered the tiny face and peered into the wondering, bright eyes. The pain caused by Many Horses' death and the slurs against his leadership faded away. He held the baby high above his head and uttered a short silent prayer of thanksgiving to Father Sky.

Quiet Woman bustled up to seize the bundle. "Have you lost your senses? Bright light is bad for little eyes. Help your daughter down. We must get daughter and baby inside. Running Turtle, fetch water. Bring in wood. We must make the lodge warm."

Granny, who waited at the tipi entrance, would not let them by until she had a look at the baby, too. "Eeh! Eeh!" she clucked. "Isn't he a pretty one!"

Lone Wolf attempted to follow the women and baby into the lodge but Quiet Woman pushed him away. "Look to the horses," she ordered. "This is woman's work." She carefully cleaned both mother and child, fed them and made them comfortable in a corner of the lodge. Hardly did she complete the task when the trappers, led by Black Hair, thundered into camp.

Still musty and bloodied from beaver skinning, Black Hair thrust his way under the tipi flap. He made for the pallet where Raven Wing and his baby son lay. He knelt at the new mother's side and tenderly took her hand to kiss each finger tip. Embarrassed by the show of emotion before the watching audience, Raven Wing withdrew her hand and motioned to the bundle nestled in the buffalo robes. Black Hair picked up the baby. Ignoring Quiet Woman's protests and Granny's clucks of disapproval, he carried the baby outside. Under the bright spring sun, he unwrapped the child down to his bare skin. He made certain of its male parts and then examined each little finger and toe.

"He's a first rate youngster," he announced. "He shall be called Michael." Proudly, he displayed his naked son to his trapper friends. They came close and eyed the baby silently, awed by the tiny man and the miracle of birth. Like a trapped cottontail, the baby lay still, watchful, waiting to see what his captors would do.

"He's a tough little varmint," Tomahawk Head observed. "There he is, bare as a picked bird, an' not a cry or a shiver."

"Yuh better git the little tyke under cover," No Hair On Head warned. "After all, he ain't been in this world long."

The big man rewrapped the baby and handed him to Quiet Woman who anxiously stood waiting. Hurriedly, she took him back into the warmth of the lodge. "Men!" she exclaimed. "They feel it was all their doing, bringing a youngster onto Mother Earth."

"Don't be hard on them," Granny chided. "It takes two to make a baby. Men must make a fuss over their part."

"This is an occasion for a smoke," Lone Wolf proclaimed. He sent Running Turtle for his pipe. Before Lone Wolf could reach for the tobacco, the mountain man with the corn colored hair handed him his pouch.

"It is indeed a special occasion and calls for a special smoke. This is a mixture of tobacco from the land called Virginia and sweet grass from buffalo country. May the young fellow grow up to have the best qualities of both lands," said Buck Stone.

"Amen," No Hair On Head added. "By the looks of him, the young un'll be arm wrestlin' his pa afore he's two. I 'spect already he's lookin' forward ta his first rendezvous."

When Vision Seeker translated the words of the trappers, Lone Wolf smiled and nodded. This was indeed a big day. He glanced across the camp where a crowd had gathered to gawk and gossip. Lone Wolf caught sight of Weasel Face. He suddenly felt sorry for him. Like himself, he had lost his first son but he didn't have a grandson to take his place.

Lone Wolf made a ceremony out of tamping the tobacco mixture into the red pipestone bowl. He motioned for Raven Wing's mate to sit in the place of honor on Lone Wolf's left so he would receive the pipe first. The new father sat proudly looking around the circle of smokers. When Lone Wolf handed him the pipe the big man puffed so strongly he choked. He coughed until No Hair On Head clapped him on the back.

Vision Seeker observed his *soyappo* brother's coughing fit with alarm. It was not a good omen. He attempted to think clearly but his mind was still staggered by the enormity of Many Horses' tragic death. To lose a blood brother, especially one so close to him, was a terrible blow. He could not shake a feeling of guilt. If he had been on hand to help with the herd his brother still would be alive. The very thought made him feel sick to his stomach.

Now here was this ominous sign -- Raven Wing's mate choking on a puff of smoke. Did it mean evil would befall the big *soyappo*, Raven Wing or their baby son? When it came his turn to take the pipe Vision Seeker took two puffs, slowly expelling the smoke to watch it swirl into the air. Once before, when the *soyappos* first had arrived, a terrifying vision had appeared to him in a puff of smoke. But this day the breeze caught the wisps of gray and blew them away before Vision Seeker could read anything that might signify misfortune.

Ignorant of his son's foreboding thoughts, Lone Wolf beckoned him to act as interpreter. Now that he had a grandson it was more important than ever to return to the home lodge. He informed the trappers of his intention to make the trek back to Lapwai. He invited them to travel along. He didn't expect all of them to make the journey, but he did count on Black Hair to accompany his wife and child.

The trappers smoked and glanced uneasily at each other. They did not want to disappoint their host, but traipsing across the mountains to Lapwai did not fit into their plans. There were weeks of the trapping season left. After that, there was the journey to the rendezvous to dispose of the winter's catch of pelts.

Finally, Buck Stone spoke. "It is important we remain in the mountains until the Season of Long Grass," he said in the Nimpau dialect of Shahaptian learned from Vision Seeker and Raven Wing. "There are many beaver left in the streams. We must remain to harvest as many as we can. Afterward we will travel to the rendezvous place while the price of beaver skins is good. Once the beaver skins are gone we can do other things, like visit Lapwai."

Lone Wolf attempted to hide his disappointment. He did understand. He knew the importance of beaver skins and what good things they bought. For half a beaver skin he would wait and go to the rendezvous with them. He quickly put the thought behind him. He had to do what was right for his people. Since the day of the storm Weasel Face had kept them aroused. He would not let anyone forget the suffering they endured or the lives and horses that were lost. Weasel Face kept reminding the people these things would not have happened if they had joined him when he wanted to take the Lolo Trail home.

Lone Wolf glanced at his son-in-law. The only member of the *soyappos* he really wanted to make the trip to Lapwai was Raven Wing's new mate. It was proper that he, Lone Wolf, leader of the band, make the entry into Lapwai with his new son and one and only grandson. Surely, the big *soyappo* would not let him down.

"The long lodge awaits us in Lapwai," Lone Wolf said hopefully. "We must make a special place for mother and son."

Vision Seeker appeared not to take notice but he heard every word and caught every expression. His heart saddened for Lone Wolf. It was easy to see the big man with the black mane did not want to leave his trapper friends. When he spoke the big man confirmed Vision Seeker's thoughts. He would take Raven Wing and her newborn back to the trapping grounds, he said. When trapping was finished they would travel to the rendezvous with the season's catch to trade for the many things his family needed to set up their Lapwai home.

Raven Wing, who sat in the shadows nursing her son, remained silent. The thought of rearing her infant son in the trappers' unsavory quarters made her feel ill and she had no desire for more beaver skins or trade goods. Her son was now her most precious possession. The thought of the long trip to the rendezvous site made her shudder. It was rumored the Blackfeet were still raiding enemy villages and herds. What would prevent them from attacking the trappers? The Blackfeet would love to carry off her precious baby son.

Early the next morning Vision Seeker and Running Turtle went to bring in the pack mares. It was the Season of First Grass. The animals had started to fill out. With no work over the winter they were so frisky and full of life, it took hours to separate the pack mares from the riding mounts and lead them into camp. When the brothers returned the trappers already had departed. Vision Seeker could tell from the set expressions on his parent's faces there had been trouble. When he went in to eat the morning meal he was astonished to see Raven Wing inside the lodge.

"You did not go with your mate?" he foolishly asked.

Quiet Woman answered instead. With a wag of her hand and a raised eyebrow, her expression said not all was well. She motioned for him to sit and handed him a bowl of gruel.

Raven Wing, who sat in the shadows, stared straight ahead. Vision Seeker ate in silence. His sister's face looked as dark and ominous as a thunder cloud. Granny was the only one who appeared her usual tranquil self.

"Two crows and one ear of corn make for quarrels," she said when Vision Seeker glanced her way. She chuckled, her toothless mouth creased in a grin. "Youth and age never agree," she added before Lone Wolf silenced her with a glare.

Later Raven Wing spoke of the troubled morning. "My man likes beaver skins more than he does me or our son," she complained bitterly. "He stays with his *soyappo* friends to trap more beaver, then goes to the place called rendezvous. Our son will be crawling before he sees his father again."

"Now, now," Quiet Woman soothed. "When your man does come he will bring many good things."

"I have enough good things. What will our people think when I return with a child and no mate?"

"Perhaps if I ride after the trappers and ask him, Black Hair will change his mind," Vision Seeker offered. "He often listens to me."

"No! I will not plead with him. A man must do what he thinks best." Raven Wing spoke with a vehemence that took her parents and Vision Seeker by surprise.

"I have to go to the trappers' camp anyway and bring back my catch of beaver pelts," Vision Seeker insisted. "I will speak to him then."

"You do not need beaver skins. Let Black Hair look after them," Raven Wing snapped.

Vision Seeker glanced at his father. Lone Wolf frowned and looked away. Vision Seeker thoughtfully walked out to collect the few horses that remained in the pasture. Raven Wing's

marriage had done strange things. Last year at this time Lone
Wolf and Raven Wing could not wait to get their hands on beaver
skins and all the froofraw the beaver skins would bring. Now
they turned their backs on them like they were evil things.

IX

When passion enters at the foregate,
wisdom goes out the postern.

English Proverb

It was nearing midday when Lone Wolf led the column of hunters and their families away from the Sun River encampment. Lone Wolf was in no hurry. The trail was still dangerous. Deep snow banks left by the winters' storms cloaked the north slopes of valleys and mountain sides. Rushing streams burst out of the forests on every hillside. Even for sure-footed Nimpau ponies the footing was treacherous.

It was a heart-wrenching time for Lone Wolf. The morning of departure he walked down the bank of Sun River to his firstborn's final resting place. For a long moment he stood, as silent and still as the stones that covered the grave. Finally, he knelt and softly spoke. "Son, we leave this place but we do not say good-bye. You ride with us every step of the way to Lapwai."

As the column got underway Lone Wolf continued to look back. He had hopes his new son, Black Hair, would change his mind and join them. It was a small hope but he clung to it until the column arrived at the Bitterroot River junction and began the climb to Lolo Pass. At the hot springs near the summit he ordered a halt where, in spite of Weasel Face's protests, the travelers tarried several days.

The bubbling waters, some so hot they burned the hand, provided a pleasant place to relax and catch up on repairing worn garments and broken equipment. In the warm pools women washed clothes, bathed their children and immersed themselves in the soothing waters. A particular hot water hole attracted the men. They erected a shelter over the pool, soaked themselves in the hot water, then, shrieking and hooting, they ran across the trail to plunge into an ice cold creek that rushed down snow packed

mountain slopes. From a distance Raven Wing watched the naked bodies flit from hot pool to the creek and back again. Suddenly she felt a keen yearning for her mate. Her nerve ends tingled
as she remembered the thrill of his warm strong body touching
hers.

To ease the journey for Raven Wing and her newborn,
Lone Wolf kept each day's travel short. It would do no good to
lose his daughter and would be disastrous to lose his only grandson. Yet, the nearer the column approached Lapwai Valley, the
quicker did Lone Wolf hurry. Every day the travelers were aroused
earlier and kept on the trail longer. No one appeared to mind.
Horses and dogs sensed they were nearing home. Horses picked
up their gait. The dogs ran ahead to bark and chase squirrels and
chipmunks out of the way.

For Quiet Woman the return trip did not bring the joy she
expected. When the familiar bare hills rising above Lapwai Valley came into view, she uttered a keening moan. Her first son,
Many Horses, never would return to the homeland he loved. Never
again would his shadow fall on the hillside where he had watched
over his four-legged friends. Never again would his moccasined
feet trod the Lapwai Valley pasture fields.

Quiet Woman wiped at the corners of her eyes. She inspected the sleeping Buffalo Boy and tucked the blanket beneath
his chin. She attempted to smile. The little tyke had come to
replace her lost son. But the thought only made her feel worse.
She could not stifle a final heart-wrenching cry that rose unbid-
den to her throat. No matter how many men children came to the
lodge, none ever could fill the terrible vacant space in her heart.
The loss of a firstborn left a hurt no medicine could heal.

When the travelers entered Lapwai Valley Quiet Woman's
mood brightened. Friends and relatives poured from their lodges.
Excited dogs and children chased each other around the village.
Youthful riders raced their mounts up the valley to spread the
news. Helpful village women came to relieve the pack animals
of their burdens. Before the horses were driven away to pasture,

lodge fires began to blaze and the pleasing aroma of food cooking filled the air.

Lone Wolf, who entered the village ahead of the rest, stood to one side watching as friends and relatives crowded around Raven Wing to catch a glimpse of the newest member of the clan. The new mother basked in the attention. She proudly held her baby son aloft for everyone to view. Buffalo Boy seemed to enjoy the attention too. He waved his short arms and cooed. Perhaps it was just as well Raven Wing's mate remained behind, Lone Wolf thought. His massive presence would have made the villagers shy and dampened the welcome.

The first few weeks back in Lapwai Valley went swiftly. The travelers were so busy they hardly had time to turn around. From early morning until late at night the village was a beehive of activity. People rushed in and out of each other's lodges like lost ants searching for their homes. The people who had remained behind were anxious to discover what they had missed, badgering the returning families to relate their experiences. The returnees were just as eager to hear what had happened in Lapwai during their absence.

Lodges and equipment needed repair. Then there was the business of preparing for the upcoming winter months. Food and supplies had to be collected and harvested from the slopes, fields and streams. Soon after the hunters arrived, the women and children trekked to the south slopes of the hills. Here, rocky ledges caught the heat of the spring and early summer sun to make kouse plants flourish. After a winter diet of meat, pemmican and camas cakes, everyone savored the taste of the succulent kouse root.

During the high heat of summer whole families, even entire bands, went into the foothills to gather wild onions, carrots, and edible roots. In the thickets along creek beds women and children sought out berry bushes. Wading into the thorny shoots, they picked the fruit and carried it back to camp in baskets. Much of this sweet bounty was pressed into cakes and packed away for use during winter months.

When the snow runoffs ceased the salmon started their run. Every stream carried the silver flashing bodies that had come home to spawn. The men speared, netted and even caught them bare-handed. Along the banks women busily cleaned the catch and sliced the fish into strips and laid them out on racks to dry in the sun.

Shortly afterward came the camas bulb harvest in which every able-bodied person took part. Bands from all over the Nimpau homeland traveled to the camas meadows to dig for the nourishing bulbs which, as long as anyone could remember, had been a staple food of the tribe.

When Vision Seeker and Running Turtle brought in the pack animals to prepare for the trip to the camas grounds, Raven Wing suddenly decided not to go. She had no desire to dig for camas bulbs with the women while the men took their leisure in gambling, horse racing and games. Now that she was a wife and mother, it would not be proper for her to join the men as she formerly had done. In firm tones she told Lone Wolf she would remain in the village with the elders and Bad Foot, the boy whose appendage had not been right since birth.

Lone Wolf swallowed his disappointment. He wanted to show off his grandson, especially to the White Bird band who had refused to make the trip to the rendezvous and had no knowledge of Raven Wing's marriage or motherhood. He started to speak, order his willful daughter to go, but the warning frowns of Quiet Woman and Granny deterred him. Raven Wing was no longer his to command. Lone Wolf held his tongue but silently fumed. He wished his *soyappo* son would appear and take his stubborn wife in hand. He did not like the thought of leaving his only grandson in the care of elders and the youngster, Bad Foot.

Raven Wing enjoyed the quietness of the nearly empty lodge. Every day she played with Buffalo Boy and inspected him from head to toe. She searched for defects but found none. His skin, hair, especially his eyes, were lighter than she wished but he had a strong, sturdy build. This pleased her. She wanted him to grow into a hunter and warrior of great skill and courage. Would the Boston blood in his veins cause it not to be so? She brushed the disagreeable thought aside.

One pleasant afternoon, as she lazily strolled along the creek bank, three horsemen rode up the valley. One rider sat his mount like a mountain man. Raven Wing's heart beat quickened. It was Black Hair! She started to dash back to the lodge for Baby Buffalo Boy, then changed her mind. Her mate had waited this long, he could wait a bit longer. She selfishly wanted all of his attention for the first while. She smoothed her hair and ran forward.

Suddenly, she stopped. It was not her mate. These people were strangers. Abashed by her forwardness, she sidled back and attempted to hide behind a clump of willows. Like a cornered bird, she held her breath, waiting for the horsemen to pass. Instead, when the riders came abreast, they stopped. The man who rode like a mountain man, dismounted. He handed the reins of his horse to a companion. Straight for the clump of willows he strode, softly whistling. Raven Wing turned to run. Before she could escape the horseman seized her by the arm.

"Aha!" the man exclaimed. "If it isn't the Bear Lake beauty. I knew someday we would meet again."

Raven Wing's heart pounded so hard it squeaked. This was the tall dark faced man who made bumps rise on her skin and sent her blood racing. She wanted to run but the power of his bold eyes held her captive.

"Do not be frightened, little one," he said. "I only wish to know you better. What are you called?"

"Raven Wing," she answered against her will. The narrow mustache, no larger than an eyebrow, looked so neat and interesting. Why didn't all hairy faces do that? She mentally shook herself. "What is the matter with me, thinking of such things at a time like this?"

"Raven Wing! Beautiful! I could not have named you better."

The voice had the caress of a spring breeze. No one except her *soyappo* mate paid her compliments like this. She missed them. She could listen to words like these all day. The man reached out to caress the black wing of hair. His other hand still gripped her arm. Raven Wing ducked away. The forwardness of the stranger frightened her. What would he do next?

The thought of what it might be brought blood racing to her head making her dizzy. The time their lips had touched and the little mustache had tickled her nose, flashed through her mind. She uttered a scream, tore her self free from his grasp and ran as fast as she could for the safety of the long lodge. The dark, tall man's mocking laughter followed her. Inside the lodge Raven Wing dropped breathlessly on the sleeping pallet. She pulled Buffalo Boy to her breast and held him tightly, trying to calm the pounding of her heart.

What was this man doing in Lapwai? Francois was his name, she remembered Black Hair say . . . a French Canadian who had once trapped for the Redcoats of Hudson's Bay. Now he was a free trapper like Buck Stone and Black Hair. This man was dangerous. He had the power to excite her like no man ever had. For the first time since Lone Wolf and his band left for the camas grounds Raven Wing wished she had gone along. If she ever needed the protection of her family, now was the time. To keep herself safe Raven Wing vowed not to venture outside the lodge until the dark faced man was gone.

Buffalo Boy began to whimper. He was hungry. She nursed him, noticing with distaste the blue veins that appeared on her milk filled breasts. "Ah!" she thought, "to be slim and attractive again." She quickly squashed the thought. What difference did it make how she looked? She had her mate. But after bouncing the baby on her shoulder and putting him to sleep, she dug into a pack and took out a small mirror. She combed her hair and smoothed her eyebrows. The old couple at the end of the lodge watched, startled by her strange behavior.

"Aiiee!" Raven Wing uttered aloud. Why didn't people

mind their own business. She laid down beside Baby Buffalo Boy and tried to regain her composure. It was no use. Even the chatter of blue jays and rustle of the busy chipmunks and squirrels touched her every nerve. Finally, she drifted off into troubled sleep. She awoke to hear man-made sounds that came from somewhere in the nearly vacant village. Raven Wing's first thought was of the three strangers. Had they ridden on? Was this a party of horsemen returning from the camas grounds? Perhaps it was Black Hair!

Raven Wing quickly sat up, gave her hair a token brush and ran outside. She stopped to stare. Less than an arrow flight away two of the three strangers were busily erecting a tipi. The man named Francois gathered stones from the creek bank to make a fire pit. He caught sight of Raven Wing. He called out and waved. She ducked back inside the lodge, her heart pounding in her throat. The old folks at the far end of the lodge glanced up in alarm. Raven Wing attempted to calm herself. She was as jumpy as a hare caught in one of Running Turtle's horse hair snares.

That night Raven Wing slept badly and so did Buffalo Boy. She awakened feeling out of sorts and wondered why. It was that man. The thought of the smooth dark skin, the neat mustache and the eyes that looked like they would devour her, sent her blood racing again. How she wished for the presence of her family. She needed to feel the stolid firmness of Quiet Woman, the thoughtful counsel of Granny, most of all the protection of Black Hair's arms. She even would swallow her pride and endure her domineering father.

Late in the morning, after Baby Buffalo Boy had been bathed, fed and lulled to sleep, Raven Wing made up her mind to rid herself of the spell the man Francois cast upon her. She strode down the creek bank. The new lodge was set back from the creek. For a moment she stopped to stare, wondering what was going on inside. Who were these people? Why were they there? The tipi flap opened. Before she could turn away the dark faced stranger emerged. He did not act surprised. It was almost as if he expected her.

Raven Wing started to speak. Her tongue failed her. She stood helpless before the bold black eyes. He came forward; his voice uttered soothing, enticing words. The stranger's hand reached out to her. The touch sent shivers darting up her spine. Before she could resist, he roughly pulled her to him. She did not feel surprised even when he led her to the tipi lodge and carried her inside. Time stood still as he did things that made her body and mind wild. Only momentarily did a small voice shout that she was no better than a camp woman who sold herself for a length of calico or spool of thread.

X

Deceiving those that trust us, is more than a sin.
Anonymous

After leaving Lone Wolf's hunting camp on Sun River, Buck Stone's band of trappers returned to the beaver streams. For weeks they continued to toil on their trap lines. Then almost overnight, when they made the rounds, they found no beaver. The traps were empty. The streams they worked had been trapped dry.

"'Pears ta me, it's time ta leave," baldheaded Deacon observed. "As the sayin' goes, there's no profit in floggin' the stuffin's outta a dead horse."

Buck Stone agreed. The next day they pulled their traps and began the task of curing the last green pelts. To make certain everyone received his fair share of the winter's catch, they took an inventory, sorted the pelts by grades, divided them into piles and finally pressed them into easily transportable packs. Vision Seeker's share they set aside.

I suppose yuh'll be wantin' ta handle yer Injun brother's catch?" Deacon asked Little Ned.

The big man nodded. It was strange Vision Seeker had not returned for his pelts. Lone Wolf was certain to have insisted on it. He thought back to the bargaining for Raven Wing. Lone Wolf had attempted to deal him out of every last one of his pelts. What had happened to the avaricious side of the fellow? Something told him not all was well with his Nimpau relatives. He should not have left his bride. He never would forgive himself if something happened to her or their baby son.

It was a bountiful beaver harvest. Even hard to please Hawk Beak had to admit it was a successful season. "Now, if the price of beaver is good we'll be in tall clover fer sure," he said, sizing up his stack of skins.

Little Ned brushed away his fears for his family. The prosperous season seemed to vindicate his decision to remain east of the mountains. His catch was one of his best ever. He could afford handsome gifts for every member of the Lone Wolf family and be able to send money to his folks in the east. Yet, he had to plan well. There were so many things he wanted to do for Raven Wing and Michael, the name he insisted on calling his new son.

In his daydreams he saw the boy going east to school, maybe eventually Harvard College. He would be no neglected half-breed like most mountain men's offspring. He would see to it he had every advantage a New Englander's child should have. He would send money to St. Louis with the trader, Sublette, and open a bank account for the sole purpose of educating his son. Before parting with Raven Wing he had attempted to explain the need for making all the money he could while trapping still was good. Some day soon the beaver would be gone.

Throughout the Rocky Mountains trappers like Little Ned were cashing in on the rich harvest of pelts. In the northern regions Hudson's Bay sent great brigades of men to set traps by the hundreds. Along the North Pacific shores it was said ship loads of Russians came each winter to capture and slaughter beaver, otter, seals, foxes and other fur bearing animals for their skins. Little Ned told Raven Wing of these things but she did not understand. She saw no need to save or plan for the future. Mother Earth had always provided. She would do so next year and the next, for as long as they lived, Raven Wing argued. The subject of sending their son away to school never had been discussed.

As the time for departure came Little Ned found himself getting impatient. He wanted to get to the rendezvous, get his business done and be off for Lapwai. His little son would be scampering around like a wild colt before he knew it. He was missing out on one of the most joyous periods of fatherhood.

Everything seemed intent on frustrating the trappers. The pelts taken last were still green and would not dry. When it was finally decided they were cured sufficiently, the mules could not be controlled. The well rested animals fought, bit, kicked and hee-hawed as pack saddles were strapped on their backs. When the loads were in place, they bucked and crow-hopped. One shaggy animal dislodged its packs and disappeared into a thicket of brush. Before the men could run it down and recover the packs, the rest of the animals became out of hand, running in circles, snorting and hee-hawing. Only when Hawk Beak seized the shaggy ring leader by the nostrils and bit down on its ear with his big teeth did the mules quiet down.

"There's nothin' more aggravatin' than a stuborn, ornery mule," No Hair commiserated. During the effort to get the mules under control his cap had flown off and was trampled by churning hooves. A cloud of mosquitoes descended to feast on the inviting bald head. His companions laughed as he furiously waved his arms to keep the swarming insects away. "Yuh think it funny, do yuh? Let me tell yuh, thet's tender skin. These critters're big as buzzards with stingers like hornets. Yah! Yah! Git away from me noggin. Tarnation! Where's me blinkin' cap? Next time I'll tie it on with a chin strap."

Getting started on the right trail also became a problem. The trappers did not know the exact location of the rendezvous. Buck Stone said it was on the stream called Popo Agie, (meaning Head River in the Crow language). Hawk Beak insisted it was north, in Wind River country. No Hair Deacon said they were both wrong, it was on Bear Lake again.

To make certain they didn't miss the summer fur fair, the trappers took the trail that skirted the western foothills of the great peaks the French named the Tetons. They passed near Pierre's Hole where the rendezvous in '32 would occur. They wended their way through Teton Pass to follow the Green River. At South Pass they crossed the divide into Sweetwater country. They just about had given up finding the rendezvous when they spotted a herd of horses grazing in a valley. Soon spirals of campfire smoke appeared. Then they heard the boisterous sounds that could come only from a group of mountain men on a spree. Someone shot off a gun. "Whoopee!" came a shout. A US flag went up. More shots and more shouting echoed back from the hills.

"I'll be danged!" Deacon exclaimed. "We've arrived in time ta celebrate the Fourth of July, in the year of Our Lord, 1829!"

The little brigade was soon surrounded by the celebrants. "Hey! Yer late," a slurred voice shouted. "We been here fer a week."

One greeting after another came from the buckskin clad crowd. "I'll be damned if it ain't thet ol' crowbait, Hawk Beak Tom Nelson. I thought the Blackfeet got yuh last year. Buck Stone, yuh ol' son of a gun, from the looks of yer packs yuh've trapped out the whole blisterin' northern mountains. If'n it ain't Little Ned. Where the hell's yer Nez Perce filly, yuh ain't ditched her already, hev yuh? Deacon Walton, No Hair On Head I hear yer called by yer Injun friends. Yuh unfrocked preacher, yer fatter, uglier an' dirtier'n ever. When yuh plannin' on yer first bath?"

The new arrivals made their way into the village of tents and lean-tos. On the outskirts were several tipis. Indian women were scraping fresh hides, staking them out and slicing meat to hang on racks to dry. Two lads dressed only in breechcloths rode ponies through camp shouting and waving lances made of sticks. A cluster of camp dogs lay sleeping in the sun. A row of little faces peeked from under the tipi coverings to stare at the white men having fun. The sight of the youngsters made Little Ned's heart lurch. He thought of his son. At this rendezvous there would be no carousing for him. He had to get his business done, get home and see to his family.

"What's the price of beaver skins?" he shouted.

"Five dollars a pound fer prime," someone answered. "Might as well give yuh a kick with a frozen boot."

#

At the camas meadows Lone Wolf also was anxious for the camas bulb harvest to end. He could not concentrate on the horse races. Gambling did not interest him and he was too old to enjoy the games. He sat and smoked and talked with the White

Birds, the Wallowa, Asotins and a small band of visiting Flatheads. He wanted to brag about his new son and grandson but Weasel Face always was on hand. Much to Lone Wolf's disgust, the narrow-eyed man always seemed to turn the conversation to the disastrous winter in buffalo country, broadly hinting that the tragedies never would have happened if he had been the leader of the party.

More and more, Lone Wolf kept himself apart, not even joining in talk of the hairy faces' Great Spirit Book and the great power it was supposed to possess, a subject close to his heart. Members of the Asotin and White Bird bands were interested particularly in two Indian youth who, it was rumored, were returning after four years of instructions at the Red River Mission School run by the Black Robes (Anglicans) of Hudson's Bay.

"Flathead people say the Black Robes do not have the true religion. It is the Long Robes (Catholic) who know the way to the hairy faces' spirit world called 'heaven'," a voice reported.

"Ah! The Flatheads. How can they have such knowledge?" one of the horse herders retorted. "They would not know a Black Robe from a speckled bird egg."

The argument over which religion was best went on and on until Rabbit Skin Leggings of the White Bird band suggested the only way to learn the truth was to send emissaries east and talk to teachers of the Great Spirit Book. He offered to make the journey if others would accompany him.

Vision Seeker also did not take part in the fun and games or discussions. Raven Wing's refusal to accompany the Lapwai band to the camas meadows troubled him. It was not good for a woman and a small child to stay in the near vacant village without protection. Raiders would not harm the elders and Bad Foot, the crippled boy who tended the elders, but they would delight in taking captive a young, healthy woman. A male child prisoner would be an even greater coup. Regardless of her stubbornness, Lone Wolf should have ordered Raven Wing to come with them.

On the excuse he wanted to inspect the herd left in the

home pasture, Vision Seeker rode back to Lapwai. He gave the horses a cursory look and hurried on to the long lodge. He entered to find Buffalo Boy alone. The baby lay on the sleeping pallet, kicking his legs and waving his tiny arms, his face nearly purple with anger. Raven Wing was nowhere to be seen.

"Here! This will not do," Vision Seeker said. He picked up the baby and made clucking sounds as he had seen Granny do. Buffalo Boy howled all the louder. He was hungry, Vision Seeker decided. He went to the far end of the long lodge and questioned his decrepit aunt and uncle. They knew not where Raven Wing was and had nothing to offer in the way of food for the baby. Bad Foot finally told him Raven Wing had left the lodge that morning. She went while the baby slept. He did not know where.

#

Events seemed to pave the way for Raven Wing's illicit love affair. Shortly after their arrival, Francois' companions departed. They took the trail down the Kooskooskie and across the plateau to the great Chinook trading place on the Columbia River at the falls of The Dalles. The two lovers had the newly erected tipi lodge to themselves. They established a routine. Raven Wing fed, cleaned and put the baby to sleep in the morning. She then slipped out of the long lodge and walked quickly to the tipi lodge where Francois impatiently waited. Some days, as today, they were together for hours.

#

Vision Seeker made a little broth, dipped his finger in it. The baby glared at the finger and continued to howl. Vision Seeker thrust the finger into the open mouth. Buffalo Boy choked, tasted the broth and began to suck. It was not a satisfactory substitute for mother's milk but after a few moments Buffalo Boy grew quiet. Vision Seeker cleaned the baby and rocked him to sleep. All the while the icy grip on his heart tightened. Something had happened to Raven Wing. She loved the child, and no mother went off for hours leaving her newborn untended. There was no evidence of struggle. Could she have gone for water, slipped and fallen into the river? He covered the baby and began the frantic search for his sister.

He started down the creek bank. Immediately, he picked up her tracks. She had gone toward the river. Then the tracks led away from the creek bank. The footsteps were spaced as if she had been in a hurry. Like a bird whose nest was threatened, had she been decoying danger away from her baby in the long lodge? The thought made Vision Seeker quicken his step. Then he caught sight of the new tipi lodge. The tracks led straight to its entrance. Perplexed, Vision Seeker stopped. What was the lodge doing here? Had his brother with the black mane returned? No! He would not have left Baby Buffalo Boy alone. Something very strange had happened. Somehow the tipi was involved.

Vision Seeker dodged into the trees and crept nearer. He heard voices. He stopped to listen. A strange male voice spoke. Then came an answer. It was Raven Wing. Vision Seeker froze. Who could the stranger be? He searched the nearby grove of trees for a horse. There it was, a tall black stallion. Whose was it? It looked familiar but he could not place it. He took a step nearer. He slid the knife from its sheath and paused again. He could hear much clearer. Vision Seeker inwardly groaned. The couple inside the tipi made the unmistakable sounds of love.

Vision Seeker could not believe his ears. His sister, Raven Wing, married with a son, was acting like a wanton camp woman. She, who had resisted the advances of every eligible male in the tribe, had taken up with a stranger. What was worse, she had cunningly planned the whole affair. She did not feel up to taking in the camas harvest this year, she told her parents. Instead, she remained behind, waiting for her lover to appear. The deception made Vision Seeker feel ill. He glanced down at the skinning knife. He had half a notion to slice away the tipi covering and pull Raven Wing out by the hair.

Instead, Vision Seeker returned to the lodge, looked in on the still sleeping Buffalo Boy and thoughtfully polished the razor-edged knife blade. He had to get rid of the stranger but how was he to do it and not expose Raven Wing's illicit behavior? He asked the half blind aunt to keep her one good eye on the baby. He had to get away and think things out. Whatever he did, he had to do it without betraying his sister. If Lone Wolf and Quiet Woman discovered their daughter's wantonness they would be devastated. Lone Wolf might lose control of himself, take his gun and shoot Raven Wing's lover dead and banish his daughter from the lodge.

"Aiiee!" Vision Seeker groaned. The whole village, the whole tribe, could get involved. Lone Wolf would for certain lose his place as leader of the Lapwai band. As he mounted and started up the valley, a rider leading a string of pack mules came down the far creek bank. Vision Seeker reined his mount to a stop. He knew the horse. He knew the mules. His mouth suddenly went so dry he could not swallow. The horseman sat tall in the saddle. He wore a wide-brimmed black hat.

"Agh!" Vision Seeker groaned. His new brother could not have arrived at a worse time. Hardly without realizing what he was doing, Vision Seeker kicked his mount into a gallop, uttering a wild war cry, he raced for the man with the black mane and the string of pack mules. His only hope was Raven Wing would get the message. It was up to her to get back to the long lodge and her baby before all the thunder and lightening in the sky descended to destroy her marriage.

#

Raven Wing long had feared such a moment. Each day she vowed not to visit Francois' tipi again. Each day the spell of the dark-faced man pulled her to him. Almost as though she expected it, Vision Seeker's cry of warning pierced her consciousness. Without a stitch of clothing on, she leapt up. Keeping herself hidden behind the fringe of willows that lined the creek bank, she raced to the long lodge. Ignoring the stares of Bad Foot and the old couple, Raven Wing slipped into the quill decorated elk skin wedding dress, grabbed Buffalo Boy and ran to greet her husband.

XI

Like war, love is easy to begin but hard to stop.

H. L. Mencken

Black Hair lifted Buffalo Boy into the saddle beside him. The big mountain man was covered with trail dust but he could not wait to hold his son. This was the moment he had dreamed about since the unhappy parting with Raven Wing on the Sun River hunting grounds.

"Ah! How the young man has grown." The little boy gazed at his father with wide eyes, then wrapped his tiny hand around one of the big man's thick fingers. The father was delighted. "Ah, ha! You want to shake hands? This is as fine a welcome home any man could have." He swung down and enclosed both wife and son in his arms. His heart overflowed with love. How wonderful it was to have an adoring wife and handsome, healthy child!

Vision Seeker, who watched, swung his quirt and gave his mount a vicious slap, something he never, never did, and galloped away. He rode high into the hills that surrounded the valley. His sister's act of loving wife made him sick to his stomach. She arose from her lover's arms and welcomed her husband with no more shame than a buffalo cow that received one bull after another. He could not stand by and let her get away with such outrageous behavior. But what could he do that would not expose Raven Wing's infidelities to her mate and the Lone Wolf family?

The remainder of the day Vision Seeker kept to himself, mulling over plans to rid Lapwai Valley of the seducer of his sister. Only at dusk did he return to the village. Before entering the long lodge, he studied the location of the stranger's tipi. Its presence seemed to taunt him. "Herein was seduced your sister, now what are you going to do about it?" it seemed to say.

There was no one in sight. Only a black horse tethered nearby told him that Raven Wing's lover was still there. He yet had to see the man, but he had a premonition they had met before, but where? The interloper was no happenstance traveler. The sleek horse was owned by a man who thought well of himself. He had to be extremely cunning. Somehow he had known in advance that Raven Wing was alone. Of course! They had planned this meeting.

The treachery that had occurred almost under his nose, made bile rise up in Vision Seeker's throat until he thought he would choke. Not only was he disgusted with his sister, but also himself. Raven Wing had done the crass deed, but he was guilty, too. He was her brother. He should have protected her from harm . . . kept her from this terrible temptation. He stared at the new tipi lodge until it became a brown blur. It was like a boil on his nose. One could not avoid its painful presence. The quicker he removed it from sight, the better off everyone would be. A plan began to take form in his mind.

The man with the black mane greeted him in his usual friendly manner. "Where have you been, brother? I brought your winter's catch," he pointed to a stack of beaver pelts. "I thought you would rather have pelts than money, I trust I guessed right."

Vision Seeker winced. Black Hair's kindness was like a dagger thrust to the heart. He glanced at Raven Wing. She was busy cooking and did not look up. "Thank you. Welcome to Lapwai," Vision Seeker said. "I hope you find this a happy place. You may find the long lodge strange."

"Of course I'm happy! With wife and child by my side, how could I be otherwise?" The big mountain man glanced down the length of the building. "However, the accommodations are somewhat different than I expected."

Actually, Black Hair was appalled. The lodge reminded him of a subterranean cavern. It was half sunken into the earth. Mats and grasses held in place by poles and tree branches completed the sides and covered the roof. Networks of spider webs hung in the corners. He guessed the dark, dank building to be 100 feet or more in length. Although it was nearly vacant, he counted places for 20 fires which probably meant 20 families made it their home. He could not imagine the confusion that must take place: howling babies, quarrelsome youngsters, scolding parents, waspish grannies, gossipy old women plus the fumes and cooking odors of 20 fires. Inwardly, he flinched. Yet, he didn't let his dismay show. He invited Vision Seeker to sit and busied himself helping Raven Wing with the evening meal.

Vision Seeker reluctantly hunkered down. He avoided looking at Raven Wing. She appeared so innocent and Black Hair so entranced, it made him uncomfortable to be in their presence. After they had eaten, the big mountain man overwhelmed them with gifts. Vision Seeker received a new wide blade knife, a gun with a short barrel that Black Hair said was called "pistol", a bridle for his horse and a supply of lead and powder. The man with the black mane gave Raven Wing a necklace, a beaded comb to wear in her hair and several lengths of red calico and printed gingham. Buffalo Boy received a toy bear, a ball and a colorful rattle. The wealth of gifts stunned Vision Seeker. He glanced at Raven Wing. She flushed and looked away.

"I must see to the horses," Vision Seeker said. He had to get away before his white brother noticed the distress he felt. He picked up his sleeping robe. "Tonight, I will sleep on the hill."

Black Hair Ned gave him a grateful glance. "Thank you, Raven Wing and I have much to talk about."

Late that night Vision Seeker aroused himself from the warm sleeping robe. He shivered. There was a chill in the air but he could not rest until he carried out his plan. He adjusted his hunting shirt, made certain the knife Black Hair had given him was in its sheath at his belt and took the trail down the hill and into the valley. Beyond the long lodge he paused. His eyes searched the area around the stranger's tipi. The black stallion tethered in the locust patch lifted its ears and stamped its hooves.

Vision Seeker walked softly and quietly forward until the newly erected tipi loomed before him. He took the knife his mountain man brother had given him. He had sharpened it until the blade sliced a hair into two pieces. He gripped the bone handle with a grunt of satisfaction. It seemed fitting to set things straight with Black Hair's gift.

At the rear of the tipi lodge Vision Seeker paused again. From inside came the rhythmic sound of fitful snoring. Vision Seeker dropped to his hands and knees. Carefully, he crawled forward. Next to the tipi he stopped to listen. The sleeper inside continued snoring. Vision Seeker pressed the sharp point of the knife into the thin tipi lodge covering. Carefully, he drew the blade down making a long cut in the tipi wall. The ripping sound was loud in the quiet of the night. The snoring stopped. Vision Seeker sat back and waited.

Soon heavy breathing started again. Vision Seeker made the slit larger, large enough to allow his body to enter. He thrust his head in and waited until his eyes adjusted to the darkness. He could make out the sleeping form, the head not an arm's length away. He slid through the opening and crawled to where Raven Wing's lover lay. In a single motion, he straddled the body and seized the stranger by the hair. He pressed the sharp blade against his throat. For a moment he feared he had pressed too hard. Warm blood trickled down the bone handle and dripped from his fingers. His captive did not struggle. He lay paralyzed, too terrified to move.

"I come with a warning," Vision Seeker hissed. "If you are not gone by morning you will not leave this camp alive."

To give emphasis to his words, he pressed down on the knife blade. The flow of blood increased. "Do you understand? If you are not gone by daybreak you will not see the next sunrise." To make his intentions absolutely clear, he carved off the man's left ear lobe, held the piece of flesh above his face and let the blood drip into the victim's eyes.

As quickly as he had entered the lodge, Vision Seeker was gone. He slipped through the opening and through the trees. A stone's throw from the tipi he stopped to look back. Out of the tipi burst the stranger, half dressed, a rifle in his hand. He glanced around wildly. Seeing nothing, he ran for his horse. Smelling fresh blood, the stallion snorted and reared.

For a moment Vision Seeker thought the animal would break free, but the stranger viciously jerked the horse's head down and snubbed it to a tree. Hurriedly, he saddled. Without bothering to reenter the tipi or collect his belongings, the man mounted and raced away in a thunder of hooves. Through the vacant village the rider galloped, swerving onto the trail to the west. A couple of camp dogs ran out to bark, then all was silent.

Vision Seeker walked back up the hillside to where he had left his own mount. He rolled up his sleeping robe, tied it behind the saddle and rode toward the camas grounds. The encounter with the stranger pleased him. It also bothered him. Anyone bold enough to set up a tipi lodge in a strange camp and seduce village women was no stranger to mischief. He would not be easily frightened. The indignity the stranger suffered would weigh heavily on his mind. He surely would return. When he did he was certain to take his revenge.

However, the thought of meeting up with the stranger was not nearly as worrisome as Raven Wing's behavior. What had possessed her? She had a good man, but betrayed him. Raven Wing had succumbed to the stranger, apparently going willingly to his tipi. What was to prevent her from doing something like this again and again? What more could he do to keep her from doing such shameful things? All the way back to the camas meadows these troublesome thoughts nagged at Vision Seeker like a sore tooth.

At the camas grounds the campers still were eating the morning meal. Before joining the family, Vision Seeker unsaddled and wiped down his mount. Running Turtle came out to help and hurry him up. Lone Wolf wanted to have a report of what he had seen in the valley. News of Black Hair's return was received with delight. Lone Wolf nodded his approval. He had half feared his *soyappo* son might have abandoned his wife and child. Quiet

Woman clapped her hands delightedly. She was happy for Raven
Wing. Granny clucked like a satisfied setting hen. She knew all
along the big *soyappo* would return. Running Turtle asked what
gifts his new brother had brought. He hoped for an iron shooting
stick.

Vision Seeker sat down to eat. The excitement created by
Black Hair's return left him depressed. How differently his family would react if they knew the inapprehensible behavior of their
daughter. Then an even more terrifying thought came to mind.
On some future day they were bound to find out . . . The consequences were too unnerving to contemplate.

XII

We had neither devil nor hell in our religion until the white man brought them to us.

Ohiyesa, Dakota

A rider from the village of the Asotin band brought news that quickly pushed talk of Black Hair's arrival into the background. The two Indian youth sent to the mission school at Red River had returned to their homelands. J. H. Pelly and Nicholas Gary, the Anglican missionaries called Black Robes had named them. Pelly came from the Kutenai tribe, Gary from the Spokan; both were sons of tribal leaders. The missionaries taught the students reading, writing, history and geography. In the summers the youths learned to plant and tend crops and every day they received religious instruction. They were baptized according to the Black Robes' way. On returning home they wore the clothes of the hairy faced ones. They carried leather bound copies of the Great Spirit Book and spoke the language of the hairy faces better than their own.

The camas harvesters stopped work to question the messenger. They wanted to know every detail. They were upset. No member of their tribe had been chosen to attend the mission school. This was not right. The Nimpau always had been the leaders of the Northwest tribes. Although their Cayuse relatives brought the first horses to the plateau, it was the Nimpau who bred and developed this precious animal into the colorful, sure-footed Appaloosa. These prized animals were coveted by horsemen even in the lands of the Lakota and Dakota. Now, the Kutenai and Spokan had the power of the white man's Great Spirit Book and the Nimpau did not. It was a blow to their pride.

In the lodges and around the campfires of those who remained at the camas harvest, discussions of the two mission trained youth went on late into the night. Vision Seeker was besieged by questions. He knew the language of the hairy faces, had trapped and lived with them. What had he learned about the Great Spirit Book which revealed the pathway to heaven? His friend, No Hair On Head, carried "The Book" with him wherever he went. Did he use this great power to bring Many Horses back to life? Vision Seeker did his best to answer the questions but had little success in satisfying everyone's curiosity. He remembered what Black Hair had said about missionaries; they were the people who taught the power of the Great Spirit Book. He finally told the questioners if the people wanted to learn about this power, they had to ask missionaries to come teach them.

Lone Wolf listened thoughtfully to all that was said. It greatly annoyed him that the Black Robes had overlooked the Nimpau. Since before the great flood that covered Mother Earth his people had held sway in the lands that lay between the waters without end in the west and the great mountains that rose in the east. The influence of the Nimpau was recognized in every village and trading center along the great river Columbia -- even in isolated encampments beyond the buffalo hunting grounds.

What worthy things had the Kutenai or Spokan ever done? He could not think of a single one. But if the Kutenai and Spokan received the power of the white man's Great Spirit Book, what would happen to the Nimpau? Would their position as the most powerful nation in the Northwest wither away? Should his people seek the teachers of the white man's religion, journey to the River of Many Canoes and invite them to Lapwai? Perhaps he should send Vision Seeker. He knew the ways and language of the *soyappo*. Lone Wolf brushed the thought aside. No, he could not chance losing another son. Someone else had to go.

That evening Lone Wolf sat and smoked with the leader of the White Bird band. He spoke of the missionaries and the need to bring them from the east. The White Bird headman puffed thoughtfully on the pipe. They, too, had dreams of possessing the Great Spirit Book. He glanced at his friend who also was his brother-in-law. He envied him. He now had a *soyappo* son. If this new son used his influence, the Lapwai band easily could gain this great power. Ah! He had to proceed carefully. If the Lapwai band possessed the power of the Great Spirit Book his White Bird band must acquire it, too. Who could he depend upon? Oh, yes, he knew just the person.

"Perhaps we should speak with Rabbit Skin Leggings," the White Bird suggested. "He has visited with the young men trained by the Black Robes. They told him many things about the white man's heaven and hell. He may know how to get the help we need."

Lone Wolf nodded. His mind was busy. Should he ask his *soyappo* son to make the trip to the land beyond the River of Many Canoes? Yes! That was the answer. Black Hair was the man to send. He knew the language and ways of these eastern people. He would know how to go about bringing back a teacher of the Great Spirit Book. Yet, he might refuse. His new son had a mind of his own and then, there was Raven Wing to manage. She was certain to be against the whole idea. He had better bide his time, listen to the White Birds and learn of their plans.

That night Rabbit Skin Leggings came and sat in council with the White Bird and Lapwai leaders. He respectfully listened to what they had to say. In turn he spoke of his visit with the two mission trained youth. The Black Robes had taught the two mission youth well. They spoke of the many good things in the Great Spirit Book. The Book also contained many frightening things, the youth warned. It told of the place called "hell" into which sinners were cast to burn forever and ever, plus a day. The screaming and gnashing of teeth was awesome. Again and again the Black Robes warned them, this was where people who broke the laws of the Great Spirit Book went when they left Mother Earth.

"This is serious business," Rabbit Skin Leggings finally said. "If we ask for the power of the Great Spirit Book, we must accept what it says and live by its laws."

Lone Wolf agreed. Any great power had to be managed wisely, anyone with half a brain knew that.

"The Great Spirit Book will bring a change to our people that is hard to imagine," Rabbit Skin Leggings continued. "To follow its teachings the Black Robes say Indian people must quit their hunting and trading travels. They must make their livelihood by cutting Mother Earth's skin to plant things like maize, wheat and a root called potato."

"That's foolish thinking," Lone Wolf said. "Do not the Black Robes know the fields in their season furnish camas bulbs, berries, pasture for horses and other good things? The streams bring fish and the mountains are plentiful with game. Mother Earth gives us everything necessary for life. Why should our people torture her by cutting her skin? If we do, she might withhold all the good things she has given our people since the beginning of time. Perhaps these missionary teachers and the Great Spirit Book are not good for us."

"You see things clearly, Lapwai friend," Rabbit Skin Leggings said. "If we are to bring teachers of the Great Spirit Book into our midst, our people must have a great thirst for it. The power it contains could do our people much harm."

Lone Wolf smoked and stared into the fire. He had not thought of the damage the *soyappo* religion might cause. Perhaps they should not be in a hurry. Let the Spokan and Kutenai try the religion first. If harm descended on them, they deserved it for trying to best the Nimpau. Lone Wolf nodded to Rabbit Skin Leggings. "We hear your words. Your counsel is good. I do not think we need these people called 'missionaries'. What they teach is not good. It is a serious matter to harm Mother Earth."

Lone Wolf dismissed the Great Spirit Book from his mind. However, over the coming months he was reminded again and again of the power the Kutenai and Spokan possessed. Spokan Garry traveled from village to village telling about the hairy faced one's God and his disciple, Jesus. He spoke of heaven and hell and taught the Ten Commandments. He read from the Great Spirit Book and told his listeners what they must do to gain entrance to the white man's wonderful heaven. Many Nimpau tribesmen went to hear these messages. They came away of two minds. Some thought the Great Spirit Book went against the ways of their people. Others were intrigued. Heaven, the place the Black Robes said believers went when they left Mother Earth, sounded wonderful.

"Why do we not seek this power possessed by the Kutenai and Spokan?" people began to ask. "Why do we let the Kutenai and Spokan have all these good things?" Weasel Face was quick to capitalize on this. "Do you not see? Our leader is old and blind. He does not see these good things that should belong to our people."

In the Lone Wolf camp there were other things besides Weasel Face and talk of the Great Spirit Book to cause concern. Raven Wing was again with child. Quiet Woman's countenance was more somber than usual. She did not think it wise to have a second child so soon after the first. Whenever he appeared she gave her son with the black mane stern glances of disapproval.

Raven Wing, herself, was appalled. How could this have happened? At first she had no idea whose child it was. She tried to believe it was Black Hair's. Deep inside she knew it was not. She found herself giving Vision Seeker apprehensive glances. Surely he knew of her wanton indiscretions. She never forgot his warning shout. It was all that kept her sinful actions from being exposed. Of course, her brother did not do it solely to protect her. Vision Seeker wanted to protect Black Hair, and keep disgrace from Lone Wolf's lodge.

Raven Wing sighed. How could it have happened? It seemed like a dream. The tall dark man appeared out of nowhere. They had their torrid moments of love, then her lover disappeared as quickly as he had appeared. No one saw him. No one spoke of him. Except for the seed in her belly and Vision Seeker's accusing eyes, the man she knew as Francois might as well never have been in Lapwai. The empty tipi was the only visible reminder of the frenzied, exciting moments they had spent together. In a way Raven Wing was glad Francois was gone. She knew if he were around, she could not resist him. Just the thought of him made her blood race with excitement.

#

As the Season of Falling Leaves approached, talk of the Great Spirit Book faded. Lapwai villagers turned their attentions to inexplicable happenings that were taking place in the valley. In addition to the eerie tipi that had appeared while they were at the camas meadows, a dusky figure had been seen slipping in and around the village at night. Strips of salmon left to dry and baskets of camas cakes had disappeared. Once a hank of venison vanished into thin air. A strange three-legged, one-eyed dog with empty eye socket and leg stump dripping blood, was found in the pasture. Several camp dogs strayed away and were not seen again.

At night herders reported strange lights on the far hillside, sometimes bright and sometimes dim. Villagers spoke of investigating, but the lights appeared in the vicinity of the rocky den where rattlesnakes clustered together in huge coils to hibernate during the cold season.

The sight of the vacant tipi sitting in their midst troubled people most. As far as anyone could tell, no one ever entered or left it. Village dogs were equally curious. They circled it, smelled it and barked at it without effect. Raven Wing, who had spent the camas season in the long lodge, was asked about it. It mysteriously appeared overnight, she replied.

Raven Wing was as curious about the tipi and its occupants as anyone one in the village. What had happened to Francois? Where did he and his friends go? Surely they would be back. One did not abandon a good tipi. The dress she had left behind when she ran naked to the home lodge was what bothered her most. She had worn it often. If it was found in the tipi, most anyone in the home lodge would know it belonged to her.

Running Turtle, who had completed his vision quest and thought himself a bold warrior, went to investigate. He entered the tipi and searched the interior. He reported that it contained a buffalo robe and some camping gear. There was dried blood on a fringed buckskin garment that looked like someone's dress. Blood also was smeared on the buffalo robe and on the tipi covering near the entrance flaps. In the rear of the tipi there was a cut large enough for a man to slip through. The news made Raven Wing suck in her breath so sharply, Quiet Woman gave her a worried glance. Had the baby started to kick already?

Shortly after Running Turtle made his report, the village was routed out in the dark hours of morning. "Fire! Fire!" the night guard shouted. The strange tipi was ablaze. The dry tipi coverings and poles burned so quickly and fiercely villagers fought to keep the flames from running wild through nearby trees.

Vision Seeker, who led the effort to keep the fire under control, burned his arm. When Raven Wing applied buffalo grease to the wound, she gave her brother a searching look. Had he set the fire? The expression on her brother's face told her nothing.

SPOKAN GARY
Native missionary who spread the word of
"THE GREAT SPIRIT BOOK"
Sketch by Gustavus Sohon, courtesy Washington State Historical Society

REVEREND HENRY SPALDING
Presbyterian missionary who eventually came to teach
"THE GREAT SPIRIT BOOK"
From THE NEZ PERCES SINCE LEWIS AND CLARK by Kate C. McBeth

XIII

Every sin brings its punishment with it.
Outlandish Proverbs

Throughout the Season of Falling Leaves and the Season of Falling Snow, Raven Wing lived in a state of fear and anxiety. The slightest mishap made her irritable. Big Black Hair did his best to please her. His solicitous attention only increased her irritation. How could he be so kind when she had been unfaithful? As the weight in her belly grew she knew for certain it was her lover's child. Each night she turned her back on her mate to face the blank lodge wall. Her married life, which began with such promise, had become a nightmare. She was tied to one man, in love with another. Soon she would have had a child by each one, husband and lover.

Black Hair knew something was wrong but he had no idea what bothered his mate. He could understand Quiet Woman's concern about Raven Wing's pregnancy. For the life of him he could not imagine how it had occurred. He had taken every precaution. He knew full well how dangerous, under the best of conditions, childbirth was. After all, he had lost his first wife in childbirth and had no desire to lose Raven Wing in similar manner. On several occasions he sought Vision Seeker's advice on how to make Raven Wing happy. His brother-in-law was no help. "Do not worry," he said. "She will be all right when the second child is born."

Raven Wing's second delivery was far different from Buffalo Boy's harsh entry on Mother Earth. The weather was sunny and warm. The mother lay on a soft buffalo robe padded pallet. Against Raven Wing's wishes, Granny and Quiet Woman stood by, watching over her like hawks on the hunt. A second child coming so soon after the first, made them fear for her life. The men were shooed away. Vision Seeker took himself to the pasture and remained there all day. Running Turtle was told by Quiet Woman to leave and stay in the lodge set apart for teenage males. Big Black Hair fared no better. Quiet Woman declined his help. He would know in good time when the newborn arrived. Lone Wolf strutted around the village, proudly announcing the news. Another male child soon would grace his lodge.

When the delivery was over and the child lay by her side, Raven Wing smiled to herself. Locked away in her heart she held a secret too priceless ever to reveal. This son had been conceived in a frenzy of passion that still made her blood race. Each time she looked at the rosy faced baby, those glorious moments when he was conceived were relived.

Nervously, she watched her mate pick up the tiny bundle and take it into the sunlight to better examine the newborn. What if some mark identified the father? What would Big Black Hair do if he discovered it was not his child? How long would Vision Seeker keep their secret? For the moment Raven Wing's fears were put to rest. Vision Seeker did not appear to see the little boy, he had left on a visit to the White Bird band.

After completing his inspection, Black Hair congratulated her on his fine son, kissed her on the forehead and gently placed the precious bundle in the crook of her arm. "We'll call my second son, John," he said.

Raven Wing smiled. "He must also have a Nimpau name." To please her father and Quiet Woman, she called him Young Wolf, the name of her baby brother who had been swept away in the swollen Kimooenim (Snake River).

For Black Hair, life in the long lodge settled down to a tedious routine. From early morning until late at night, the children absorbed Raven Wing's attention. Black Hair was told to get out of the way or brushed aside as though he was not there. The big mountain man found himself longing for the isolation and freedom he had enjoyed on the trap lines. He missed the easy camaraderie of Buck Stone, No Hair Deacon and Hawk Beak Nelson. He detested the cramped life in Lone Wolf's long lodge.

He never was alone with his family. It was like living in a zoo. Everyone watched every move they made, and then loudly voiced their approval or disapproval for the benefit of lodge occupants who had an obstructed view.

Besides suffering the inquisitive stares and disapproving commentaries, the sounds of daily living were enough to ruin one's ears. The shrieks of children, barking of dogs and, at times, 20 or more pestles and mortars pounding kouse root into flour, created more clamor than the forge and boiler factory near the big man's former New England home.

In desperation, Black Hair cleared a piece of land and began to build a regular cabin of his own, a quiet place free from the ever present smell of fish and lodge fire smoke. The building project went slowly. Proper logs for the cabin walls had to be brought from a long distance. Nevertheless, the mountain man patiently continued. Gradually, the cabin began to take form.

Members of the long lodge were aghast at the manner in which the big white man approached the task. He built a platform first. With a sharp hand ax and knife, Big Black Hair planed smooth the rounded surface of the log planking. This alone took him weeks to accomplish. Down from the hillside he brought flat stones and, with a mixture of mud and straw, made an entryway and a fireplace. Villagers looked on in disbelief. What a lot of work. What a waste of time.

Finally, the big man started on the walls, hewing and notching, fitting one log on top of another. When the walls were head high and chinked and watertight, the roof went on. Instead, of using brush and matting like any sensible lodge builder, Black Hair erected a ridge pole. From this centerpiece dozens of smaller poles, held in place by strips of buckskin, extended down to overlap the top layer of logs that formed the walls. Over these platforms of poles were laid overlapping slabs split as thin as the width of a finger. These were held in place by pitch and resins.

On the day after the roof was finished, it rained. The villagers were astonished to find not a drop of water fell inside.

Even so, they went away bemused. People lived together for protection and company. It was not good to go off alone like a solitary family of hibernating bear. Besides, like many tasks this big man did, it was women's work to fix up a lodge.

Only after she heard others speak of the strange log lodge did Raven Wing arrive to visit her mate and watch him toil. She was not impressed. The strange rock thing called "fireplace", where Big Black Hair said they would make their fires and cook, did not look good. She much rather would have the fire in the center of the lodge and smoke hole in the ceiling.

The only one who appreciated Black Hair's labors was Running Turtle. He helped wherever and whenever he could. Sometimes he and Black Hair spent all day planing and smoothing one end of a log. Running Turtle found the big man's quiet, steady company comforting. Although he just had completed his vision quest and discovered his *Wyakin*, the guardian spirit that would protect and guide him through life, it did little to raise him in the eyes of village youth. He had wanted to take the name, Buffalo Slayer. When he announced his intention Lone Wolf scoffed. "Look at you. You're as short and round as a turtle. A name like Buffalo Slayer does not fit you."

Running Turtle sadly realized his father was right. People still made fun of him for his short stature and clumsy manner, so he remained Running Turtle. To escape the taunts of his peers he asked his brother with the black mane if he could help around the cabin. Grateful for any assistance, the mountain man gladly welcomed him. The arrangement was beneficial to both. Working with the big man kept Running Turtle's tormentors at a distance. Besides, Running Turtle found the work interesting. He was learning many helpful things while his former playmates wasted away their time in idleness and games.

Running Turtle was anxious, especially to have the big man teach him how to handle guns so he could slay buffaloes with the deadly accuracy of Tomahawk Head. To satisfy the youth, Black Hair took him away from camp for a shooting lesson. In a vacant draw they set up a target. They fired a couple of shots, then abruptly stopped. Near their target a ragged buckskin clad figure staggered out of the brush. A tangle of dirty hair fell to his shoulders. A scraggly beard, matted and filled with burrs, covered the lower part of his face. It looked as if it never had been washed or combed, yet did not hide a badly inflamed wound. The man's right cheek was red and swollen, the skin so tight it appeared it would split open. Ugly red streaks ran from his hair to the bridge of his nose. He barely was coherent and almost too weak to walk.

Black Hair studied the man. There was something about the tall cadaverous person that was familiar. It took him a while to realize he knew this fellow. This tattered, staggering, wounded creature was the French Canadian trapper, Francois -- the suave, brash trapper who had accosted Raven Wing at the Bear Lake rendezvous.

"Hmm!" Ned grunted to himself. Now that several years had passed, the incident seemed trivial. It was only one of many such happenings that had occurred at rendezvous. Francois was in trouble, perhaps would die if his wounds were left unattended. Raven Wing's mate sat the delirious man down to examine the inflamed flesh. Something terrible had happened to the right side of his face, half his ear was missing, a recently healed scar ran down his cheek. The inflammation came from a wound that had happened fairly recently, perhaps the claw of a mountain cat or that of a bear or perhaps a badger, sniffing blood, had attacked the man while he slept. Whatever caused the wound, it festered and had not been cared for properly. It was yellow with putrefaction. The man himself, skin and bones, probably had not had a square meal in weeks.

Black Hair sent Running Turtle to the pasture to fetch a horse. When Running Turtle returned the big man helped the French Canadian mount the animal and led him toward the village. On the way they encountered Vision Seeker. Vision Seeker pulled his mount to a stop. He stared at the injured, ragged stranger, his gaze hard and cold, then abruptly reined his horse around and galloped away without uttering a word.

"What's the matter with him?" Black Hair Ned muttered to himself. If ever he had seen hate in any man's eyes, it was in those of Vision Seeker. He thought back to the Bear Lake rendezvous. Yes, there had been words exchanged between Vision Seeker and Francois, but it wasn't like Vision Seeker to bear a grudge over a small incident like that.

Although the cabin, only partially was finished, Ned decided it best to take the sick man there. He had trouble enough with Raven Wing without explaining why he chose to play the Good Samaritan to a Hudson's Bay trapper he barely knew. She probably would not understand, but it was something he had to do. It was the code of the mountains to give a fellow member of the mountain man fraternity a helping hand, especially when needed in the depths of the high country wilderness.

The big mountain man built a fire in the newly completed fireplace. From a cut of dried venison he made broth. He forced some of it down the throat of the wounded man. It seemed to give the French Canadian trapper strength. He stared wildly about. He attempted to get to his feet and then sank back.

"You're not going anywhere, leastwise not for awhile," Black Hair Ned said. He examined the inflamed ear and reopened scar that ran down the right cheek. It was said Jedediah Smith had received a similar wound when he tangled with a grizzly. The bear's big jaws had caught his head in their vise like grip. In breaking free the mountain man lost an ear and half his scalp. "I was mighty lucky at that," Jed had said. "I could've lost me head."

Black Hair sent Running Turtle for his pack in the lodge. While the lad was gone Ned boiled water. With a clean cloth he soaked the infected area. Carefully, he pressed yellow pus from the wound and scraped the poisoned tissue away. Running Turtle, who had returned, watched breathlessly. Only old women and medicine people did such things and usually allowed no one to watch, certainly not callow youth.

Black Hair Ned finished by putting a healing salve on the wound and carefully bandaging it. He glanced at Running Turtle and shook his head. He was not at all certain his doctoring would pull the man through. Francois lay on the pallet of bulrushes as lifeless as if dead.

"The stranger has the sickness of death," Running Turtle told Raven Wing later in the long lodge. "Black Hair says he may pass to the other side before morning."

"Humph!" Raven Wing muttered. She was annoyed. She might as well have no mate at all. Ever since her man started building the log lodge she barely saw him except at meal time and at bed time. He did not talk to her or play with the boys as he formerly had done. Except for Granny and Quiet Woman, all the work in caring for the children fell on her. The dark, noisy, smell-laden lodge also was getting on her nerves. Why should her husband stay outside all day and leave her inside? One bright sunny morning she could stand it no longer. She bound Young Wolf in a cradle board and took toddler Buffalo Boy by the hand. The three of them meandered up the trail toward the unfinished cabin.

Raven Wing's mate had his patient sitting outside where he had the benefit of the warm sun. He had replaced the bandage, cut Francois' hair and trimmed the scraggly beard. He finished tending his patient just as Raven Wing and her two baby sons came around a bend in the trail. Delighted, the big man rushed to meet them. He lifted Buffalo Boy to his shoulder and took Raven Wing by the hand. It was only her second visit to the cabin site. He was anxious for her to see all the new work he had done.

Raven Wing followed her mate. For the first time in days she suddenly felt alive. It was so good to be in the sun, out of the gloom, smoke and incessant chatter of the long lodge. She ran an appreciative eye over the log cabin. Living here would have its advantages, she thought. It would keep her away from the disapproving eyes of Lone Wolf who was not satisfied with the way she handled her sons.

As she came near she caught sight of the man sitting in the sun. There was something familiar about the head, the way it tilted to one side, as though listening to the whisper of the wind. The stranger turned. Dazzling teeth flashed in the sunlight. Before Raven Wing could clap a hand to her mouth an animal like cry escaped her lips. She grabbed Buffalo Boy and ran back down the trail. Bobbing in the cradle board, Baby Young Wolf began to howl.

Perplexed, the big man watched them disappear. "Women!" he uttered more to himself than to Francois. "How do you explain them?"

Francois shrugged his shoulders. "Perhaps your woman saw something she did not expect."

"Yeah!" Black Hair Ned said grimly. Indians had long memories. Raven Wing had not forgotten Francois' long ago advances at Bear Lake. He should have thought of that. The man was on the mend. In another week he would send him on his way. To make certain he left the country for good, he personally would see to it Francois attended the trappers' summer fur fair. He wanted to see all of his old friends anyway. The meeting this year was near the headwaters of Wind River. Perhaps Buck Stone would need another trapper for his brigade and take Francois off his hands. Unaware of his mate's unfaithfulness, the big man with the black mane blithely went ahead making plans.

XIV

Oh what a tangled web we weave,
when first we practice to deceive.

Sir Walter Scott, LOCHINVAR

Raven Wing's distress upon seeing her lover again did not go unnoticed by family members. Quiet Woman gave her daughter a sharp look and muttered to herself. "I knew those babies came too fast. She is not herself. Why should the sight of a stranger upset her so?"

"Pay no attention. Young mothers are like flighty colts," Granny said with the wisdom of 80 years. "Her babies are like fledglings. She fears a hawk may come and steal one from the nest."

Running Turtle, who had been with Black Hair when the stranger staggered out of the brush, repeated the story of the event until his mother told him to hush. "Why do you make such a fuss? Talk! Talk! You are worse than a magpie. Go outside. Do something useful. See where this man came from. Why is he wounded? Is he the stealer who takes our provisions and makes strange lights on Snake Hill?"

Running Turtle left the lodge in a huff. Why was everyone carrying on so? Raven Wing looked as sour as if she had swallowed a toad and his mother acted like a snore-nosed bear. How was he going to find out what caused the man to lose half an ear? He already knew where he came from, down the hill and out of brush. Why did no one listen? That was what he had been telling everybody all along.

Running Turtle went to the cabin. Maybe he could find out from the stranger what had happened. Black Hair was on the doorstep mending a bridle. Running Turtle sat down alongside him. He glanced at the cabin door. The stranger was not in sight.

"He's asleep," Black Hair said. "Don't bother him. He

needs all the rest he can get."

"What happened to him? That ear . . . ?

"I don't know and I don't particularly care," Black Hair answered sharply. "Maybe he fell asleep and a porcupine chewed on him. Anything is apt to happen when you live in the open."

"Ah!" Running Turtle looked at Black Hair in surprise. His *soyappo* brother acted as upset as did Raven Wing and Quiet Woman. He always spoke in a quiet, polite manner. For some reason the big man did not want to talk about the stranger. Running Turtle walked away puzzled and hurt. What was the matter with everybody? There was something going on he did not understand. The presence of the stranger who stumbled down off the hill distressed the whole family. Even Vision Seeker acted oddly, coming in only at meal time, looking like a thunder cloud.

Running Turtle returned to where the stranger was first seen. Armed with a club made out of a locust limb, he attempted to follow the stranger's path through the brush and weeds. Days had past. Any tracks the intruder left were obliterated. A few broken branches and flattened weeds caught his eye. They led to an ancient jack rabbit run that ascended the slope toward the rocky, snake-infested hillside. To give himself courage, Running Turtle hummed and chanted a war song. To frighten away snakes, he swung the club back and forth rattling the dry brush.

He topped a rise and came to a hollow surrounded by rocks. A thick-bodied diamondback wriggled from the weeds. It lifted its ugly head, the forked black tongue darting menacingly back and forth. In his fright Running Turtle stumbled over a bush. He quickly picked himself up and glanced fearfully around. At this time of year snakes ran in pairs. He hurried up the hillside only to encounter a barrier of rocks. He was about to turn back when he spotted the stranger's camp at the face of a cave.

Running Turtle banged the club against the ground. Another diamondback scurried out of his path. When it was out of sight, Running Turtle walked closer to inspect the cave. It contained a fire pit, a worn, half-burned saddle blanket, a cooking pot, scraps of cloth and woven hemp. But what caught Running Turtle's attention were the piles of bones. Staring up at him were a row of dog skulls! In the crevices of the rocks were the skeletal heads and vertebrae bones of dozens of snakes. His stomach heaved. He turned about and quickly ran down the slope. At every step he envisioned rattlers coiling to strike. He arrived at the bottom of the hill breathless. He knew no more than before except the stranger had lived on the hillside for months, apparently existing mostly on camp dogs and snakes.

Running Turtle's report sent Lapwai villagers' tongues wagging. Weasel Face declared the stranger was responsible for all the mysterious happenings: flickering lights on the hillside, disappearance of camp dogs, loss of dried fish and venison, burning of the mystery tipi and the strange figure flitting through the village. Most of the villagers agreed with Weasel Face. Youngsters and inquisitive adults walked up the trail to Big Black Hair's cabin to sneak a look at the snake eating man accused of doing all the mischief.

Talk of the stranger barely died away when another topic titillated village gossips. Spokan Garry and Kutenai Pelly had returned to Red River mission school. They took with them a group of Indian youth, one of them came from the Nimpau village of Kamiah. The Black Robes gave him the name Ellis. In years to come the education Ellis received at the mission school would get him named chief of the tribe.

The elders were pleased one of their own finally had been chosen to learn the ways of the Great Spirit Book; they also were impatient. The Black Robes would keep the youth four years. That was a long time to wait to acquire the power of The Book.

"This is not good. What has become of our people? We stand around like robins waiting for worms to pop from the ground. In the old days we would track down this great power and bring it home," the White Bird leader argued. He had come to Lone Wolf's lodge, traveling north with Rabbit Skin Leggings. The two White Bird members sat in a circle with Lone Wolf and Vision Seeker.

They had smoked and now waited for Quiet Woman to prepare food.

Quiet Woman shuffled the cooking pots around with only half her mind on what she was doing. Every day she became more and more concerned about Raven Wing. Since her daughter rushed back from visiting Black Hair's new lodge, she had not acted right. She ignored her babies and spent hours staring at the blank lodge walls. Nothing Quiet Woman did took her out of her trance. Now Lone Wolf wanted eats for these White Birds. Why did he bother with them? When they needed something they always came to Lapwai. They depended on Lone Wolf for everything, buffalo hunts, trading trips and now they wanted him to help them get the white man's Great Spirit Book.

Quiet Woman noisily slammed the cookware down. Why didn't they stay at home and mind their own business? Talk-talk-talk! Did these men not have better things to do? She mixed a bowl of dried buffalo meat and kouse root. It looked unsavory and tasted worse. She did not care. She laid it before them anyway. She was sick and tired of people who came into the lodge at all times of the day expecting to be fed.

Quiet Woman moved away from the circle of men who dipped their hands into the bowl. She did not want to hear complaints about the food and did not need any more talk about the white man's religion. If this *soyappo* Great Spirit Book cleansed people's hearts so thoroughly, why did their bodies smell up the lodge like the stink sack of a skunk? She gave an involuntary shudder. She doubted if the *soyappo* called No Hair On Head bathed once a year. From childhood her people made it a practice to cleanse themselves regularly with sweat baths. If the hairy faced ones' religion revealed how to cleanse their hearts why did it not show them how to cleanse their bodies as well?

In spite of her dour thoughts and dislike of the talk, Quiet Woman found herself listening to the conversation. The White Birds were asking Vision Seeker to lead a party to acquire the Great Spirit Book. Quiet Woman scowled. Second Son should not have spent so much time with the hairy faced trappers. Learning their words and the secrets of talking paper was not good. Because he knew these things, the White Birds insisted he was the best man to make the trip east to a place called St. Louis. Why should Vision Seeker go? Why did not the White Birds go themselves? Crossing the plains was dangerous. It meant traveling through the lands of the Blackfeet, Crow and Sioux. Coup happy warriors would love to kill and plunder trespassers of any tribe.

Quiet Woman's fears were groundless. When asked to lead a party in search of the Great Spirit Book, Vision Seeker declined. "You do me great honor. A person more worthy than I should make this journey." Vision Seeker spoke sincerely. He did not feel up to the task. He also did not want to leave Lapwai. With Raven Wing's lover present, he had to guard her. If he did not, there was no telling what foolish things his wayward sister might do.

Vision Seeker also was aware of the dangers of the journey. To make it safely through the lands of their traditional enemies, he advised that the messengers place themselves under the protection of hairy faced traders who traveled down the Big Muddy (Missouri) in huge steam canoes. His brother, Black Hair, and his trapper friends, Buck Stone, No Hair On Head and Tomahawk Head had made the trip many times. Perhaps they would give the White Birds council and advise the best route to the banks of the River of Many Canoes (Mississippi). He promised to speak about this to his *soyappo* brother, Big Black Hair.

Raven Wing, who sat in the shadows of the long lodge, absently listened to the conversation. Since recognizing her lover at the cabin she had wandered about in a daze. The sight of Francois had stunned her. Her heart had pounded at her brain so hard she thought she would faint. Like a frightened goose, she had run away as fast as she could. In the safety of the lodge she had thrown Baby Young Wolf down and flung herself on the robe covered pallet. Startled by the rough treatment, Baby Young Wolf had begun to howl. Unmindful of his cries, Raven Wing had sat gasping, trying to control her emotions. Desire for her lover was stronger than the remorse she felt over the way she treated her mate. After recovering her senses her first thought had been to run to him, soothe the pain away from the ravaged face. She wanted to meet with her lover; she wanted to feel his touch and reveal to him the beautiful boy they had conceived. "Aiiee!" she groaned.

Granny, shocked at Raven Wing's behavior, had dropped her weaving. Her old bones creaking, she had picked up the baby to shush him. She began to croon a nearly forgotten lullaby:

> *"Shish! Shish! Baby! Sleep!*
> *Your father's gone a-hunting!*
> *Soon! You will have plenty to eat."*

Remembering all of this, Raven Wing berated herself. She almost had given away the secret she promised herself she never would reveal. She now went outside where she could be alone. In vain, she attempted to compose herself. She had to rid her mind of lustful thoughts. She had a fine mate, two healthy sons and an array of possessions that made her the envy of all the women in Lapwai Valley. Yet, the only restraint that kept her from rushing to the wounded man were the watchful eyes of Vision Seeker and the fear of exposing her treachery to Black Hair.

She feared her brother's wrath most, not for herself but for her lover. There was no doubt of it, Vision Seeker had driven Francois from Lapwai. So far he had protected her, keeping her secret safe. It must have been he who burned the tipi, destroying the incriminating dress she left behind.

"Aiiee!" she inwardly groaned. How did she get herself into such a terrible fix? She could not help herself. The tall dark man with the bold black eyes had a hold over her she could not break.

XV

*We believed that the spirit pervades all creatures and that every
creature possesses a soul . . . the tree, the waterfall,
the grizzly bear . . . each is an embodied force,
and as such an object of reverence.*

Ohiyesa, Dakota

Black Hair also was interested in Running Turtle's report on the stranger's campsite. He could not believe his ears. "What was the matter with the man, living off of snakes and dogs? Why didn't he come down, ask for food and have his wound tended like a sensible person?" he ranted. "What could he possibly be afraid of? There's something strange been going on. Let's go up the hill. I want to see what's there."

The mountain man, who had been chopping wood, buried the ax blade in a stump and strode up the slope. Running Turtle followed apprehensively. The way the big man waded through dried weeds and brush could stir up every rattler on the hillside. In front of the cave Big Black Hair strode back and forth, bones and skulls crackling underfoot. "I don't understand it. Why should this guy roost up here like a vulture watching over the valley? From the looks of it, he's been here for months. What brought him here? Why did he stay? It doesn't make sense, rattlesnakes and dogs. Ugh! The idiot must have a cast iron stomach." Big Black Hair strode down the slope so fast Running Turtle had to skid and slide to keep pace.

The discovery was the last straw for mountain man Ned. For days the injured man had strained his patience. More than once he had caught the French Canadian watching him with a contemptuous expression on his face. Then there were the snide remarks. "I see you don't spend much time with your woman," he once commented. Another time Francois said with a sly grin, "It must give a man a good feeling to have two fine sons." He even had the audacity to ask their ages, where they were born and their names.

The man's impertinence and rudeness knew no limits. Not once did he offer a word of thanks or appreciation for all the care and attention his host had tendered. It was almost as if he believed it was due him. Just that morning Francois had complained about his sleeping pallet, the housing and the grub.

"Dammit, I'll be glad to get into the outdoors and breathe fresh air again," he said. "I feel like I have been sleeping on a sack filled with horseshoes, and what I wouldn't give for a good old buffalo steak."

"You're lucky to be alive," Black Hair Ned had retorted.

All the way down the hill the irritations Ned had suffered at the hands of Francois boiled to the surface, until he was ready to throttle the French Canadian. He hated the sight of him. He never should have bothered with him. He should have turned him over to the medicine man. The only bright thought was Francois nearly was healed. Soon he could kick him out, send him on his way. The quicker he got the odious trapper away from Lapwai, the better.

The big mountain man slowed to a walk and kicked angrily at a clump of brush. Two blue-tailed lizards scurried away. Running Turtle caught up and watched his *soyappo* brother apprehensively. He still could not understand why everyone was so upset. The snake eating man had done no great harm; he stole some provisions and killed a few camp dogs, but anyone lost and homeless might do the same. Secretly, Running Turtle enjoyed having him around. Francois' presence gave him a sense of importance. Every time he visited the village he was quizzed about the snake eater. When people wanted news of the stranger, Running Turtle acted as town crier.

Mountain man Ned was not the only one making plans to rid the village of the Hudson's Bay trapper. Long before his *soyappo* brother learned of Francois' hillside campsite, Vision Seeker had figured out the man probably never had left. He must have lived on the hillside all winter. Did he and Raven Wing meet to continue their adulteress love affair? The thought made Vision Seeker wild with fury. He blamed himself. When they first met at the Bear Lake rendezvous, he knew he should have killed the bold-eyed man on the spot. To do it now, would cause all sorts of problems. When the evil man got well and left his brother's lodge, he would strike.

Vision Seeker convinced himself that the lovers had not been able to carry on their illicit affair. If they had, Raven Wing was far more clever than he thought. From the way Raven Wing acted, she was as surprised as anyone that the man Francois was still around. On the day she discovered his presence, Vision Seeker had returned from inspecting the herd and was about to advise Lone Wolf to move the horses to summer pasture when Raven Wing rushed into the long lodge. She was in such a state everyone turned to gawk. He and his father had stopped their conversation and watched in astonishment as Raven Wing threw the babies down and flung herself on the sleeping pallet, uttering a moan. Like the haunting cry of a loon, it had carried the length of the long lodge. Surely, she would not have acted this way if she had known her lover had been in the valley all spring and winter.

Shortly before Running Turtle and Black Hair returned from inspecting Francois' skeleton ridden campsite, Vision Seeker rode high into the barren hills on the opposite side of the valley. At the crest of the ridge he stopped to sit on a flat rock warmed by the sun to watch the horses graze in the valley below. Many Horses often had sat in this same spot to inspect and count the herd. From this vantage point, Vision Seeker had a clear view of Black Hair's cabin. He watched his *soyappo* brother and Running Turtle come down the far hillside. He knew at once where they had been. Was Black Hair suspicious? Had he learned anything? Vision Seeker's conscience bothered him. Was he doing right by keeping his brother in the dark? Should he tell him what really had happened, why the man lost half his ear? No, that would not solve anything, probably cause more trouble. Raven

Wing was his sister. No matter what she had done he could not expose her.

Suddenly an idea popped into Vision Seeker's mind. It was so simple yet so brilliant, momentarily he was stunned. He knew exactly how to solve the problem. He swung up on his horse and galloped downhill and across the valley straight for Big Black Hair's cabin. He should not rush things. Perhaps his idea was not as simple as he thought. What if Black Hair refused to go along? He splashed across the creek and up the hillside. He caught his *soyappo* brother coming out of the cabin. The mountain man glanced up in surprise.

"What brings you here, brother? I haven't seen you in days. From the look on your face you have something on your mind."

Vision Seeker smiled. "You are most wise. Let us talk. Over there." With his chin and lips he pointed away from the cabin. Above all, he had to avoid alerting Francois.

Black Hair came down the steps. They walked a short way in silence. Now that he had his brother by himself, Vision Seeker did not know how to begin. He went over his plan again. "Lone Wolf and the White Birds are sending a party to the River of Many Canoes," Vision Seeker finally blurted.

"They still hanker after missionaries, is that it?" Black Hair mused. "I suppose your father won't rest until they arrive."

Vision Seeker sighed. "Father wants what is best for the people. . . ." Vision Seeker hesitated. Black Hair never had shown enthusiasm for the Bible. When Lone Wolf questioned him about inviting missionaries to come and live in Lapwai Valley, the big man had tipped back his wide brimmed hat and snorted in disgust. "You don't know when you are well off," he said and refused to discuss the matter further.

In the months they spent together in the trapper's quarters the big man listened to Deacon Walton's biblical exhortations with a half smile, as though he was not convinced but did not want to offend his friend by arguing. Black Hair was likely to think the emissaries' journey to St. Louis a foolish waste of time. His Boston brother surprised him.

"You want someone to help them on their way, is that it?"

Vision Seeker remained silent. He should not appear too eager. Everything hinged on his *soyappo* brother. With Black Hair gone, he could deal with Raven Wing's snake eating lover any way he wanted.

"I'll be glad to help," Black Hair said. "In fact I'll travel with them to the rendezvous and see them safely on their way through enemy lands. I'm certain traders traveling east will be happy to have their company." The big mountain man secretly was delighted. It was like killing two birds with one stone. Any help he gave the party bound for St. Louis would please Lone Wolf, and he had planned to rid himself of Francois by going to the rendezvous anyhow. Now he wouldn't have to make up an excuse to mollify Raven Wing and would not have to travel with the obnoxious trapper by himself.

Lone Wolf was pleased indeed with his *soyappo* son's offer to help. He sent a messenger south to inform the White Birds of the good news. A few days later the White Bird leader, Rabbit Skin Leggings and White Bird band elders appeared in Lapwai to lay plans for the trek east. Black Hair sat with them. For hours they smoked and discussed the journey.

"Hostiles should present no problem," the big mountain man assured the council members. He had several friends in mind who would deliver the emissaries directly to the rooms of the American Fur Company in St. Louis. Someone there was certain to help them accomplish their mission. Black Hair also suggested they meet with General Clark who, 25 years previously, had passed through the land of the Nimpau with Meriwether Lewis. The old man lived in St. Louis. He was certain to remember the Nimpau and would do what he could to repay the kindness they had tendered the explorers.

Plans to launch the party on its way rapidly went ahead. Yet, as the day of the departure approached, dissension reared its ugly head. There was dispute as to who should make the journey. Red Elk of the Wallowa band thought he should go. Tamootsin, whose village was west of the Snake, heard about the effort to acquire the Great Spirit Book and wanted to join the emissaries. People who lived around the camas meadows on the Kamiah and Weippe Prairie thought their eloquent leader, Bat Who Flies in the Daytime, should be included and, in Lapwai Valley, a number of youth clamored to make the trip. Meetings were held. Speeches were made and arguments debated. A group of young Lapwai men decided the Lapwai band should send their own delegation to St. Louis to seek the Great Spirit Book. They asked Vision Seeker if he would lead them. Vision Seeker refused. He was getting disgusted with the entire affair.

"The ancients named us Nimpau. Only one party of us should make this journey," he argued. "If two groups of Nimpau appear it will look bad, like we are not one people. As long as we are Nimpau why should we care who makes this trip? If the power of the Great Spirit Book comes to our tribal lands, the Lapwai band will receive its share."

"The White Birds and others will get the power and we will have nothing," the leader of the young men answered. They dispersed to grumble and harangue among themselves.

Finally the day of departure was set. The previous afternoon the White Bird contingent arrived in Lapwai, and camped overnight near the long lodge. Before sunup the chosen emissaries arose, they bridled and saddled their mounts, loaded the pack animals and were ready to start. In spite of dissension among the youth, everyone in Lapwai turned out to see the party of travelers off. Lone Wolf, wearing his special bear claw necklace, solemnly made his way through the gathering carrying the ceremonial pipe. No moment like this should pass without prayer. Clasping the pipe in both hands, Lone Wolf stood facing the dawn. Raising his eyes to the first rays of the sun, he saluted Father Sky, the four directions: east, south, west, north and Mother Earth. He took two puffs and handed the pipe to the White Bird leader. The

White Bird held it high above his and said a silent prayer. Much to the gathering's astonishment, a flock of chattering magpies flew up from a grove of nearby trees. The black and white birds swirled overhead only to disappear into a mist that hung over the river. Vision Seeker shivered. This was not a good omen.

To assure safe passage, amulets were tied to the bridles of the travelers' mounts and sacred objects placed in their saddle bags. Thunder Eyes and other medicine men, who regarded the whole venture as an insult, looked on and scoffed. How foolish to ask the old gods for protection for these messengers who went in search of new gods. This was sacrilege of the worst kind. The people who did these things would suffer in due time, perhaps bring the wrath of the Great Spirit down on the whole tribe.

Among the emissaries chosen to make the journey to St. Louis was Black Eagle, an elderly brave who had visited with Lewis and Clark on the explorers' eastward journey in 1806. He was certain to be remembered by General William Clark. Another elder was Man of the Morning. In the party were the two younger men, Rabbit Skin Leggings, the White Bird leader's friend, and No Horns on His Head, a youth not yet 20. At the last hour another elder, a man from Flathead country, joined the group. He would travel only two days then return to say he was too old to keep up.

Before the ceremony was completed, Black Hair arrived, followed by Francois. Vision Seeker was stunned. Surely his brother was not taking Francois on the journey! It was like inviting a poisonous snake into his lodge. The French Canadian was certain to be deadly with a knife. There would be a dozen nights on the trail when the slippery creature would not hesitate to strike. Vision Seeker felt ill. His plan to deal with Francois had fallen through. His *soyappo* brother would not solve the problem. He was too kind, too soft. He would take the man who seduced his mate to the rendezvous, and set him free. In time, the snake eater would return. What devilment would he do then? The thought was too grim to contemplate.

The waiting crowd studied the stranger who ate snakes and dogs. For many it was the first time to set eyes on the man who had stumbled out of the hillside brush, but he looked far different from the emaciated, delirious person he had been on that day. Much of his ear was missing, but the wound had healed. His face and body had filled out, and he wore a pair of Black Hair's clean buckskins and sat his spare horse. The French Canadian's arrogant eyes gazed back at the curious gathering, a slight sneer on the thin lips.

"All right, if everyone is ready, let's hit the trail." Black Hair raised his arm and pointed to the east. He saluted Lone Wolf and the White Bird leader, and reined his mount up the Kooskooskie. As he passed the gathering he glanced over the faces searching for Raven Wing. He was disappointed. She had not come to see him off.

Until they were well up the trail, Vision Seeker and other horsemen escorted the emissaries and finally said a last farewell. It was not a cheery parting. Just as the two groups separated a dark cloud slid over the barren hills to cover the sun. A chilling breeze swept off the rushing waters of the Kooskooskie. Vision Seeker shivered. He wanted to have a last word with Big Black Hair, but his *soyappo* brother already was well up the trail. He turned back to the village and rode up the hillside. He dismounted at the lookout point where he and Many Horses liked to watch over the herd. He laid against the sun warmed soil to stare at the sky where the dark cloud still hid the sun. From its folds, a shaft of bright light broke through to shine on a field of white. Startled, Vision Seeker sat bolt upright. In the square of white the forms of two men emerged. They lay in narrow rectangular boxes. Each one held a cross in his hand. The figures and boxes grew fainter and fainter until all traces of them disappeared. Only the two crosses remained.

Vision Seeker rubbed his eyes and looked again. "Ah!" he chided himself. The crosses were sailing hawks outlined against a distant cloud. The men and boxes were only in his imagination. Yet, a sense of foreboding gripped him. The cool breeze stiffened. The hawks dipped to disappear beyond the horizon. Rain began to fall. Shivering, Vision Seeker aroused himself. The day was filled with too many signs to dismiss. Did they predict trouble? Would the travelers face perils on the trail? Were Thunder Eyes and the other medicine men right? Were the messengers on an evil mission? Would disaster strike them and the tribe?

Still deeply troubled, Vision Seeker rode toward the village. On the way his sharp eyes picked up a movement in the trees. He reined to a stop. It was gone. Then he saw it again. A figure in buckskin. He grimaced. It was Raven Wing. She had hoped to get a last glance of Francois. Did the woman have no pride at all?

Raven Wing did not see her brother. She was too upset. She had no idea Francois was leaving. She secretly had hoped somehow to show him their beautiful son. The disappointment made her a groan. A pair of blue jays fluttered out of a tree and flew away squawking.

#

Summer passed quickly. The elders who sent the messengers for the Great Spirit Book did not let their interest in this power of the *soyappos* dampen their enthusiasm for the old ways. When salmon came up the streams in bountiful supply, the head of each band called his people together. In a ceremony as old as time, each headman led his followers in a dance around the sun pole. Holding a salmon above his head, he turned in the direction the sun takes as it crosses Mother Earth from east to west.

In Lapwai the ceremony was led by Lone Wolf. "Great Father Sun! Shine down on this fish," he chanted. The gathering joined in to sing words of thanksgiving for the bountiful harvest of salmon. They dug a hole in Mother Earth and offered the fish to her as a gift.

More feasts and ceremonies were held. When deer and other wild game appeared in plenty, the tribe gave thanks and danced. When the berries ripened and were picked and when the harvests of roots and bulbs were completed, the people came together to dance and give thanks. It was such a glorious time, Vision Seeker wondered why his tribesmen felt compelled to send for the Great Spirit Book. They already had all the gifts Mother Earth provided. Did they expect to possess every good thing of the next world, too? Vision Seeker frowned. Desiring too much was not good.

XVI

*Too much kindness to a man is not profitable,
for he becomes ungrateful.*

Turkish Proverb

When final good-byes had been said and the well-wishers departed, the column bound for Wind River rendezvous started up the Lolo Trail. Black Hair Ned ordered Francois to bring up the rear. He was sick of the man and wanted him as far away as possible.

"I'm unarmed," Francois complained. "If hostiles attack I'm a dead pigeon."

"Don't worry. You'll be safe. We're not in enemy territory," Ned replied tersely.

Francois dropped back. He asked Rabbit Skin Leggings if he had a spare gun. The White Bird looked the other way. Francois went to the next man, No Horns on His Head. He brushed past the French Canadian as though he had not heard. Each man in the column refused to speak. Snake eater! Dog eater! The man was unclean. They did not want anything to do with him. His mere presence made them uneasy. He was arrogant and quarrelsome. The disrespectful way he acted toward their leader, Big Black Hair, irked them. It could mean trouble. This was no way to begin a long journey but it was too late to turn back. All they could do was watch and be prepared for whatever happened. They wouldn't be surprised to see the two *soyappo* go for each other like rutting buck elk.

Little Ned was fully aware of the bad example he and Francois set. Yet, he could not bring himself to act otherwise. Since visiting the French Canadian's camp on the hillside he hardly could stomach him. A snake, dog eater and thief . . . Yes, there were times when one did anything to survive but the man had been within a stone's throw of a village of friendly Indians. Rather than seek help he had sneaked in to steal and plunder, acts repugnant to the true mountain man.

The hillside findings also raised a myriad of questions. How did the damned fellow get there? What possessed him to spend endless months in that snake infested place? How did he come by his wounds? He had quizzed him, but the fellow was as elusive as the reptiles he ate. From what little he could glean, the French Canadian had been on a trip up the Kooskooskie. His horse shied, dumping him into a pile of jagged rocks. Little Ned had a feeling the story was false. A man did not lose half an ear from getting bucked off, but why should he tell such an unbelievable story? There was an unwholesome, uncanny mystery surrounding the entire affair.

After an hour on the trail, Little Ned turned in the saddle to look back. Francois rode along sullenly, a scowl on his face. He glanced up. For a brief second their gazes locked. Even at that distance, the big mountain man could see hate smoldering in the French Canadian's dark eyes.

Little Ned turned back to face the front. He did not look forward to the trip. If he hadn't wanted to get rid of Francois so badly, he would have refused to go. For days Raven Wing had behaved strangely. She was like a fledgling, ready to try its wings and fly away from its nest. He finally reasoned the presence of Francois had her upset. He attempted to assure her, there was nothing to fear. He was on guard day and night. She had turned away as if she didn't believe him.

He had said good-bye to Raven Wing in the long lodge. It was not a satisfactory leave taking. As usual, everyone listened and watched. Raven Wing had been more nervous than ever and acted like a skittish colt. She was worried about her younger son. She claimed he had a bad cough. That didn't make sense, the youngster was as lively as ever, his sharp brown eyes bright as a chipmunk's.

For the first time ever, Little Ned had resented his young son. There was a bond between him and his mother that did not exist with Michael. The knowledge made him sad. To make up for Raven Wing's neglect, he had ruffled First Son's hair, taken him by the hand and led him outside. He was a handsome, stout fellow who looked so manly in his little fringed buckskin shirt and pantaloons that Little Ned, himself, had stitched for the boy. The mountain man's heart felt like it would burst with pride.

"While I'm gone, you're the man of the family," he had said. "Can you handle the job?"

The boy did not understand but solemnly nodded anyway. He gave his father a shy smile and looked at the fascinating horses that stood nervously waiting, jerking their heads and champing at their bits. For a moment the big mountain man had hesitated. It was as if a powerful hand had held him fast. He knelt down to better study the boy's trusting face. Would he be safe? He pulled the boy to him and held him tightly. Why didn't Raven Wing love this lad like she should? He searched the memories of the past but no answer came to him. It was just one of those things that happened. Even in the animal world it was not uncommon for a mother to favor one offspring over another.

Little Ned released his son and had mounted up. He still had to get Francois who waited at the cabin. He gave Michael a last wave and reined across the creek. The boy called to him, but the noise of the horse threshing through the water swept the words away unheard. When the mountain man turned back for a final look, Michael had disappeared into the lodge. He felt hurt. Not a one of his family had been there to see him ride away.

Ned rode far ahead of the column. He was in a hurry to complete the journey. There was so much to do when he returned to Lapwai. Somehow he had to make Raven Wing happy. Perhaps at the rendezvous he would find something that would please her, maybe a furnishing for the cabin that soon would be their home. Also, the quicker he arrived on Wind River the sooner he would get rid of Francois. The emissaries disliked Francois and he disliked them. Any moment one or the other might get out of hand and shed blood.

The nights were the worst. Even though surrounded by friendly Nimpau, Little Ned could not let down his guard. The cold stare of Francois followed his every move. The French-Canadian made no attempt to help make camp but seemed to take pleasure in getting in the way. After everyone had rolled up in their sleeping robes, Francois continued to sit upright. From the dark, taciturn mask of a face, his watchful eyes glowed like those of a wild beast. Although he kept his loaded Hawken close at his side, Little Ned did not feel safe. Night after night he barely got a few minutes of sleep.

In spite of Little Ned's fears, the journey passed safely. Francois continued his surly behavior but kept to himself. As the days passed he acted as though, he too, was anxious to get the trip over. However, at the rendezvous site, Little Ned's party encountered utter confusion. Supply trains from the east had not arrived. Disgruntled trappers sat in groups complaining to anyone who would listen. When Little Ned and his party rode in they uttered a round of good-natured curses. They thought they were advance riders of a pack train from St. Louis.

"Consarn it, where're all the goods?" a white-bearded trapper tartly asked. "We been sittin' here dry as ducks in a desert waitin' fer somethin' ta wet our whistles; anythin'll do. Moonshine, sour mash, corn squeezin's, we ain't perticular."

"Yeah, what're yuh doin' here? Yuh ain't even got any skins." A trapper named Slim finally extracted Little Ned from the crowd and took him into his lean-to where another old timer named Gus the Wolfman sat patching a hunting shirt.

"So yer outta this racket, are yuh?" Gus asked. He wore a capote made of wolf skins which gave him the name, Wolfman. "Well, yer damned smart. Look at us. We're at the mercy of those damned Easterners. All those galoots have ta do all winter is count their money and stock up fer the comin' summer. Now, look at 'em. They ain't here, probably stopped ta powwow with the Blackfeet or Crow an' didn't give us a thought. If they ever git here we ought to string 'em up by the nose so by Jehoshaphat next time they'll be on their toes."

"Yeah!" agreed a rough looking old codger Little Ned didn't know. He wore a bearskin cap and puffed on a sour smelling pipe that made him sputter and cough. "I been reduced ta smokin' dry weeds, don't satisfy worth a damn."

A third man took a chaw and spit, nailing a running ant. "What a pitiful state this trappin' business has become. Ah, I say, lookit! A bunch of flop ears're comin'. Maybeso, these folks'll hev some blinkin' firewater."

These newcomers were none other than Buck Stone and his partners. No Hair Deacon was the first to spot Little Ned. "Well, I swan. Look what the cats've dragged in!" He jumped off his mule and clapped his big trapper friend on the back. "By granny, yer the only smart one around. Look at our packs. They're 'bout as flat as one of Hawk Beak's flapjacks. "Where's the little woman and thet strappin' lad? Yuh mean yuh didn't bring yer family? An' who the hell's thet? Ain't he the Frenchie, the fella yuh had a dust-up with at Bear Lake rendezvous? How come yer travelin' with him? He's lost half a' ear. What the hell's goin' on? Didja take a swing at him with yer hatchet?"

Little Ned attempted to answer but Buck Stone and Hawk Beak descended. More greetings. More questions. More trappers drifted in. Later the big mountain man set up camp with Buck Stone's band. Rabbit Skin Leggings and his companions threw up shelters on one side of the creek, the trappers on the other bank. Little Ned introduced the four emissaries and explained their desire to continue east to St. Louis.

Reluctantly, he also introduced Francois. Now that he had met up with his old friends, Little Ned had second thoughts about asking Buck Stone to take the truculent French Canadian on as a trapping partner. It was not fair to push the insolent snake eater onto an enemy, let alone his best friends.

For some reason Buck Stone took an interest in the French Canadian. He asked him about his trapping experience. Francois, after a surly start, began to talk freely of winters spent in the

Canadian wilderness and Northern Rockies.

Buck was impressed. "We're thinking on going north of the Flathead range, maybe Kutenai, do you know that country?"

Francois nodded. "Yep, know it like the back of my hand. That's Hudson's Bay country. I wouldn't suggest going there. They don't take to free trappers coming in, neither do the Blackfeet. They can be mighty feisty."

Hawk Beak, who had been listening, broke in. "They haven't seen the likes of real trappers. We'll slip in an' out before they'll know what hit 'em."

Francois gave Hawk Beak a skeptical glance. "If you're thinking of going into that country you'd better have good firearms and know how to use them."

"Don't worry 'bout us. What 'bout yerself?" Hawk Beak retorted.

"Give me that Hawken an' I'll show you." Expertly, Francois threw the long barreled rifle to his shoulder and shot at a magpie flying overhead. The head of the bird disappeared in an explosion of feathers. The rest of the body fluttered down to land in a gray bearded trapper's lap. "Hell's fire! Now I've seen everything. It's rainin' headless magpies," the old man exclaimed.

"Yeah! Well yer passable." Hawk Beak observed dryly. "Guess we'd better not ask if yuh kin use a knife. More'n likely yuh'd demonstrate by liftin' some galoot's scalp."

The next morning Francois again asked to borrow Hawk Beak's Hawken. When Hawk Beak protested, he promised to bring back fresh camp meat. Reluctantly, Hawk Beak let him have the rifle and powder and shot.

"What's with him?" Hawk Beak asked Little Ned. "He don't have a weapon and nothin' else as far as I kin see. He was a real dandy at Bear Creek, riding a big black with a saddle so heavy with silver it took a derrick to heave it on a horse's back. Ain't thet horse an' rig yers? Sure looks it."

"Yep, it's mine," the big trapper said, then told the story of Francois stumbling out of the Lapwai hills. "There's something mighty mysterious about the fellow. There he was within an arrow flight of an Indian village but didn't seek help. Then when I fixed him up, he acted like I had done him a disfavor. I have a feeling he's hiding something -- something that has to do with me."

"What do yuh suppose happened to thet ear? Looks almost like someone took a chaw out of it?" Hawk Beak speculated. "But I'll be consarned if he cain't shoot. I 'spect I'll have to try him out. Yuh plannin' on takin' him on, Buck?"

"Dunno, don't especially like the sound of him. Let's see if he comes back with something for the pot."

Near dusk Francois returned. From the saddle hung the carcasses of two antelope. He swung down and handed Hawk Beak his rifle. "Would've had another kill but your Hawken pulls a bit to the left."

#

The encampment of trappers who had come to replenish their supplies and sell their winter catches, grew more furious by the day. With no trade goods there was little reason to stay. One morning Gus the Wolfman and his trappers packed up and left. In the afternoon another disgruntled band of men drifted away. Then a wholesale evacuation occurred. Even Buck Stone said it was time to move on. He made arrangements with Lucien Fontenelle to take their pelts down the Missouri River and bank their money in St. Louis.

"I reckon that's the best way out of this mess," Buck said. "If we're going up in the tall timber we've got to get moving. Snow will be up to our belt buckles before we know it."

"Taking Francois with you?" Little Ned asked.

"Yeah, we'll give him a try. I have my doubts about him but he knows the country and has a dead eye. I would rather have you, want to change your mind and come along?"

The big man shook his head. "Can't. I'm a married man, must take care of the family."

Nevertheless, with a heavy heart, Little Ned watched his

friends prepare to depart. He let Francois take his extra horse and riding equipment. The arrogant French Canadian didn't utter a word of thanks or show any appreciation for having been taken in and nursed back to health. Instead, as he mounted to ride away, he looked back to give his benefactor a smug glance of disdain. Little Ned had the distinct feeling his Good Samaritan efforts would one day return to haunt him.

The big trapper had good reason to be apprehensive. Francois finally was free to give vent to the rage that consumed him. He slashed viciously at the gift horse, drawing blood. Bitter rage flooded up nearly to choke him. Every hurt and indignity that had been caused by this big mountain man Indian people called "Black Hair", floated to the surface.

"Aagh!" the furious French Canadian swore to himself. One of these days that shock of black hair would hang from his personal coup stick. Even the loss of half his ear, he blamed on the big trapper. Then, there was the death of his horse. On fleeing into the hills, it had broken a leg and he had to shoot it. To keep from starving, he was forced to butcher the beautiful body and eat a haunch -- every torturous bite increasing the rage that filled his heart.

Not only did he lose the horse, but also the intricately silver decorated saddle which was his pride and joy. After leaving what remained of his horse's carcass, largely consumed by coyotes and buzzards, he had lugged the saddle with him as long as he could, then, to stave off starvation, was forced to cut it into bits and boil the leather. The silver he had hidden in the hills. One day he would go back. Ah, yes, . . . when . . . the thought of sweet revenge made his thin lips curve into a cruel smile.

XVII

Ye shall seek me, and shall not find me:
and where I am, thither ye cannot come.

Jesus, John 7:34

While the trappers voiced their frustrations and made plans to leave, the emissaries bound for St. Louis patiently waited. Big Black Hair introduced Rabbit Skin Leggings and his companions to Lucian Fontenelle, leader of a brigade of American Fur Company trappers bound for St. Louis. Fontenelle, was a man of few words. Because of his reticent nature and educated talk, some thought him a snob. Actually, he had a big heart. He sympathized with the emissaries' plight. He took to Rabbit Skin Leggings with his big face and dark intelligent eyes. Here was a man who thought deeply, a committed person who would not accept defeat.

Fontenelle knew Indian nature better than most of his counterparts. He had an Indian wife and named his first son Logan, after the famous chief of the Mingo tribe. He also was Roman Catholic. He understood the Nimpau's desire to acquire the Great Spirit Book. He spoke to Rabbit Skin Leggings of the Long Robes in St. Louis. He would see that the emissaries met with the bishop who would give them audience. He knew General Clark. He would accompany the emissaries to his offices.

However, Lucian Fontenelle voiced apprehension to Little Ned. "It is dangerous," he said. "These people don't know what they're in for. Accustomed to living in the highlands of the Northwest, I don't know how they'll manage wintering in the lowlands of the Mississippi River Valley. It won't be easy for them to adjust to the climate and our way of living."

Fontenelle knew of what he spoke. His own wife was never comfortable in the house he provided. For months at a time she would leave to return to her father's tipi lodge. "I'll be happy to take these fellows along but they're in for plenty of surprises," he again cautioned Little Ned. "Strange food, different drinking water, surrounded by four walls, living cheek to jowl with strangers, who knows how it will affect them, especially the two older men. Hell, they could take sick and die. I'm not even used to it. Each time I come home after a spell out west I get a gut ache, run for the outhouse like my bowels were on fire."

"They've set their minds on going," the big mountain man said. "If you won't take them, they'll be worse off. They'll go by themselves."

"Yep, that's the hell of it. They've set their minds on bringing back the Great Spirit Book and they won't stop until they do it. The poor innocents. It's like throwing Daniel into the lion's den. Maybe, like him, they'll get lucky and do the impossible."

The previous year, 1830, William Sublette had made history by using wagons to haul supplies to the summer rendezvous from St. Louis. Sublette started out with 81 men mounted on mules, 10 high-sided Murphy wagons drawn by five mules each, and several lighter wagons, called Dearborns, with only one mule pulling. Old timers thought Sublette crazy. Wagons had no place in the mountain wilderness. Yet, in the following decade one caravan of wagons after another would be crossing the continent. Sublette had shown it could be done.

Fontenelle's eastbound caravan in 1831 included some of the same wagons that had made the first trip west. Instead of supplies and trade goods, they were loaded with bales of pelts. The emissaries, who looked on these strange contraptions as "land canoes", rode out front to avoid the dust churned up by the iron-tired wheels. Soon, other discomforts were encountered. From the cool green mountains, the column descended into great plains, barren of trees. The air was hot and humid. The rushing streams they were accustomed to, filled with cold, clear water, were replaced with warm, muddy water that barely moved and was bitter to the taste. They ran into Indian bands who lived in huts made of mud, weeds and brush. They were warned to stay away from these people. They carried diseases that were fatal to newcomers from the west.

In St. Louis, Fontenelle kept his word. He took the emissaries to the Roman Catholic cathedral where he introduced them to Bishop Joseph Rosati. The unsophisticated Indians were overwhelmed by the trappings of this man of God and the great medicine lodge in which he held forth. They did not understand the sign of the cross he made over their heads nor the strange language he used in conducting the ceremonies. The words were unlike any they heard coming from the lips of their trapper and trader companions.

Then, as Fontenelle feared, a strange illness struck the two older men. Black Eagle and Man of the Morning took to their deathbeds. To give them spiritual comfort, the Catholic fathers placed a cross in each dying man's hands. After they died, Man of the Morning and Black Eagle, still holding the crosses, were buried in the church graveyard.

Rabbit Skin Leggings and No Horns on His Head, were heartbroken. They walked away from the cemetery in silence. They came to the wide river the *soyappos* called "Mississippi" and watched the turgid water with eyes blinded by tears. Darkness fell; still they remained on the river bank. The sound of the waters rushing on the way to the sea had a soothing effect. When the first fingers of dawn appeared Rabbit Skin Leggings glanced at the wan face of No Horns on His Head and quickly looked away. It was unkind to observe one's grief. He turned from the river to brace himself for the painful days ahead.

"We go now," he said. "The elders would not be pleased if we do not complete our mission."

They wended their way back to the big lodge of the Long Robes. The men in black prepared them a meal. The Indian guests were too sick at heart to eat but politely consumed what was put before them. What were they to do? The two elders they had counted on for counsel were gone. They were young, inexperienced, in strange surroundings and ignorant in the ways of the people. The Long Robes, sensing their distress, did their best to help. They sympathized with them, prayed for them but they made it known they had no people to send west to instruct the Nimpau in the secrets of the Great Spirit Book.

Rabbit Skin Leggings and No Horns on His Head quietly talked things over. "We must do what we came to do," Rabbit Skin Leggings said. "If the Long Robes won't help, we must find people who will."

Each young man packed his pitiful possessions in a blanket roll and, after thanking his hosts, left the lodge of the Long Robes. They stopped on the way to stand over the graves of Black Eagle and Man of the Morning. They murmured silent prayers asking spirits of the elders for guidance, then the youths made their way down cobblestone streets, aghast at the crowds, the noise and confusion. In the center of the city, they stood helplessly on a street corner looking this way and that, until one of Fontenelle's trappers recognized their plight and came to their rescue.

Although busy planning and preparing for the following summer's trip back to the Rocky Mountains, Fontenelle took time to introduce Rabbit Skin Leggings and No Horns on His Head to General William Clark. The old man, who 25 years previously had visited the Nimpau homeland, greeted the two youths kindly but was of little practical help. Although he was superintendent of Indian affairs in St. Louis, he explained his jurisdiction did not extend to the lands of the Northwest.

Since they had no where else to go, Rabbit Skin Leggings and No Horns on His Head hung around the offices of the American Fur Company. Unaccustomed to the daily presence of Indians, the company employees were nervous. They avoided the two Nimpau as much as possible. No one bothered to take the time to talk to them or understand their needs.

Rabbit Skin Leggings and No Horns on His Head did not give up. They had come to recruit teachers of the Great Spirit Book and did not intend to return without them. They cornered anyone who would give them a few minutes. Soon people dodged into convenient doorways to avoid them or rushed past too important and full of business to stop. Self-righteous folk who wanted to add to their score in the playing field of the Lord, heard of their plight and sought them out. These sanctimonious individuals, more interested in embellishing their own souls than saving the souls of their fellow man, told of the magnificent glories of the Great Spirit World. They spoke through interpreters who neither understood the word of God nor the Nimpau language. These misguided zealots informed the awestruck youths there was a star brighter than the sun that lighted the path to a wondrous place called "heaven". The light, they said, was the secret power of The Book. Upon death those who possessed this mysterious power would go to heaven where there was no pain and the streets and lodges dazzled with silver and gold.

The gullible young men listened with open mouths. What they did not understand they filled in for themselves. Late into the night they discussed what they learned until they could repeat every word by heart. The more Rabbit Skin Leggings and No Horns on His Head learned, the more they realized they could not return home until this great power was in their hands.

In early spring the large steam canoe that would take the two Nimpau tribesmen up the Big Muddy on the return journey to their homeland, made ready to leave. The emissaries had been given copies of The Book but what good were they? They could not read and neither could their people. They needed teachers called "missionaries" but no one agreed to come, not even the Long Robes who had treated them so kindly. Rabbit Skin Leggings and No Horns on His Head faced the terrible task of returning to their homeland in disgrace, empty-handed.

The big steam canoe was loaded. Any moment embarking whistles would blow, the gangway disappear, engine bells jingle and the nose of the river craft would plow into the river. Rabbit Skin Leggings and No Horns on His Head were at their wits ends. How could they leave? How could they disappoint their good friends back home? Still, they did not give up. They made one last desperate plea for help. Following the customs of their tribe, they carefully memorized words of truth and eloquence. They went to the offices of the American Fur Company to deliver a last appeal for teachers of the Great Spirit Book. It was a plea that would not receive immediate response but, in time, would forever change the lives of Northwest Indian tribes.

A newspaper man who was present transcribed the words spoken that day. Unfortunately, he was not able to appreciate the eloquent nuances or fully understand all that was said, but he managed to convey a message that, in one form or another, would be delivered in Sunday pulpits all over the east. The reporter was too busy writing to see who said what, but this is the crux of what he recorded:

"We come to you over a trail of many moons from the setting sun. We come seeking the light of your Great Spirit Book, for our people dwell in darkness. We made our way to you with strong arms, through many enemies and strange lands, hoping to carry much back to our people. We now leave. Our strong arms are weary. Our strong arms are empty. Two fathers who came with us, men of many winters and many wars, we leave to sleep the big sleep by the waters of your River of Many Canoes.

"Our people sent us to get the book of the Great Spirit, and teachers you call 'missionaries' to tell us its secrets. You offer us many things, but you do not give us what we need most, those who will help us understand The Great Spirit Book's mysteries. When we tell our people that we have failed in our mission, no word will be spoken. One by one they will rise, and go away in silence. Our people will die in darkness. Your Great Spirit Book's secrets will lie hidden beneath its covers. Without its light, how can our people see the pathway to the place you call 'heaven'?"

Finished, Rabbit Skin Leggings and No Horns on His Head stood silent. Their faces impassive, their dark eyes challenging the crowd. The audience shifted uncomfortably. The words these aborigines spoke were like arrow shafts aimed at the heart. The Christian listeners were abashed. Still, no one came forward or said a word in reply. Sick at heart, the two emissaries departed. The mission which their tribal brothers had launched with such high hopes, had failed.

On March 26, 1832, the Indian youth boarded the Yellowstone, the American Fur Company steamboat that carried supplies for the annual trappers' rendezvous. Before leaving St. Louis No Horns on His Head took sick. To protect himself from the damp river cold, he wandered about the large steam canoe with blankets wrapped around his shoulders. To ward off evil spirits in the enemy lands of the Crow, Blackfeet and Sioux, he wore two strands of lucky beads around his neck and a charm fastened to a braid in his hair. His precautions were in vain. Near the mouth of the Yellowstone River, No Horns on His Head went to his reward and was buried on the bank of the river Indians called "The Big Muddy".

The death of his last companion weighed heavily on Rabbit Skin Leggings. He had to return home and face the elders alone. He had to dash their hopes by reporting failure. He had to explain why all of his companions had fallen by the trail, why he, alone, was the only survivor. It was more than he could bear. Rabbit Skin Leggings journeyed as far as buffalo country where he encountered a party of Flatheads.

"Why go home?" the Flathead leader asked. "Stay a while with us and hunt the buffalo."

Rabbit Skin Leggings succumbed. A hunt was what he needed to revive his spirits. Most of all, it would put off the dreaded moment when he had to announce the mission's failure to the tribe. Again, bad luck dogged the White Bird emissary. He wintered in buffalo country hunting with his Flathead friends. The following spring found the hunting party camped in Blackfeet territory. A roaming band of Blackfeet set up camp nearby. Itching to make coups, youthful members of the Flathead party decided to raid the Blackfeet herd. Rabbit Skin Leggings rode with

them. The riders approached the Blackfeet camp through a narrow canyon. In the depths of the canyon, Blackfeet warriors lay
waiting. They chased the raiding party into a cul de sac where
they methodically slaughtered them. A Flathead member of the
raiders who had become separated from the group, discovered
the gruesome killing grounds. In a frenzied orgy the Blackfeet
had beheaded their victims. Among the headless bodies was that
of the ill-fated White Bird, Rabbit Skin Leggings.

RABBIT SKIN LEGGINGS

From painting by George Catlin, 1832 -- courtesy Smithsonian Institute

XVIII

All happy families resemble one another;
every unhappy family is unhappy in its own way.
Leo Tolstoy, ANNA KARENINA

In the Nimpau homeland, the elders who sent Rabbit Skin Leggings, No Horns on His Head, Man of the Morning and Black Eagle to St. Louis, marked each day that passed on bleached lengths of buckskin. The black marks inched across the white background straight as a bear heading for a honey tree. Families in the long lodge also kept track. Every night after the evening meal, youths vied for the honor of marking the calendar. The watchers estimated the distance the emissaries had traveled and attempted to guess what they had done that day.

"I dreamed they camped at a place called 'split rock' (Devil's Gate)," Granny announced one evening. "They have crossed the high mountains and are on the flat lands. From here on the trail is dusty and water not good."

"What do you know about it, old woman?" Weasel Face, who overheard, scoffed. "How many treks have you made across the flat lands?"

Granny did not reply. She did not like Weasel Face any better than did her son, Lone Wolf. He talked when he should be silent. What Weasel Face did not know was once she had been a prisoner and slave of the Cheyenne. She had spent more seasons than she could count in their camps. In those days the Cheyenne people were always on the move, traveling from the south where rivers carved great red cliffs in rocky barren land, to the north where thick dark forests cloaked sacred mountains called "Black Hills" and "Bighorns". Granny made no attempt to put Weasel Face straight. He was not worth the trouble.

As the Season of Deep Snow faded away and the Season of Melting Snow arrived, the Lapwai elders who had sent the emissaries on their way became impatient. Along with the Flatheads, they decided to form a welcoming committee. A select group of riders would meet the four Nimpau men and the missionaries who would accompany them. The elders discussed the matter with Big Black Hair. He assured them, since the messengers departed from the rendezvous with Fontenelle's brigade, they undoubtedly would return with his supply train. This year the summer fur fair was scheduled to take place at Pierre's Hole.

Soon elaborate plans were underway to greet Rabbit Skin Leggings, No Horns on His Head, Black Eagle and Man of the Morning. The emissaries and the missionary guests would be met at the Pierre's Hole rendezvous site, and accompanied to the Nimpau homeland with great pomp and ceremony. Pierre's Hole was an appropriate setting for launching the triumphal march. Towering above it to the east were the cathedral like peaks called *Les Trois Tetons*. The central peak, Grand Teton, was a landmark known by tribes from the Great Plains to the Pacific Ocean. It was like a guardian sentinel, watching over the region. The sight of it gave travelers a spiritual, comfortable feeling. If one could see the Grand Teton, one never was lost.

The three Tetons and surrounding foothills produced one of Mother Earth's most precious gifts; cold, clear waters welled up to form streams which flowed in all directions. The Yellowstone River started north, through the land of the Big Smokes, to form the headwaters of the Big Muddy. To the south Green River began its journey to join the Colorado on its way to the Gulf of California. To the west, Henry's Fork, Lewis Fork and other tributaries of the Snake, started their trek to the Columbia and the Pacific.

At first it was decided only a few men of importance should journey to Pierre's Hole. The camas meadows people selected Bat Who Flies in the Daytime, to represent them. Because of the eloquent way he spoke, he was called "Lawyer" by the Redcoats of Hudson's Bay. Also from the camas meadow region came Tackensuatis, the bumptious warrior who soon would gain fame with the name, "Rotten Belly".

The choice of the two men was not unanimous. There was much grumbling. Why should these two Kamiah people have the honor of escorting the Great Spirit Book and its teachers to Nimpauland? Lame Horse, the White Bird leader, said he had to be included. Lone Wolf insisted a member of his band should be present. He had no intention of allowing Lawyer, Tackensuatis and Lame Horse to take credit for bringing this great power to the Nimpau. His *soyappo* son, Black Hair, had sent the messengers on their way. It was only right he be a member of the party that went to escort them home.

Lone Wolf also was anxious to have his son-in-law leave for other reasons. Since the mountain man had completed the cabin and taken Raven Wing there to live, he hardly ever saw his two grandsons. Lone Wolf did not like to visit the log cabin. In his opinion, it was not a proper home. The familiar odors of fish and smoke were absent. It was quiet: no barking dogs; no women pounding kouse root; and it was too far away to enjoy the music of the creek. Besides, one could not ride up and tether a horse at the lodge entrance. Running the length of the place was a pole fence that protected a patch of worthless plants Black Hair called "flower garden".

By sending Black Hair with the welcoming committee, Lone Wolf hoped Raven Wing would bring her sons to stay in the long lodge. This would give him the opportunity to instruct them in the ways of his people. He wanted to teach the boys the legends and customs of the old days. He wanted them to respect the traditions of the Nimpau. He had the great fear his grandsons would grow up to think and act like their Boston father. For many moons, this onerous thought had weighed heavily on his mind.

The mountain man understood his father-in-law's desires and his fears. He had offended Lone Wolf by taking Raven Wing and his sons away. To make matters worse, Running Turtle also deserted the home lodge. During the warm weather Lone Wolf's youngest son slept under a shelter on the back side of the cabin.

He also earned his father's disapproval by working in the garden Lone Wolf disdained. The miracle of sowing seeds to bring plants sprouting from Mother Earth entranced Running Turtle. Often he sat for hours watching the tender shoots inch out of the ground. Sometimes he lazed away a full day watching butterflies and bees flit from one flower to another. The touch of Mother Earth comforted him. To get close to her, he removed his moccasins to feel the warm soil between his toes. For some reason he could not explain, the act gave him a wondrous sense of peace and contentment, as though, like the plants, he drew strength and stature from the earth on which he stood.

The number of people desiring to make the trip to Pierre's Hole quickly multiplied. Every able-bodied man in the tribe seemed to want to greet the missionaries and accompany them to the Nimpau homeland. By the time the column arrived at the rendezvous site, almost 1,000 Nimpau and Flatheads had joined up. The awaiting trappers and traders were aghast. It was the greatest gathering of Indian people, ever, for a summer fur fair. The vast array of tipi lodges covered a huge meadow and disappeared into a stand of tall spruce and pine. In addition to the Nimpau and Flathead contingents, Shoshones, Utes and even a band of Crow set up lodges in the valley below the majestic Three Tetons.

Buck Stone and his small brigade of trappers were on hand. When the vast array of horsemen arrived, they gawked like schoolboys, stunned at the sight of Little Ned leading the great band of Indian riders from west of the Rockies. After the first ribald greetings and backslapping, the big mountain man's trapper friends wanted to know what it was that brought him and his army of horsemen to the rendezvous.

"'Pon my word, I ain't never seed a gatherin' like this," No Hair Deacon declared. "Every Injun in the Northwest must be here." He forgot himself and took off his fur cap to run a hand over his hairless head. A deer fly took that moment to descend and light on the shiny, pink surface and thrust its bill into the tempting flesh.

"Gol damn! Take 'em home! They brought these flyin' buggers armed with stingers like porcupine needles." He slapped at the fly. Unharmed, it buzzed away. "Look at it. It sucked enuff blood ta last the varmint a week."

"Yuh crazy galoot, why didja take yer cap off? Yer lucky a flock of geese didn't flop on yer noggin. Yer pate looks like the surface of a scummy pond," Hawk Beak scolded.

The familiar banter made Little Ned feel right at home. When Buck Stone suggested he make camp with them, he promptly accepted. The only sour note was the smug French Canadian, Francois. When he came in from tethering the horses, he greeted the big mountain man with a curt nod. All evening he sat by the campfire sharpening a skinning knife. When he finished, with a snap of the wrist he threw the knife straight at a nearby tree trunk where the blade quivered until he pulled it out. He then strode away making directly for the Indian camp.

"What's the matter with him?" Little Ned asked. "He acts like I carried the plague."

"Don't pay him no mind," Hawk Beak said. "He's been like thet all winter, but he sure kin find beaver. We had one of our best catches ever. He ain't too sociable, an' never ask him about thet ear. I did. He damn near lifted me hair."

"Yeah, somethin's eatin' on him," No Hair Deacon observed. "He keeps by hisself. Sometimes I git the feelin' he's got a hate fer the whole human race. We got inta a little dust-up with a party of Blackfeet. He must've shot a dozen. He went around scalpin' an' choppin' at every carcass he could find. Brought back a string of scalps, hung 'em up an' cured 'em like beaver pelts."

That night, when the camp grew quiet, Francois returned. Little Ned, half asleep, watched him prepare for bed. Francois planted his knife in the ground at the head of his sleeping robe. He took off his moccasins and placed them on either side of it. He examined the load in his rifle and carefully placed it within easy reach. Then, before lying down, he glanced around at each sleeping form, his gaze resting longest on Little Ned.

The trappers awakened the next morning to find Francois gone. After a leisurely breakfast of pan bread, bacon and coffee, Little Ned excused himself and went in search of old friends. Every trapper in the west seemed to be on hand. Young Jim Meek was there. So were the Sublette brothers, Milton and William. David Jackson and Tom Fitzpatrick were camped together. They spoke quietly of the previous Fourth of July when they had been with their friend, Jedediah Smith. Jed, who always carried a Bible and said his prayers as regular as clockwork, had been killed.

"Yep, 'twas on the Cimarron. We hadn't seen a speck of water fer three days," Jackson explained. "Ol' Jed spied a dry hole an' was diggin', tryin' ta hit wet. A band of Comanche came lopin' over the hill. Shot him dead afore he could bring his Hawken ta bear. Poor ol Jed, all his prayin' an' Bible readin' finally let him down."

The news hit the trapper assembly hard. Jedediah Smith was considered invincible. In his early years, he had been attacked by a grizzly. Although the bear clamped his powerful jaws on Jed's head, tearing off half his scalp and one ear, the hardy mountain man had survived. Three years later, while trapping in Oregon's rugged Umpqua country, Jedediah's brigade of trappers was jumped by a war party. Twenty-four of his men were slain. Horses, furs, trapping gear, everything was lost. Miraculously, Jedediah and one horse survived.

"People been makin' fun of my Bible readin an' prayin' fer years," Jedediah said afterward. "But I tell yuh, when 24 unbelievers die and the one believer lives, that tells yuh somun up there was watchin' over this believer's hide."

The news of Jedediah Smith's death also struck the Indian encampment hard. They had looked upon the Bible toting mountain man with awe. Here was a man who possessed the Great Spirit Book and knew its secrets. Over him watched an angel more powerful than their own *Wyakin*, the guardian spirit that guided each Nimpau man through life.

The shocking news did not discourage the Indians' determination to acquire the Great Spirit Book. They could not wait
for the emissaries returning from St. Louis to appear. Where
were they? Why did they not arrive? Had something gone wrong?
Lawyer, Tackensuatis, Lame Horse and other leaders pestered
traders from the east with these questions. No one knew for certain what had happened to the emissaries.

Lucian Fontenelle and his caravan of supplies were still
on the road they were told. Soon they should appear along with
the Nimpau emissaries and their missionaries. Little Ned, who
felt responsible for the Nimpau, sat with them often, telling them
not to worry. He had no doubt Fontenelle's caravan would arrive. His greatest fear was the impatient Indian contingent would
leave the rendezvous and start east in search of Rabbit Skin Leggings and his companions. If they did, they were certain to run
into hostiles. The Blackfeet were on the war path. Young Joe
Meek, who had accompanied a brigade of trappers into this for-
bidden region, had been set upon and had to flee for his life,
leaving clothes, traps, pelts, everything behind.

Besides worry over his Nimpau companions, Little Ned
was distracted by other troubling matters. Among the traders
was a group new to the rendezvous. The leader of one caravan
was Nathaniel Wyeth who came from Cambridge, Massachusetts,
very near Little Ned's New England home town. Among Wyeth's
group were 11 other men who lived in the same vicinity. Little
Ned spent hours talking with them, seeking news of friends and
relatives. He was anxious to find someone who could tell him
about his parents and the twins he had sired.

For years Little Ned had closed his mind to his New England offspring, a boy and girl he left in care of his parents. He
counted back. The twins would be 10 years old. The thought
saddened him. The years had passed so quickly. His children
soon would be adults. He should have returned to see them. Every
time he decided to make the journey, for some reason his legs

refused to take him. Just the thought of the old home place brought back the terrible, searing pain. Never could he look upon his New England children without thinking of his first wife, the lovely woman who gave her life bringing the twins into the world.

To keep these disturbing memories at bay, Little Ned traded for a jug of fiery alcohol and went to a hilltop to drink and brood. The firewater did not improve his state of mind. Feelings of guilt and sorrow overwhelmed him. He was no better than a bull elk leaving the offspring he had sired to grow up on their own while he romped in the hills with a herd of males.

He took another pull at the jug and bitterly laughed. What would his companions think if they knew of his double family? What would Raven Wing and the Lone Wolf family do if they knew? He shoved the half empty jug aside and quickly sobered. He shouldn't even think about New England. His life was Raven Wing and their sons. He was lucky she had agreed to move into the new lodge.

For a while the change had made her nervous. Now, she seemed to like it as well as he did. Over the winter months they experienced a passionate relationship he never imagined could have taken place. On the pallet of bulrushes and buffalo robes, she performed acts of wantonness that pleased him, at the same time, shocked him. After all, she was the mother of his two boys. She should act like a woman with responsibilities. He decided he should have a heart-to-heart talk with her when he returned home.

XIX

A few more passing suns will see us here no more. . . .
The antelope have gone; the buffalo wallows are empty.
Only the wail of the coyote is heard.

Plenty Coups, Crow

Everyone at the rendezvous was aware Rabbit Skin Leggings, No Horns on His Head, Black Eagle and Man of the Morning, accompanied by missionaries, were expected. The emissaries pending return with mèn of the cloth was the talk of the summer fur fair.

"Yuh'd better git yer sinnin' over with quick," Bible quoting No Hair Deacon warned. "There's a bunch of parsons comin'. It's the souls of Injuns thet worries 'em but when they see this bunch of backsliders they'll fer sure land on us'ns with both feet. We're supposed ta be settin' examples fer the heathen Injun. I'm doin' right good but look at the rest of yuh, carousin' like billy goats in a batch of corn squeezin's."

The mountain men, having been cooped up for months in stuffy shelters deep in the mountains, came to the rendezvous to cut loose, have fun. They joked, laughed and pulled tricks on each other like playful youngsters. Liquor, served in camp kettles and guzzled in great quantities, washed away all inhibitions. A trapper, cuddling a pot of firewater, staggered to his feet. He teetered back and forth, waving a finger at No Hair Deacon. "There's no call fer lectures an' no call fer parsons. We kin do our own savin' an' baptizin'." He put his fingers in the pot and sprinkled drops of liquor on the head of his redheaded companion. "Yuh ol' sinnei, I baptize yuh in the name of the Father, the Son and the Holy Ghost." He stumbled. The pot tipped on its side, the reeking contents sloshed over the shoulders and down the neck of his partner.

"Yuh blisterin' bustard!" Before Red could mop the liquor from his eyes and struggle to his feet, a glowing ember from the campfire popped into the air. The volatile fumes burst into flames. The redhead's clothes became a sheet of fire. Hawk Beak, who had been enjoying the repartee, quickly seized a buffalo robe, wrapped it around the redhead, smothering the flames.

Mouthing curses, the redhead freed himself and went after his drunken friend. "What kind of baptizin' is thet?" he stormed, his beard and hair singed to a crisp. He took a swing at his tormentor and fell to his knees.

"Stop it! Stop it!" Hawk Beak ordered. "What's the matter with yuh? Yer actin' like a couple of fallin' down drunks. Yer goin' to give us all a bad name."

The near calamity had a sobering affect. "Maybe we do need some parsons here after all," someone said. "Least-wise some of yuh coots need ta learn ta hold yer leequor."

"I certainly agree," Nathaniel Wyeth, the new man from Cambridge, Massachusetts, said in disgust. He and his men, fresh from New England, were appalled by the rough horseplay. They had come west with the dream of becoming wealthy in the fur trade. This introduction to the harum-scarum mountain men took them by surprise. Not only were they a rough, obnoxious lot, but not a one of them appeared to have gained riches from their trap lines. There was Buck Stone, a Harvard College graduate, acting as uncivilized as the rest, and without a bean to his name. The newcomers shook their heads in dismay. If a few years in the wilderness turned men like him into booze hounds, and impoverished them like this, they wanted no part of it.

Nathaniel Wyeth had sense enough to realize his men were upset. He was not about to let the rendezvous revelers ruin his plans. He had sent a ship with supplies and equipment on the long voyage around Cape Horn. It was imperative he meet it when it arrived on the Pacific coast. He had enlisted Little Ned to help him trade with the Nimpau for horses, dried meat and other provisions; he also had induced Milton Sublette to guide his caravan west. Therefore, he did not wait for the rendezvous to end, but left while it still was in full swing. A number of trappers, including Buck Stone's brigade, Little Ned and a band of his Nimpau companions, saw Wyeth's party off. They rode several miles, giving advice, trading insults and handing around jugs for last minute swigs.

Wyeth's group and the accompanying entourage, barely had passed from view of the rendezvous when they caught sight of a body of horsemen approaching from the east. "It's Lucian Fontenelle's supply train," a trapper announced.

The sighting of the newcomers excited the Nimpau. Finally, the moment to welcome Rabbit Skin Leggings, No Horns on His Head, Black Eagle and Man of the Morning had arrived. Lame Horse shouted to his men to prepare themselves. The White Bird leader urged his mount forward. He wanted to be the first to meet with the teachers of the Great Spirit Book.

"Hold up! Hold up!" Wyeth said, studying the arrivals with a spyglass. "That's no supply train . . . not Luician Fontenelle, anyway . . . more likely a band of Indians."

Buck Stone took the spyglass. "Yep, looks like a camp on the move. Women and children are bringing up the rear, many of them on foot. Wonder what they're up to? I suppose they got word of the rendezvous and are on their way there."

Abruptly, the approaching Indian column stopped. A band of horsemen galloped ahead shooting firearms, waving their arms and shouting. Just out of rifle range the advancing horsemen pulled up. Wyeth's men, new to the ways of the west, lept off their mounts, dropped flat on the ground, cocked and sighted their rifles.

"Take it easy," Buck Stone cautioned. "Whether friendly or warlike, that's their way of saying howdy."

Antoine Godin, an Iroquois half blood who had accompanied the Wyeth party from the rendezvous site, walked up to peer through the spyglass. "I don't like it. They ain't actin' peaceful."

One of the approaching column's leaders rode forward

carrying a long-stemmed pipe. A bright orange colored blanket hung around his waist, covering his thighs and the midsection of the horse. He stopped and held up the long-stemmed pipe, putting it to his mouth as if to smoke. "Says he wants ta smoke the peace pipe," No Hair Deacon said. "Maybeso, wants ta palaver 'bout joinin' the rendezvous. Won't do no harm ta talk. Those people might hev somethin' good ta trade."

"Thet's a band of Blackfeet," an old timer said. "Gettin' friendly with 'em's 'bout the same as crawlin' inta a den of rattle-snakes. Anybody palaverin' had better keep his eyes skinned. Could be the rascal wavin' the pipe has a firearm hid 'neath thet fancy blanket."

"Those ain't Blackfeet. I recognize thet bustard. It's ol' Bailoh of the Gros Ventre. The treacherous varmint ran off with some of our pack animals a few weeks back," another trapper reported.

"That son of a. . . . He scalped my old man!" Antoine Godin, the Iroquois half blood, exclaimed. "I'll parley with him in the only language he knows." He looked to a youthful Flat-head who carried a rifle. "Is that thing loaded? You want to count a coup?"

The Flathead smiled.

"All right let's go. When I tell you to shoot. You shoot. Understood?" The two men raced out to meet with the Gros Ventre leader. Godin came up on one side of him, the Flathead on the other. The Gros Ventre warily reined his horse back. Before he could escape, Godin was on him. He grabbed the rider's arm and turned to the Flathead. The observers heard him shout, "Shoot the bustard!"

The Flathead did as ordered. He fired. The impact of the bullet knocked the Gros Ventre rider from his horse. Godin quickly swung down to scalp the victim. He came up with the bloodied hank of hair, the pipe and the orange colored blanket. Uttering blood curdling war cries, he and the Flathead raced back to the safety of Wyeth's column.

The cold-blooded killing left both sides shocked. New to the frontier, Wyeth and his New Englanders could not believe their eyes. It was one thing to engage the red men in battle, quite another to shoot down one who came in peace, armed only with a pipe. The Gros Ventre were equally horrified. To shoot their leader in cold blood in front of everyone was unimaginable, but the pipe was a sacred tribal possession. To see it taken in such a humiliating fashion made the warriors appear as helpless as a collection of old women. Shooting wildly and shouting defiance, the slain man's companions galloped straight toward Wyeth's column. When they came within rifle range they abruptly wheeled about. The women and children took cover in a nearby cottonwood grove. The warriors milled angrily around in the foreground making battle plans.

Outnumbered by the Gros Ventre, Wyeth's men and the well-wishers who had accompanied them, retreated into the protection of a ravine. Two riders galloped off to get help from the rendezvous encampment. Soon a party of trappers led by Bill Sublette galloped up. Right behind them came a band of Flatheads and close on their heels, a band of Nimpau led by Lawyer and Tackensuatis.

Upon seeing the reinforcements, the Gros Ventre fell back to fortify themselves in the cottonwoods. Expecting to catch the enemy unprepared, the new arrivals galloped headlong toward the besieged warriors. For a moment the action was fast and furious. The Gros Ventre fire was deadly. Three horses went down. An enemy bullet caught Bill Sublette in the shoulder. Another broke his Indian companion's arm. A trapper suffered a belly wound and lay dying. A Gros Ventre warrior dashed out to take his scalp. Buck Stone raised up to shoot only to have his rifle misfire. The warrior turned on him with a war club. Francois shot the Gros Ventre full in the face. With a victory cry, the French Canadian fell upon the slain warrior and severed his scalp.

Frustrated by failure to dislodge the enemy, the trappers withdrew and laid plans to burn out the Gros Ventre. Their Indian allies argued hotly against it. They claimed the Gros Ventre carried with them many possessions. A fire would destroy them, leaving the Nimpau, Flatheads and other Indian attackers without victory plunder.

The enemy, protected by a barricade of logs, sensed victory. "Ho! Buzzard food! Polecats! Sightless moles! How easy you fall," an English speaking voice taunted. "You kill one man, we kill many! You better go quick. Our brothers Blackfeet come. We take furs, horses, trade goods. Everything soon be ours."

The trappers fired one volley after another into the cottonwoods, still the taunting voice continued. "You think that fellow is telling the truth?" Wyeth asked. He feared for his train of supplies. If a force of Blackfeet were on the way, he could lose everything.

"Probably braggin' talk, tryin' to scare us away," murderer Antoine Godin, the Iroquois half blood. He rose up and aimed at a movement behind the barricade. There was a sharp yelp of pain. An answering shot clipped a tail from Godin's ermine cap.

"Yuh'd better pull yer head down or yuh'll be shakin' hands with St. Peter," No Hair Deacon warned.

"Yeah, I think we should all draw back an' palaver a bit," Hawk Beak said. "I don't aim to lose my scalp here at Pierre's Hole or my goods and duffel neither. Yuh don't suppose this war party thet's comin' will hit the rendezvous? We left it almost unguarded."

"By gum! Thet's why these varmints're makin' so much fuss, tryin' ta hold us here while their Blackfeet brothers raid our camp," an excited voice exclaimed.

The Pierre's Hole gang hurriedly mounted and rode hell bent back to the rendezvous site. When they got there they found everything as they had left it. By this time dusk had fallen. The fighters and their mounts were exhausted. The combatants stopped to rest, bind their wounds, liquor up and wait for morning.

The next day the Pierre's Hole rendezvous gang returned to the battle field to find it silent. Buzzards circled overhead. A pair of coyotes darted through the grass. A flock of noisy magpies rose up to fly away. Buck Stone, in the lead, held up his hand to halt. "Either our friends are gone, or waiting to give us hell. We had best be ready."

The riders pressed cautiously forward into the cottonwood grove and behind the barricade defenses. No opposition greeted them. Dead horses and a scattering of discarded weapons and sundry items were all they found. The Nimpau and Flatheads were furious. The Gros Ventre were gone and had taken everything of value with them. In high dungeon, the Indians trailed the escaping enemy, killing and mutilating stragglers who fell in their path. A wounded woman, who sat guarding the body of her dead mate, was shot down without mercy.

The battle's aftermath left Little Ned sick to his stomach. Lawyer had taken a bullet in the hip that left him with a permanent limp. Tackensuatis received a stomach wound that never would heal. Before long, the infection emitted a foul odor which earned him the name "Rotten Belly", a label that clung to him for the rest of his life. In all, 10 Nimpau warriors died on the battlefield, and scores more came away wounded.

The irony of the situation made Little Ned cringe. The welcoming committee, which had set out to meet the emissaries and missionaries and escort them and the Great Spirit Book in triumph to their homeland, instead had taken to the battlefield. Like savages, they had killed and had been killed.

Worse was to come. In a few days Lucian Fontenelle and his caravan appeared, arriving in the dead of night. Although exhausted from the battle, suffering from their wounds, distraught over loss of warriors and plunder, the Indian encampment still managed to quickly arouse itself. Lame Horse, the White Bird leader, and his men hurried to be first in line to greet the arrivals. They were stunned by what they heard. Black Eagle, Man of The Morning and No Horns on His Head were dead. Rabbit Skin

Leggings was missing. Teachers of the Great Spirit Book had refused to come. The glorious celebration that was planned was replaced by a grievous wake.

NO HORNS ON HIS HEAD

From painting by George Catlin, 1832 -- courtesy Smithsonian Institute

RAVEN WING

XX

They were taught . . . to look when there was apparently noth-
ing to see, and to listen when all seemingly was quite.
A child that can't sit still is a half-developed child.

Luther Standing Bear, Lakota

The atmosphere in the trapper/trader segment of the rendezvous encampment was little better than that in the Indian section.
A popular mountain man named Sinclair, along with four others, had
been killed, and a dozen men had been wounded. It was a battle none
of them would forget. Even the suave dandy, Antoine Godin, who
started it all by murdering the Gros Ventre leader, was sobered.

"I guess I shouldn't have killed that old boy like I did," he
confessed. "I thought of my dead pa and couldn't help myself."

"Shucks! Yuh did what yuh thought best. Those bustards
had it comin'," a cadaverous, dirty, tobacco-chewing trapper re-
marked. "If yuh hadn't started it, they'd probably done caused
trouble anyhow. Yuh know how sneaky those Gros Ventre are;
yuh cain't trust 'em as far as yuh kin spit."

Little Ned, who sat with his old trapping companions, remained silent. The bloodletting left him shaken. It was so sense-
less. Mother Nature's beautiful Teton setting had become a killing ground. More than a dozen lay dead on either side and the
combatants would be hard pressed to say why they died. The
camaraderie he always felt when surrounded by his old trapper
partners was gone. He tried to reason why. He came to the con-
clusion it was the presence of the swarthy French Canadian. For
hours, Francois sat beside the campfire combing out the hair of
the scalps he had taken. When they were clean, he tied them to a
miniature scalp pole which he placed next to the rest of his plunder. Even rough and ready Hawk Beak took affront.

"How many of those bloody scalps didja take from womin
and children?" Francois did not answer. He busily whetted his

curved scalping knife. When it glittered like a piece of glass, he carefully sheathed it as though placing a precious jewel in its case. Little Ned had seen him on the trail of the departing enemy. Francois had scalped several of the dead left behind. The big mountain man also thought sinister Francois had a hand in the death of the woman who guarded her dead mate. One of the trophies on the scalp pole had long hair sprinkled with gray.

Bile rose up in Little Ned's throat. To think that he, playing the Good Samaritan, had taken this scalp-happy half-breed in, healed him and then wished him off on his trapper friends to do things like this. Of course, the unsavory Canuck did save Buck Stone's life. Perhaps that was the reason the good Lord induced him to nurse the French Canadian back to health.

The disconsolate Nimpau broke camp and started the long trek home. Lawyer lay in a travois to protect his hip wound. Tackensuatis, soon to be known as Rotten Belly, disdained the drag poles and rode hunched over like an old man with a bad stomach ache. Yet, in spite of their wounds, Lawyer and Tackensuatis considered the Battle of Pierre's Hole a great Nimpau victory. They had met an enemy that outnumbered them and sent it fleeing. Every night when the column stopped, they chanted victory songs. The warriors formed a circle to drum and dance.

Little Ned did not join in the victory celebrations. He saw through the facade his companions erected. They were trying to keep up their spirits. In their hearts, they knew they had not achieved victory. Instead, they had been defeated. The desire for revenge, the greed for plunder and the terrible drive to count coups, had turned them into savages. The journey to Pierre's Hole had gained them nothing except sorrow, shame and frustration.

Homecoming was a torturous affair. Accounts of the victory over the Gros Ventre were glumly received. The missing men, the grievous wounds and the disappointing news that the emissaries sent to St. Louis had failed to return and acquire teachers of the hairy faces' Great Spirit Book, eliminated any thought of celebration. Lone Wolf, who stood outside the long lodge to watch the column arrive, quickly ducked back inside. He gave Quiet Woman a satisfied grunt. He had lost nothing by refusing to make the trip. In fact it made him appear wise, while those like Weasel Face, who had created a big fuss about their departure, returned looking shamefaced.

#

During the following months life in Lapwai returned to normal. Talk of acquiring the Great Spirit Book faded away. Lawyer took to his Kamiah home and kept to himself. Regardless of the efforts of the medicine men, Tackensuatis' wound did not heal. The stench drove his mate to move out of his lodge and back to her folks. "Stink! He is rotting away," she was overheard to say. She was the first one to give him the name Rotten Belly.

Black Hair Ned and Raven Wing lived quietly in their cabin. They took great pride in their growing sons. In little ways they vied with each other for the children's love and affection. In a traditional Nimpau family, it was the role of parents to prepare boys for assuming the task of preserving and transmitting tribal legends and myths. This training might also be conducted by grandparents, uncles or close friends. Since Black Hair's family lived apart from the Lone Wolf clan and her mate was foreign to the traditions of the tribe, Raven Wing took it upon herself to be the teacher of the boys' rich Nimpau heritage.

She started telling simple stories and posing thought provoking questions. Why do bees gather honey? Why do coyotes run in packs? What makes the skunk stink? The youngsters were expected to repeat the stories and come up with answers to the questions the following evening. Most important of all was the teaching of spiritual precepts.

"Always remember the Great Mystery has placed you on Mother Earth, watches you and knows your every thought," Raven Wing told her sons. Raven Wing remembered stories from childhood, mystical legends handed down from one generation to the next. She held the boys spellbound with tales of the mountain spirit, *Allalemyah*, who stood taller than a tree yet moved easily

from one place to another. Tears of blood dripped from his eyes
and the staff he carried. They were not to be afraid of him. He
was their all powerful protector. His breath started the breezes.
The thump of his footsteps created thunder. The flash of his eyes
made lightening and it was he who, personally, selected a vision
seeker's *Wyakin*, the spirit that guided each person through life.

Raven Wing related how Coyote tricked the great mon-
ster who ruled the world before there were humans. She told
how Porcupine got his quills. The sons were enchanted with the
legend of how Grizzly Bear, Rattlesnake, Toad and other creatures of the forest quarreled among themselves until they decided
just how long to make the darkness of night, and how long to
make the light of day.

Raven Wing instructed the boys that before humans arrived, animals ruled Mother Earth. The headmen were coyotes,
and the medicine men, skunks. The animals were wise; they had
visions. The animals saw the coming of people. They were worried. What will become of us they asked? They thought of ways
to protect themselves. The bear said he would hide in a cave part
of the year. The beaver said he would hide himself in the water
and make his lodge away from shore. The birds said they would
nest high in the trees. There, high above the ground, they would
be safe, see the people coming and would sound the warning for
others.

Raven Wing prepared her sons for the time when they
would join the older boys in the separate sleeping lodge. "Every
morning," she said, "you will take the sweat bath. Water will be
poured over heated stones making a mist like the river fog, but it
will be hot making you sweat like a horse that has run itself out.
Then you will plunge into the cold creek waters until you shiver
and your teeth chatter. When you can stand it no longer you will
go back into the sweat lodge and start over. That was the way of
our fathers. That is the way it will be with you. It will make you
hardy and courageous. No matter what happens in life, you will
survive."

Black Hair Ned did not attempt to dissuade Raven Wing from the regime of traditional training. He wanted his sons to be proud of their Nimpau heritage. He also wanted them to learn the English language and the things he learned as a child, especially politeness, good manners and respect for women. Secretly, he hoped one day to bring together his families, the twins in New England and his two Nimpau sons. How this was to take place, he did not know. He could not see Raven Wing traveling east and he could not imagine his New England daughter and son settling down in an Indian village. It was foolish to expect either of his families to adapt to the other's homeland and way of living.

The big mountain man kept these thoughts to himself. Raven Wing and his two Indian sons knew nothing of the twins and very little about his former New England life. He contented himself with teaching the boys the rudiments he learned from his years at school. Every day he conversed with them in English, giving them the names of every object they encountered. A patch of earth in front of the cabin became the classroom. On the bare ground he used sharp sticks to scratch out simple words which he had the boys copy. This did not prove satisfactory. He searched the mountain sides for flat stones which he used as primitive slates. With sticks of charcoal and colored clay, he wrote lessons for his youthful students to copy. Since he gave the lessons outside, his teaching efforts soon attracted attention. Groups of villagers gathered to watch the game the hairy faced man played with his boys.

At first the watchers scoffed and were amused, then they became intrigued. In a few days two boys who watched brought slates and sticks of charcoal and asked to take part. Before a week was out, Little Ned had more than a dozen students who struggled with the daily lessons. To his great pleasure, Raven Wing often came to sit by his side. She printed letters, numbers and words as faithfully as did any student. She soon became his best pupil. She began to help others with writing and figures.

She proved a surprisingly good teacher. Many students, especially beginners, would come to her, too shy to approach the big *soyappo*.

Vision Seeker, who observed this thirst for knowledge, often came to sit and watch. The big mountain man hoped Vision Seeker would help but his Nimpau brother merely sat expressionless, eyeing the efforts of the students. One day after class Vision Seeker strolled up to lean on the porch rail.

"It is a kind thing you do, teaching these youngsters," he said. "Would it not also be wise to have classes for their parents? Already there is talk. People ask each other, is it good to teach children and keep their parents ignorant? People fear the youth will stuff their heads with *soyappo* things and turn their backs on the old ways and their elders."

Big Black Hair nodded. "Yes, brother, the words you speak are wise. When people possess knowledge it always seems to create fear among the unlearned. I will be glad to teach anyone who wishes to learn, but will parents come to my humble outdoor classes? What is needed is a proper teacher and schoolhouse and teaching materials."

Vision Seeker agreed. "Ah, yes, a place where families can come and sit as if in council. Perhaps Lone Wolf and the elders might agree to build a lodge for this purpose."

That evening a rider thundered up the Kooskooskie Trail and into the valley. When he was still a half mile away, village guards sounded the alarm. Camp dogs darted out of the shadows to bark. Children ran screaming into lodges. Men seized their weapons. Anyone in such a hurry had to bring trouble. Lone Wolf, who rushed out with the others, recognized the arrival. It was a man from Asotin, as tired and windblown as his horse. Lone Wolf sent Running Turtle for a drink of cold creek water. The rider gulped it down and sat in the saddle gasping like a beached fish.

"Out with it, brother. What news do you bring?" Lone Wolf demanded impatiently. "The way your horse is lathered there must be hostiles hot on your trail."

"Many *soyappo* trappers come. They trap the Salmon River and now are on the Kimooenim. Need horses. Make big trade. Must hurry on, tell Kamiah and Weippe Prairie."

The rider stopped to catch his breath and eat of the food that had been hurriedly prepared for him to take along. Boys ran up to ask what trade goods the white men had in their packs.

"Many, many things," the man replied. "Anything you wish, they have."

A murmur of delight ran through the listening crowd. Each horse owner counted his animals, trying to determine their worth and decide on which ones he could spare. Little Ned turned away in dismay. All this fuss over gaining a few knickknacks that had no worth, except to enrich the pockets of greedy New England traders, made him sore of heart. His Nimpau friends appeared so shrewd and knowing, when actually they were innocent lambs waiting to be shorn. What would happen to them as more and more people from east of the Mississippi arrived? They would be like putty in these Easterners' hands. The small efforts he made to educate them would have as much effect as rain drops in the ocean.

Raven Wing received the news stoically. The approach of a trapping brigade made little difference to her. She had her hands full with her two sons. It was time to go to the south slopes and dig for the kouse roots, and the berry harvest soon would arrive.

Since that fatal summer when she had refused to go to the camas grounds, Raven Wing had made it a point to slave with the other women, preparing food supplies for the winters. She did it as an act of contrition to absolve her infidelities. Francois' reappearance had shaken her resolve, but after he was gone she had been more determined than ever, to break the irresistible spell the suave French Canadian had cast upon her.

As excitement began to build over the approaching trapping brigade, Raven Wing could not keep the boys under control.

Pretending they were trappers on the way down the Salmon and Kimooenim rivers, they chased each other around the house riding stick horses and waving toy spears and war clubs Grandfather Lone Wolf had carved.

"I wish the trapping brigade would hurry and get here," Raven Wing muttered to herself. "When the boys see the smelly, dirty, hairy-faced mountain men, they will change their thinking. They will go back to playing Nimpau buffalo hunters."

XXI

Rich gifts wax poor when givers prove unkind.
Shakespeare, HAMLET

For days talk of the brigade of trappers who had been sighted on the Kimooenim, kept the Nimpau homeland in a state of excitement. In Kamiah, the wounded Lawyer limped out to mount his horse and ride to Lapwai for more details. Rotten Belly, reunited with his mate and anxious not to miss any opportunity, tagged along. They sat and smoked with Lone Wolf and Lapwai elders. How many trappers were in the brigade? How many pack animals carried trade goods? When would they arrive on the Kooskooskie? How long would they stay?

These were among the topics discussed. A White Bird rider said he had counted 70 men and an equal number of pack mules. A Flathead reported having seen 100 men and a herd of animals too numerous to count. Little Ned was skeptical. A party of this size would be like a scourge of locusts. There were not enough beaver along the route to make it worth their while.

After Lawyer and Rotten Belly departed, more reports drifted in. The brigade was led by a short stout man with a bald head. He offered better prices that Hudson's Bay. It was said he and Nathaniel Wyeth, who had been involved in the Pierre's Hole shoot-out, planned to build trading posts that would compete with Hudson's Bay; the factors of Hudson's Bay were angry and had lowered their prices to meet those of the new trading company.

This fascinating news intrigued the Indian people. Scouts were sent to the trading posts. The reports of price cutting were true. "They have many good things for small price. They bargain. If you don't like first price, they give better price," one Nimpau informer reported.

The information especially pleased Lone Wolf. "Oh-ha!" he exclaimed rubbing his hands together in glee. He sent Vision

Seeker and Running Turtle to the pasture to curry the horses and trim their manes and tails. He told Quiet Woman and Granny to inspect the cookware and camp gear. He, himself, weighed powder and shot and ordered a new, larger pouch to hold tobacco. When the trading brigade arrived he wanted to be ready. This would be a trading opportunity of a lifetime.

The Nimpau sent out more scouts. Almost every day new reports of the brigade's movements drifted in. After working the Salmon River the trappers turned south to Bear River where the brigade split. One group remained encamped. Another group led by the baldheaded leader took the trail west. At the Grande Ronde Valley they stopped, held up by forest fires in the Blue Mountains. Instead of waiting to cross the Blues, the brigade turned north.

The news was so favorable Lone Wolf, who kept close track of the trappers' movements, strode to the pasture himself to inspect the herd and count the animals he wished to trade. If the brigade kept on this path, they soon would pass near Lapwai.

Word of the brigade's approach swept through the valley. Horsemen with trading stock brought their herds in from pastures in the highlands. Pole corrals were built to hold the wild, unworked animals. Those skilled in the ways of taming horses to the bridle and saddle went to work. The roping and tying and riding of the unbroken horses created great clouds of dust which hung over the valley, blanketing lodges and tree groves. Then came gloomy news. The brigade had stopped to trade with the Cayuse. Work in the valley died away. Lone Wolf's spirits fell. Only Weasel Face remained untroubled.

"Bah!" he exclaimed. "Cayuses! They know nothing of trade. The *soyappos* will get their fill of them. They steal more than they give." He and his sons continued to work with their horses. His mate rousted him and her boys out every morning sending them to the pasture.

The Weasel Face family's optimism spurred Lone Wolf into action. He could not let his obnoxious neighbor take the lead. Somehow, he had to make certain the brigade of trapper/ traders continued on to Lapwai. He sent Running Turtle for his special mount and rode up the trail to his *soyappo* son's log cabin. Black Hair saw him coming and walked out to meet him. The two grandsons ran up, chattering like magpies. They were delighted to see their grandpa. For a while, after tethering the horse, they sat on the porch overlooking the garden Lone Wolf hated. While the boys romped, the men smoked in silence. The mountain man knew his father-in-law wanted something, but he politely observed the traditional Indian custom and waited patiently until his guest spoke.

"Perhaps this Captain Bald Head is your friend who knows much about the Great Spirit Book," Lone Wolf finally said.

Black Hair Ned remained silent. Now he knew what was on Lone Wolf's mind. He could not wait for the trapping brigade to arrive in Lapwai, and wanted him to hurry them along. It would enhance Lone Wolf's prestige as leader of the band if he did. Little Ned did not like the idea of bringing a band of trappers to Lapwai. Before they left they could do all sorts of mischief.

Raven Wing came out to serve husband and father. The big mountain man watched her deft hands place baskets of food on the stools he had spent hours making. His home was running smoothly. Raven Wing finally appeared happy. Serenity had replaced the restlessness that, for so long, had possessed her. He did not want to leave. He did not want her to move back to the long lodge for even a day.

"Is it wise to bring these trappers here?" he asked. "How do we know what kind of people they are? They may bring firewater that will do much harm."

"Our people know what firewater does. They will leave it alone," Lone Wolf answered with more assurance than he felt.

The big *soyappo* glanced at the set expression on Lone Wolf's face. It had not been easy for him to come to the cabin and ask for help. To keep peace in the family he had no choice but to go. He nodded assent, angry with himself for bowing to his father-in-law's will. As he walked up the steps with Raven Wing and his sons after seeing Lone Wolf off, a terrible feeling of apprehension descended on Little Ned. Something warned him he should have refused Lone Wolf's request; he sensed disaster.

The next morning Running Turtle brought the horses around. "Lone Wolf says I can go," he said, excitement making his voice shrill. "Maybe No Hair On Head will tell more stories from the Great Spirit Book."

The big mountain man threw a few things in a bag. He rolled up a blanket, tied a thong around it and handed it and the bag to Running Turtle to fasten on the saddle. Buffalo Boy wistfully watched. His father always went places and left him at home. He was five years old. He pleaded to go along.

"We ride too! We ride too!" Young Wolf's squeaky voice added its plea. Big Black Hair looked to Raven Wing. He would like to take Buffalo Boy but he feared, if he did, it would break Young Wolf's heart and he couldn't take both boys. Raven Wing surprised him.

"Take them both," she suggested. "It is a short journey. It will be good for the boys to ride with their father." She helped the boys get ready. She would have gone along too, but it was her moon. He did not have to worry. She would be safe in the special hut for women.

The small party proceeded down the Kooskooskie to where it emptied into the Kimooenim. It was the Season of First Grass. There was a chill in the air. Water in the rivers and streams was high. Driftwood careened down to pile up on creek and river banks. The boys found the speeding debris exciting. Their eyes remained glued on the turbulent Kooskooskie. They pointed and shouted as each bobbing object came into view. When a favorite piece of debris was held up by brush, crashed against a rock or swirled around and around in the many foamy eddies, they shrieked and laughed. They looked on each piece of flotsam as if it was alive.

Running Turtle joined in the fun. He dismounted and

threw rocks at driftwood to keep it in the middle of the stream. A pair of camp dogs tagging along, cavorted and barked. Ducks, mud hens and other water birds skittered away. Flocks of black-birds and red-throated sparrows flitted out of the willows to cross the river and land on the north shore. Everyone was having so much fun Little Ned's feeling of foreboding disappeared. It was wonderful to enjoy life with his sons. He silently promised him-self to take them on more excursions like this.

At the confluence of the Kooskooskie with the Kimooenim, the big mountain man led the little party south to-ward Red Wolf Crossing where the brigade of trappers was said to be camped. Near the home village of Flint Necklace, head-man of the Asotin band of Nimpau, they came upon a herder rounding up horses. When asked about the trappers' camp he pointed with lips and chin down river. "Short ride," he said. "You make before dark."

The camp proved to be no more than a few lean-to shel-ters. Instead of 100 or more men, there were barely 20. The baldheaded leader was not No Hair Deacon, but introduced him-self as Captain Bonneville. He greeted them affably and invited them to dismount and "sit a while". He was taken with the boys. He helped them off the horses, and dropped to his knees so he could talk to them face to face.

"Aha!" he exclaimed. "Who do we have here, the chief of the Lapwai Nimpau?" he asked Young Wolf. The boy stuck his fist in his mouth and, with wonderment in his eyes, stared at the pale man's hairless head. "You like the looks of all that bare skin, do you, lad? Here, run your hand over it," the captain in-vited.

Young Wolf shyly stepped back to stand behind his fa-ther. Captain Bonneville laughed. "I don't blame you. I don't like it much either."

A group of men dressed in worn buckskins and faded homespun's left newly built campfires to gather around. They were fascinated by the two boys dressed so neatly in their little buckskin suits. One of them, taller than the rest, held back, his face a dark mask in the dim evening light. The shape of his head, his bearing, the cocky tilt of the hat were familiar. He picked up an ember to light a black cigarillo. For a moment the flame exposed a scarred cheek. An involuntary shiver raced up Little Ned's spine. It was the swarthy, snake eating French Canadian, Francois!

The party from Lapwai made camp that night with Bonneville's men. Buffalo Boy and Young Wolf were entranced by the trappers with their loud talk, heavy-barreled guns and bushy beards. They gleefully skipped around camp trailed by a bevy of dogs. As they passed Francois' lean-to, the swarthy French Canadian called out to them and invited them to sit beside the fire. They dutifully obeyed, watching the dark-faced trapper with expectant eyes. Francois did not disappoint them. After digging through a pack, he held a hand out to each boy. When he opened them, the boys gasped. Each hand held a clasp knife in a beaded sheath. Buffalo Boy immediately ran to his father to show off his prized gift.

Young Wolf tarried behind. The man who gave such exquisite gifts had won his heart. His round brown eyes carefully watched as Francois demonstrated the workings of the clasp. He smiled up at the dark man's face when the trapper told him to take care, the blade was sharp. "Nice man . . . he give knife," Young Wolf proudly exclaimed, his small voice squeaking with delight.

"Yep, it's a fine gift." Little Ned's first thought was to make the boys take the gifts back. He had no desire to be indebted to the scalp-happy French Canadian. He glanced at his sons' shining eyes and decided against it. How would he be able to explain it to them? Perhaps there was no evil intent. He had done Francois many favors. Was this his way of showing appreciation? The big mountain man could think of no other reason for the apparent softening of Francois' attitude.

The next day Captain Bonneville and his brigade broke camp and headed west, their destination the Willamette Valley.

A score or more pack animals trailed along laden with trade goods and furs. Somewhere on the banks of the Columbia they hoped to establish a trading post. Little Ned, Running Turtle and the two boys silently watched them file away.

"Nice man go. Wish he come with us," Young Wolf said wistfully as Francois passed.

#

Lone Wolf, Vision Seeker and a group of Lapwai tribesmen, rode down the Kooskooskie Trail expecting to meet a train of pack animals loaded with trade goods. When they saw only Black Hair's small party, Lone Wolf uttered a cry of dismay. "Where is Captain Bald Head?"

"They had business down river," Black Hair Ned said. He neglected to say he did not invite them to Lapwai.

"The baldheaded one trades with the Cayuse. Does he think he is too good to trade with the Nimpau?" Lone Wolf demanded.

"No, he is on his way to establish a trading post on the Columbia," Black Hair replied. "When he is settled you can go there to trade."

"Wagh!" Lone Wolf snorted. "I thought these people wanted horses. That's the way of the hairy faced ones. They say one thing and do another."

Lone Wolf was all for riding after the brigade, especially after his grandsons showed him the gifts they had received. He turned the knives over in his hand, opened and closed the blades and reluctantly handed them back. "Much too good for young boys," he said.

Vision Seeker asked to see the gifts. "Why did the man give them to you? They must be worth a beaver pelt each."

"He like us," Young Wolf piped up.

"Had funny ear," Buffalo Boy added.

Vision Seeker gave his *soyappo* brother a searching glance. Black Hair shrugged and looked away.... Francois ... The dreaded name seared Vision Seeker's mind.

When they arrived at the log cabin the boys ran to show their mother the wondrous gifts. She, too, wondered who the kind trapper was who gave such special things to young boys.

"It was the man with half an ear who lived on the hillside and ate snakes and camp dogs," Running Turtle announced.

"Oh, my!" she uttered the words without thinking. She quickly clamped her mouth shut. She had put the affair with Francois behind her. She ignored the pounding of her heart and busied herself with the housework. She had a good mate, two healthy sons and all the good things any woman could desire, she kept repeating to herself.

XXII

I fear the Greeks even when they bring gifts.
Vergil, AENEID

Disappointment over the lost trading opportunity was quickly forgotten. Once again the topic of the Great Spirit Book had Lapwai villagers' tongues clacking. Shortly after the Lone Wolf/Big Black Hair party returned empty-handed, a messenger from Flathead country arrived. A crowd soon gathered in the village square. Always eager to be informed of anything new, Lone Wolf was one of the first to greet the newcomer.

"What brings you here? Is there trouble across the mountains?" he asked. He was so anxious to hear the news he failed to notice he stood next to his adversary, Weasel Face.

"There are big happenings," the messenger announced above the hubbub. "Hairy faced teachers of the Great Spirit Book come to live in Lapwai Valley. Not Black Robes. Not Long Robes. People called 'missionaries'."

"Missionaries!" Lone Wolf took a minute to think. "Missionaries!" he repeated. "Ah, yes, teachers of the Great Spirit Book. You say they come to Lapwai?" Lone Wolf noticed Weasel Face. He pushed him aside and virtually pulled the messenger off his horse. He took the newcomer by the arm and hustled him into the long lodge. Impatiently, he clapped his hands for Quiet Woman to bring food. Immediately after the visitor finished eating, Lone Wolf brusquely motioned for her to remove the food utensils. Without inviting his guest to enjoy a sociable smoke, his pent-up thoughts tumbled forth.

"Give me straight talk. I hear many false tales about this Great Spirit Book. Our people run around in circles like dogs trying to catch their tails seeking this Book. They always end up with nothing. What makes your news any better than what we have heard before?"

The visitor shrugged. "I can only tell the words I hear. It is said these missionaries are on their way to the hairy faces' rendezvous. They seek guides to take them to the Nimpau tribal lands. Perhaps they do not come to Lapwai, perhaps to Kamiah, Asotin, Wallowa. The Flatheads believe the words true. They will go to the rendezvous. They seek them too."

"Wagh! Flatheads!" Lone Wolf exclaimed. His mind raced. To have the power of the Great Spirit Book in the hands of the Lapwai band would bring his people honor, like nothing else ever had. He would be the leader of the most prestigious band in all the Northwest. When Running Turtle came in from putting away the horses, Lone Wolf sent him rushing to fetch Vision Seeker and Black Hair. This was an emergency. They had to get to the rendezvous before the Flatheads.

When his sons arrived, Lone Wolf pulled the *soyappo* and Vision Seeker into the lodge to explain his plan. "We must keep these people called 'missionaries' in our midst. They will wish to have log lodges like yours," Lone Wolf said to Big Black Hair.

"I think we should wait and see what they desire. Perhaps they will want to live some place else, maybe with the White Birds," Vision Seeker suggested. He saw no reason to get excited.

Lone Wolf glowered. "Son, pull your head out of the clouds. Can you not see? It is important we lodge them here. If White Birds want to learn the ways of the Great Spirit Book they will have to come to Lapwai."

Lone Wolf took the matter so seriously he called a council of elders. He told them of his plans, pointing out plots of land that the missionaries could use to build their lodges. Weasel Face objected.

"Who are you to be giving away Lapwai land? It belongs to all people. When a *soyappo* builds on the land he says the land is his. He will not give it up. If he does, he puts a price on it like it was a piece of trade goods."

Lone Wolf ignored Weasel Face's objection. The matter

before them was too important to end in a quarrel. The main thing was to get the missionaries to Lapwai, then the problem of where to lodge them could be solved. He insisted the Lapwai band send a delegation to meet the missionaries and escort them safely to the valley. He selected Vision Seeker to lead the group. His son spoke the language of the hairy faces, and knew the words of the Great Spirit Book. For insurance, his *soyappo* son, Black Hair, also should go along.

Weasel Face objected, but Lone Wolf was adamant. How could the holy men resist the entreaties of his two older sons, he argued, one a hairy face himself, the other a seer of many visions? The majority of elders agreed. The assignment should be in the hands of those who knew the white man's ways. They could not endure another failure. They also agreed with Lone Wolf that the delegation should leave immediately. The Flatheads were friends of the Nimpau, but they did not deserve these teachers of the Great Spirit Book.

Vision Seeker reluctantly accepted the role as leader of the group. It was ridiculous to keep chasing after missionaries. Did his people not have any pride at all? They were like greedy children who could not stand to see others have something they did not possess. Signs told him this venture also would fail, but he could not very well refuse. If he did not go, and the missionaries did come to live with the White Birds or Flatheads, Lone Wolf never would forgive him. With apparent agreeableness he bowed to his father's will.

Big Black Hair also was dismayed. He was becoming no more than Lone Wolf's messenger boy. Besides hating to leave his family, there was much work he had planned. A fierce wind had blown down the lean-to in which he kept the winter fuel. It needed to be rebuilt. Chinking in the cabin walls had fallen out. It should be tended to before the rains came. Then there were the students . . . They were doing so well their classes should continue.

"Should I ride the mare or the spotted pony?" It was

Running Turtle who came to ask Black Hair's advice. The formerly squat lad, who suddenly had sprung up like a weed, had wheedled his father into allowing him to make the trip. Black Hair Ned dourly shook his head. He would have this pest asking questions all during the journey.

Before the Lapwai contingent could get underway, Lawyer and Rotten Belly rode in from Kamiah. Flint Necklace, the headman of the Asotin and Bonneville's friend, appeared, as did old Cut Nose, who had smoked the pipe with Lewis and Clark. The Cayuse leader, Tiloukaikt, also arrived. He wanted to see what these teachers of the Great Spirit Book looked like, he said. Weasel Face, of course, was one of the first saddled and ready to ride. Lone Wolf watched in dismay as the numbers increased. His hoped for coup was vanishing into thin air.

From the very first, everything about the trip went wrong for Big Black Hair. After he finished packing, the cinch on the pack saddle broke, pitching the load onto the ground. When he went to retrieve the pack, the balky mule kicked him in the groin. The shock of pain doubled him over, causing his hat to roll into the creek. As he grabbed at it he slipped on the muddy bank and fell into the water, wetting himself to the waist.

To make matters worse, his two sons who watched, howled with laughter. "Daddy! Daddy! You are so funny," Buffalo Boy shouted. "Momma! Momma! Come quick. Daddy is in the creek."

For the first time ever, Little Ned gave them each a good rap on their backsides. Their little faces puckered up. Big tears filled their eyes. After changing his clothes, the big mountain man finally was ready to leave. Raven Wing threw her arms around him, kissing him with such passion it bruised his lips. He was so astonished, he could not believe that it actually had happened. Never before had she shown so much emotion upon his leaving. All through the long day, the memory of Raven Wing's parting kiss and the little hurt faces of his sons rode with him.

"Ah!" he growled. He did not want to make this trip. He

should have stayed with his family. The thought crossed his mind, he might never see them again. Why did he think that? Would this rendezvous end in a battle like Pierre's Hole? Even at the end of the day, the dour thoughts that beleaguered him did not leave. He snapped at Running Turtle who asked him where he should stake out the horses.

"Don't know what's the matter with me. I'm acting like a soreheaded shrew," Black Hair said in way of an apology.

The motley column of travelers arrived at the Green River rendezvous site only to be told local pasture was so skimpy the meeting place had been moved to Ham's Fork, a half day's ride to the southwest. They arrived at the new rendezvous place tired and disgusted. The welcome they received also was disappointing. Everyone seemed out of sorts. The American Fur Company and Rocky Mountain Fur Company were at loggerheads. The companies were in competition. They challenged each other for every pelt. Furs were not as abundant as in previous years. Small fur bearing animals were being hunted into annihilation. It was obvious there was not enough business to support two trading companies. The ill-feeling between the two organizations spilled over to affect everyone.

Nathaniel Wyeth, making his second trip to the west, fell victim to the ill-starred competition. He brought a caravan of supplies for the Rocky Mountain Fur Company. Already overburdened with more goods than they could sell, the company refused to accept Wyeth's supplies. This led to more rancor and ill-feeling. The whole business left Little Ned depressed. The summer fur fair, which in the early years had been so carefree and enjoyable, was caught up in one wrangle after another.

However, the rough and tumble trappers came to have fun and were not to be denied. High jinx and carousing took over. On the surface everything appeared normal. Accompanying Wyeth's supply train were five men new to the west. Two were scientists: Thomas Nutall, a botanist, and John Townsend, an ornithologist. These two men attempted to explain their unusual professions to the bemused mountain men.

"By gum! Interested in plants, are yuh?" a graybeard trapper asked when introduced to Nutall. "Hell's fire. Yuh should be in hog heaven. Besides varmints, plants is about all we hev around here."

The role of Townsend, the ornithologist, was harder to understand. Most of the men knew something about botany but ornithology was out of their ken. "Study of birds! Hell's bells they have feathers, wings, build nests in the spring and fly south in the winter. What the hell else is there to know?" Graybeard, the trapper, snapped.

The scientists' companions were missionaries. Solemn-faced and dressed in dark clothes, they stood out like ravens in a flock of chirpy sparrows. They were led by a stoop-shouldered, slow-moving man named Jason Lee. The trappers and traders made no attempt to draw them into their fun and games. The preachers made it clear they did not want to mix with the boisterous trappers and traders.

"I say, brethren," a scruffy mountain man with beard yellowed by tobacco juice called out to the missionaries' tents, "how 'bout a prayer meetin'? Before yuh go savin' Injuns yuh kin practice on us. Whilst we're 'bout it maybeso yuh'll lead us in a hymn."

The Indian delegation saw the missionary trio in a different light. These men carried the Great Spirit Book and knew its mysteries. Every day they stationed themselves in a circle around the missionaries' campsite just to get a glimpse of these men who held such enormous power in their hands. Occasionally, the black clad men appeared to relieve themselves, fetch water from the creek or to do minor chores. They ignored the Indian delegation, noiselessly going about their business as if the red men who sought their attention were no more than bothersome insects. The delegation of men who had ridden for days to meet with these missionaries were perplexed. Didn't these black coated people have any manners, did they not know how to speak?

Among the throng of trappers and traders was Buck Stone's brigade. Little Ned found them camped on the banks of a small stream. As usual, he received a warm welcome as did Vision Seeker and Running Turtle.

"I swan," No Hair Deacon exclaimed when he saw Running Turtle. "Is this the same brave who rolled instead of walked? Look at him. He's sprung up quicker'n a mushroom. He's grown like Jack an' the beanstalk."

The offhanded compliment made Running Turtle smile and wriggle like a dog that had been praised. Never before had his changed stature received such complimentary recognition. He didn't know anything about mushrooms or Jack and the beanstalk, but acclaim coming from this man who knew the Book of Heaven had to be special.

Buck Stone, delighted to see his friends from Nimpau country, invited them to sit for a smoke. For the first time Running Turtle sat in the ceremonial circle. Vision Seeker watched him with a wary eye, but his young brother took his puffs on the pipe as if he had done it all his life.

After Vision Seeker and Running Turtle left to make camp with their Nimpau countrymen, Black Hair remained with his former partners, Buck Stone, No Hair On Head and Hawk Beak Tomahawk Head. The trappers inquired of Raven Wing and the two boys. For a while they reminisced about the winter pregnant Raven Wing spent on the trap line.

"Some filly yuh hev," No Hair marveled. "I tol' yuh she'd make a good wife. At the time yuh wasn't fer it. Look at how wrong yuh was." The trappers murmured agreement, then the conversation lagged.

"What happened to Francois?" Little Ned finally asked. "Saw him sashaying with Bonneville's party on the Snake."

"Got a bit restless, me thinks," No Hair answered. "Afta the set-to at Pierre's Hole he took off like a gut-shot cat. Didn't say good-bye're go ta hell."

"Yeah!" Hawk Beak chimed in. "Me thinks he got fussed

'cause we didn't 'preciate his scalps. Smelled worse than a gut wagon an' drew flies somethin' fierce. Tol' him straight-out, bury 'em or burn 'em. Reckon he didn't cotton to me advice. Next mornin' he'd vamoosed."

"What yuh askin' after him fer?" No Hair asked. "Didn't think yuh an' him perzactly hit it off."

"That's right but maybe he has changed his stripes. For some reason he appeared more amiable than usual -- gave the boys a pair of folding knives, no strings attached," mused Little Ned.

"I'll be consarned!" No Hair exclaimed. "How about thet? I'll bet yer boys was pleased as fleas in a house full of dogs."

"When thet bird starts bein' nice, thet's the time to watch out," Hawk Beak warned. "Made me nervous as all get out, him whettin' those knives of his every time he sat down. Figured any minute he might take the notion of slippin' one in our ribs and make off with the catch."

"Trouble with you fellows is all you see are his faults," Buck said. "He did a lot of good. Led us to good beaver streams. Kept us in camp meat and was right there when it came to a scrap."

"Yep, he sure saved yer bacon at Pierre's Hole. Thet's fer certain," No Hair agreed. "I still don't trust him. Like Hawk Beak says, when he's on his good behavior he's still thinkin' up devilment. Anyways, guess we don't hev ta worry 'bout him. Yuh say he an' thet Bonneville fellow were headin' down the Columbia. Maybeso, he'll stay in the Willamette Valley an' take up farmin'."

"Yeah! Let's hope he does," Little Ned said with such vehemence his trapper friends glanced up in surprise.

XXIII

Ye look for much, and, lo, it came to little.
BIBLE, Haggai 1:9

While Black Hair Ned visited with his trapper friends, Vision Seeker, anxious to carry out his father's wishes to escort the teachers of the Great Spirit Book to Lapwai, sought out the missionaries' campsite. Now that the missionaries were here, it would be disastrous to let them slip away. Much to his chagrin Lawyer, Rotten Belly and Tiloukaikt of the Cayuse, already were on hand. Patiently, they stood waiting for Jason Lee to appear. Only the Flatheads did not vie for the missionaries. When the Flathead contingent first arrived, Missionary Jason Lee and his companions sent word from their tents they did not wish to speak to them. They were interested in working with tribes who spoke only Sahaptin languages. This included the Nimpau and Cayuse, but excluded the Flatheads.

Even so, things did not go well. The first Nimpau delegation seeking audience with the missionaries was turned away. Jason Lee was not in the mood to meet with them. He was "indisposed", the spokesman said. The Indian men murmured among themselves. They did not have to speak with the headman. Anyone who knew the mysteries of the Great Spirit Book would do. Surely, not all three of the missionaries were "indisposed"?

After the initial rebuff, Vision Seeker and Running Turtle departed. "Perhaps these Black Coats will feel better tomorrow," Running Turtle said.

"Perhaps." Vision Seeker had no such hope. These people did not look like teachers with knowledge of the Great Spirit. They did not look like people thankful to be alive, touched by the Great Mystery that created all things on Mother Earth. Their faces were not pleasant. Lines of disapproval marred their countenance. When they spoke their lips turned down as though they had bitten

into a sour chokeberry cake. From the way they refused to ac-
knowledge the people who came to greet them, it was clear they
felt superior. They did not want anything to do with these men of
red skin.

"Wagh!" Vision Seeker uttered in disgust. Why was it
there was such a difference among the *soyappo*? Mountain men
like Big Black Hair, No Hair On Head, Tomahawk Head, Buck
Stone and their friends, were generous and friendly, and these
people who dealt with sacred things were haughty and sour-faced?
They acted like they did not like anyone, not even themselves.
Did they not know all living things were related, even to the mouse
in the field and the scolding blue jay? Yet, Vision Seeker knew
he could not give up. If the Nimpau delegation did not escort at
least one of the missionaries back to Lapwai, Lone Wolf would
be furious.

A second attempt to meet with the missionaries also failed.
This time Buck Stone and No Hair Deacon accompanied Vision
Seeker and Running Turtle. The presence of the mountain men
did little good, if anything the expressions of the Black Coats
were more sullen than before.

After the second rebuff Buck Stone pulled on his side
whiskers. "From what I understand these people to say, they aren't
yet sure what they want to do. Maybeso, they've given up the
idea of mission work. If you ask me, they don't appear too anxious to get on with the job."

"I'm thinkin' they're havin' second thoughts 'bout this
preachin' business," No Hair On Head agreed. "I seen 'em last
night on their thin shanks prayin' like all get-out, lookin' ta the
Lord fer light, I guess. Must not hev showed on 'em. Yuh kin see
by the looks of 'em they're hard-nosed, stubborn folk. They ain't
goin' ta do nothin' till the Lord gives the word."

When they returned to camp, Hawk Beak, in an attempt
to lift their spirits, offered the brothers a drink from his whiskey
jug. Vision Seeker politely refused. Running Turtle tipped the
jug up and took a swallow. He choked, coughed and spluttered.

He gasped for air until tears came to his eyes. He attempted to speak. His voice uttered an unintelligible croak. Hawk Beak laughed.

"Good, ain't it? Calls fer another, don't it!"

Vision Seeker seized the jug and threw it down so hard it cracked. The seeping liquid formed a widening pool in the sand. The rank smell of whiskey filled the air. Hawk Beak leaped to his feet. "What the hell did yuh do thet fer? Thet's pure drinkin' whiskey, cost me two whole beaver skins. Prime pelts they was, at thet!"

Vision Seeker jerked the still sputtering Running Turtle to his feet and pulled him away. "Come! We camp with our people."

Hawk Beak started after them. No Hair stuck out a moccasined foot and tripped him. "Yuh crazy idiot! Yer lucky those boys are friends. Otherwise, instead a loosin' whiskey yuh might a lost yer scalp. Ain't thet right, Little Ned?"

Little Ned did not reply. He was thinking of his two Nimpau sons. What would happen when they were offered their first taste of firewater? Would they be fortunate enough to have someone like Vision Seeker around to make them stop?

#

The missionary contingent was in as much of a quandary as were Indian men and their trapper friends. No Hair's prediction was true. Jason Lee was having second thoughts about converting the natives. The role of a missionary was far different than he had envisioned. When he first decided to be a missionary he likened himself to Paul of Nazareth. He would go into the byways and trail ways of the western wilderness spreading the word of God. He knew the task would be difficult but he was well acquainted with hard work and hardship. In his early youth he had toiled as a woodsman. Not until the age of 26, did he answer the call to the ministry. He was such a rough and insensitive appearing person, officials of the seminary were reluctant to accept him. Yet, his zeal and dedication were so impressive when the Methodists wanted a mission in Oregon Territory, the unanimous choice was Jason Lee.

Long before arriving at Ham's Fork rendezvous, Lee had his introduction to Indian people. At the start of the trek west the party, captained by Nathaniel Wyeth, encountered a pitiful village of Caws. This first experience with a frontier Indian camp appalled the fledgling missionary. The Caws swarmed around the caravan like demented children. Half naked, lice clinging to their hair, mewing like cats, they came running, holding out their hands, happy to receive scraps or leavings of any kind. They pestered the column for days. In spite of shouts and threats, they would not go away. At night Lee and his entourage stood guard in fear the aborigines would steal their boots, or any article that could be carried off. Even their milk cow the missionaries deemed was at risk.

Jason Lee's determination to bring the souls of Indian pagans into the kingdom of God was shattered. After the shocking Caw episode he questioned if these lice-infested, mewing creatures even had souls. If they did, how could he possibly save them? He prayed day and night for the answer. God could not be reached. He floundered like a drowning man. His inspiration to go west had come from reading the words of Rabbit Skin Leggings and No Horns on His Head. Their eloquent plea for teachers of the Great Spirit Book had misled him. Jason Lee expected to encounter Indians of noble bearing who would greet him with dignity, eager to receive the mysteries of the Great Spirit Book. Instead, he encountered almost inhuman creatures who, he sensed, had no higher thought than what they could beg or steal.

At the time Lee arrived for the rendezvous, the Caw experience still haunted him. He could not bring himself to face the task ahead. The circle of Indian men who surrounded the missionaries' campsite repelled him. Each delegation that vied for the missionaries' attention reminded Lee of the Caws' begging, outstretched hands. How could he live amongst these heathen savages? How could he face them every day feeling as he did? Lee commiserated with his companions who felt equally apprehensive.

"Perhaps we should go farther west," one of group suggested.

"Yes, that is the answer. Aborigines are all over Oregon Territory. Perhaps we should start in the more civilized Willamette Valley," Jason Lee decided.

The party of Nimpau, who remembered their previous failures to recruit teachers of the Great Spirit Book, could not face the prospect of another defeat. If they coaxed the missionaries with gifts and sweet words, certainly they would come to their homelands. When these holy men arrived and saw how much their people yearned to learn the secrets of the Great Spirit Book, the missionaries would stay and teach them. This was the argument put forward by Lawyer and Rotten Belly.

The enticements the Nimpau offered rudely were brushed aside. Lawyer and Rotten Belly were perplexed. The missionaries who had come west to live with them and teach them, now refused. What had changed their minds? Some blamed a group of youth who gambled, raced horses and carried on with the trappers in most undignified ways. At the height of the riotous behavior a young man corralled a stray buffalo, then chased it through camp. The frightened animal created havoc. Shelters were knocked flat. It was meal time; cooking pots tipped over, spilling their contents. The enraged buffalo gored a prize horse and charged a pack of dogs tossing one canine into an open fire, burning it so badly it had to be shot.

Little Ned, silently observed the unsuccessful efforts of his adopted people receiving one rebuff after another. He was ashamed of the treatment they received, at the same time he was disgusted with the way they accepted it and went back for more. On purpose he refrained from getting involved. It was quite clear the missionaries had little respect for either Indian men or mountain men.

Finally, Little Ned could stand aside no longer. After the

buffalo upset the camp, Little Ned went to visit Vision Seeker. "It won't hurt to give these people one more try," he said. He had met one of the missionaries who knew Pastor Barclay, the minister of his former church in the east. Perhaps this acquaintanceship would help sway the missionaries into coming to Lapwai.

The meeting started well. The missionaries were pleased to visit with someone from back home but when Little Ned spoke of the need of a mission among the Nimpau, his words fell on deaf ears. Jason Lee shook his head. "We have made up our minds. We will start with a mission in the Willamette Valley. When it is successfully established we may branch out into other areas, perhaps the plateau lands where these horse Indian friends of yours live."

That night Little Ned expressed his disappointment to his former trapping partners. Buck Stone thoughtfully puffed on his pipe. "You have to keep in mind, these missionary folk put on their pants one leg at a time just like everybody else. When you get to thinking they're infallible -- keep their word and keep the Golden Rule -- that's a mistake. If I read the tea leaves correctly, I think the good Reverend Lee has let politics sway his decision. Hudson's Bay people have been working on him. They don't want an American mission above the Columbia River. McLoughlin, the big Redcoat chief at Fort Vancouver, is on the hot seat. His bosses in London are telling him to keep Americans out. They want the land north of the Columbia for themselves as a part of Canada. Tom McKay, McLoughlin's stepson, is trying to head Jason Lee off, telling him a mission is needed in the Willamette Valley. He says the horse Indians of the plateau are not ready for conversion, claims they're nomadic people and won't settle down to plowing, cultivating and harvesting like good Christians are expected to do."

"Tom McKay's a bleedin' fish snapper, probably up ta mischief. Thinks us Protestant folk ain't sellin' the right bill of goods. Anyways, what business does he hev buttin' in like a bull in a pen of heifers?" No Hair Deacon dourly complained.

"McKay's not thinkin' of savin' Injuns' souls. He's thinkin' of the beaver skin trade," Hawk Beak Tomahawk Head added. "He don't want nothin' to upset the takin's of Hudson's Bay. Besides, from what Wyeth an' his men say, Parson Lee ain't above makin' a bit of moola fer hisself. Wherever he settles he plans to establish a tradin' post. He figgers business'll be better farther west. Look't the haul John Astor made. He came to Oregon Territory without a bean, set up a tradin' post at the mouth of the Columbia an' 'afor yuh kin say scat collected enuff beaver skins to fill a four mast schooner. I've heard tell the ol' skinflint has a place in New Yawk as big as a potentate's palace."

"Yes, there's that, too," Buck Stone agreed. "Scratch a man, even one of the cloth, and nine times out of 10 greed'll show through."

Regardless of the rebuffs they received, when Jason Lee and his companions left the rendezvous, a delegation of Nimpau led by Rotten Belly and Lawyer, went along. For two days the Indian horsemen rode alongside the missionary party hoping to change their minds. They finally parted with a halfhearted commitment from Jason Lee.

"I will come visit your villages this winter or perhaps the next or the one after that," was the missionary's evasive promise. The Nimpau, who were adept at reading what was in men's hearts, did not argue. The teacher of the Great Spirit Book spoke with a forked tongue. He had no intention of coming to live in their midst.

For the dispirited Nimpau, the trek to their homeland, seemed to take forever. They wanted to hurry but they did not want to hurry. They wanted to be in the familiar surroundings of their homeland, but hated the thought of facing friends and relatives. Instead of returning in triumph, once again they brought the sad tidings of defeat.

As they approached Lapwai Valley the column broke apart. Members of the White Bird and Kamiah bands wended their way south. Flint Necklace of the Asotins and Tiloukaikt of the Cayuse, continued on the trail west. Big Black Hair and Vision Seeker led the Lapwai party into the home village, surprised that no one came to meet them. They pulled up at the long lodge. From the interior came the high keening sound of women in mourning. Lone Wolf stood at the entrance, has face a grim mask. He glanced at his two sons, unable to speak. Vision Seeker swiftly swung down from the saddle and rushed inside, something terrible had happened.

Cold fingers of fear clutched at Little Ned's heart. Violently, he reined his horse up the trail toward the log cabin. It was dark and silent. He swung down, leaving the bridle reins to trail on the ground. The cabin door was closed. He pushed it open. A terrible feeling of dread swept over him. There was not a sign of his family's presence. He called out and paced the length of the cabin. The place was dusty and in disorder. It was so unlike Raven Wing to leave it that way. He started to run outside, then he saw it. On the mantle above the fireplace was a piece of parchment. With trembling fingers, he picked it up. On it, in Raven Wing's hand, were primitive printed letters.

"We go. Francois, father of Second Son, come. We go away. Sorry to give sadness."

Little Ned read the crudely printed words again and again. He was too stunned to grasp what the message said. Almost curiously, he turned the parchment over and over in his hands. A hopeless feeling overwhelmed him. These were the first words his Indian wife ever had written him. The painful ache in his heart told him they also were her last.

XXIV

When you get married, do not make
an idol of the woman you marry.

Sam Blow Snake, Winnebago

Little Ned sat down on the porch bench he had made especially for Raven Wing. It overlooked the bed of flowers which he also had planted especially for her. The bright sunlight and brilliant colors made the message on the parchment seem all the more unreal. It had to be a cruel joke. Perhaps Weasel Face's sons were the culprits. They knew of their father's dislike for Lone Wolf and often had come to heckle and, for a while, attend the writing classes.

It was ridiculous to believe Raven Wing had gone with the despised snake eater, Francois. How could she possibly have done that? To say he was the father of Young Wolf, did not make sense. She had seen the French Canadian only three times, twice at the Bear Lake rendezvous and, three years later, at the unfinished cabin. All three times she was frightened to death of the Hudson's Bay trapper.

Vision Seeker came up the path. He sat down and put a sympathetic hand on Big Black Hair's shoulder. Numbly, the grieving man thrust the note at his Indian brother. Vision Seeker glanced at the crudely printed words. It was to gain time only. He had a good idea of the message the parchment contained. Above the keening of Quiet Woman and Granny, Lone Wolf had told him of his sister's shocking departure. Quiet Woman and Lone Wolf had tried to stop her, but neither Raven Wing nor her lover would listen. The parents begged their daughter to leave the grandsons behind, but she had refused.

"She was like a crazy woman. She would not listen to a word we spoke," Lone Wolf reported. "The man with half an ear rules her like her *soyappo* mate should have done. If he had, this would not have happened."

Vision Seeker glanced at the note again, surprised how well the letters were formed. He also was surprised Raven Wing had taken the time to write. It was not like her to explain her actions to anyone. What a cruel twist. The first time she used the words learned from her husband, she turned them against him. Vision Seeker searched for something to say that would console his *soyappo* brother. He could think of nothing. His silence deepened the hurt. Little Ned glanced at Vision Seeker with accusing eyes.

"What do you know about this?" he hoarsely demanded. "What is this all about? Why should Raven Wing leave me after all I have done? What kind of nonsense is this? She says Young Wolf is Francois' son. How can that be? It's a mean, despicable lie."

Vision Seeker put the parchment aside. He glanced at the far horizon trying to think of how to reply. He was at fault. He should not have shielded Raven Wing. It would have been far better if Big Black Hair had ridden into the valley that first day and found Raven Wing with Francois. Perhaps he would have killed Francois, but the matter would have been settled. Now, what could be done? Vision Seeker cleared his throat. He had to speak but what could he say? No words would bind the wounds suffered that day, but he had to try.

"Your heart is big. Your love is so great it blinds you. My sister is not the innocent one you believe. Like a wild animal of the forest, she has an untamed spirit that makes her do strange things. Yes, Francois, the Hudson's Bay trapper, is the father of Young Wolf. The fathering of the child came during the Season of the Camas Harvest while you were absent at the trappers' rendezvous. The sneaky dog eater came and set up his lodge. Raven Wing went there to be with him. It is painful to hear but true. I came from the camas grounds and found them together."

"No!" The big man stood up and waved his fist in Vision Seeker's face. "You lie. It isn't so. Raven Wing is my wife and your sister. You make her no better than a camp harlot. She is the mother of my two sons. Someone in this village is evil. Is it that Weasel Face who hates your father? Who else would play such a hateful trick?"

The anguished expression on the mountain man's face made Vision Seeker turn away. He was reminded of the beaver Black Hair had clubbed to death their first winter on the trap line. The eyes of the man, and those of the rodent, had the same desperate glint. "Weasel Face did not play a joke. He could not have done it. Remember, he was on the trip with you."

"Yeah! Well, somebody has made this up," his *soyappo* brother retorted. "I won't believe otherwise until I have proof."

"How do you think the man called Francois lost half his ear? It was done by your gift knife. If anyone has played a joke on you, it is your brother, Vision Seeker. I failed to guard your lodge while you were gone. I knew this man was evil, yet I let him sneak into the valley and take your wife, and then let him get away. If I had it to do over, I would cut his throat instead of his ear. I would do anything to undo the harm I have caused."

Little Ned leaned against the railing and brushed at his eyes. The flower garden was a blurred kaleidoscope of color that seemed to mock him. If what Vision Seeker said was true, planting the flowers and the other things he had done to give Raven Wing beauty, and an easy life, had gone for naught.

Deacon and the others who complained he was wrong for treating his Raven Wing so well, had been right. He should have beaten her, withheld his gifts, made her set up the tipi lodge, take it down in the morning, and labor at every mean chore proper Indian women did for their mates. If he had, she would have remained in his lodge. There would have been no bastard child.

Little Ned groaned inwardly. No wonder Raven Wing had acted so wantonly. Every time they made love, she was thinking of snake eating Francois! The thought infuriated him so, he hammered his fist on the rail with such ferocity, it split in two.

For a second the big man's gaze fell on Vision Seeker's

impassive features. The thought of Raven Wing's unfaithfulness angered him all the more. His Indian brother had known about it all the time, yet he had kept it to himself. So that was how the Indian character worked? He clenched his fist and took a stride toward Vision Seeker, then abruptly turned. It would serve no purpose to take it out on his brother. He only had been trying to help.

The mountain man strode off the porch and down the steps. He picked up the reins of his mount that patiently waited, its tail lazily switching flies. He swung into the saddle. For a moment he sat staring at the cabin. He had built it with such high hopes, with such love and care. Now, it was an empty shell. Soon, without love or care, it would decay. He should have listened to the villagers and not set himself apart. If he had been satisfied to live in their midst, Raven Wing and his sons would not have been lured away.

He gripped the reins and dug his heels into the horse's ribs. He did not want to see the log cabin ever again. There was not a thing in it he needed. He had not unpacked from the journey to Ham's Fork rendezvous. He was ready to leave his life at Lapwai behind.

"You can give the cabin to the missionaries, if they ever come," Black Hair called over his shoulder and neck-reined the horse down the trail. Vision Seeker watched horse and rider move away without expression. He made no attempt to call out or stop the heartbroken man. If this had happened to him, he probably would have acted much the same.

At the creek Little Ned let the horse drink. He had a long way to go, but where should that be? His first thought was to ride after his family, hunt them down, retrieve his two sons and take them east. It made no difference what anyone said, Young Wolf always would be his. But where should he start the search? They had left days ago and could be anywhere, probably north. That was where the dirty snake eater came from. He knew the country. Winter fell early up there. It would not be long until snow covered the ground. Tracking them would be like finding a needle in a haystack. And what would he do when he found them, shoot Francois down like a sheep killing dog? That never would do. By now, the swarthy trapper had the boys eating out of his hand. Francois had laid his plans well. He had won the boys' hearts with the gifts of knives. He would bring more gifts. The boys would follow him anywhere.

The big mountain man forded the creek and turned toward the Kooskooskie. He rode by the long lodge but did not stop. He knew Lone Wolf and his family suffered as much as he did, perhaps even more. Not only had they lost a daughter and two precious grandsons, but also suffered loss of face. To have a stranger lure away loved ones was worse than if they had been captured by raiders. The enemy could be searched out and vengeance taken. When loved ones left on their own, this outlet was taken from them.

As sounds of the village receded, he took one last look back. The hurt expressions on his sons' faces took shape. The thought that his last act as a father had been to unjustly chastise them, made the pain in his heart more intense. For the rest of his life he would be condemned to remember their reproachful eyes filled with tears, the look they gave him when they parted for the last time after he paddled their backsides.

#

Perhaps Little Ned would have acted differently if he had known Raven Wing and their two sons were not far distant and not too happy with their new existence. The years of living with her Boston mate had accustomed Raven Wing to gentle treatment and the comfort of a snug home. After the first few days on the trail, the thrill of her lover's touch began to pale. The exciting and romantic future she had visualized was replaced by cruel reality. She was not prepared for the burdensome chores of camp life and the hardships of travel. Her muscles ached. Half the time she felt sick to her stomach. The wild love-making she had enjoyed so much was dampened by worry over what tomorrow might hold. Where would they stop next? What would they live on? When would the journey end? Questions like these plagued her until she thought she would go mad.

As the days drug by, Raven Wing felt more like a slave than a lover. For hours Francois sat in her presence, but ignored her. He turned his attention to the boys, especially his own son, Young Wolf. Although they were still very young, he started to teach them the skills of hunting, tracking and trapping. He had them listen to the lonely calls of the loon and owl, the melodious songs of the robin and meadowlark and the chirps of the chickadee and sparrow. He made the boys identify each bird's cry. When they learned to do that, he had them mimic each one until they had the call to his satisfaction.

Francois taught the boys discipline. He demanded they eat and drink sparingly. When one went on long hunts or set out to raid or do battle, food and drink was often scarce, he warned. He insisted they be observant, note the habits of the rabbit, deer, water birds, fish and other game. "How can you be a successful hunter if you do not know the ways of your prey?" he asked. Plants and trees were studied. The fruit and roots of some were edible, others had healing qualities and some were poisonous. He taught the boys to identify them on their daily treks through fields and woods.

Raven Wing was happy to have her sons receive the rigorous traditional training, but at the same time she felt cheated. It had been the pull of their son that brought Francois back to Lapwai, not his love for her. What hurt even more, was that both sons were attached to Francois. The gifts and attention he lavished on them made him their instant friend. When Francois first arrived at the Lapwai cabin, he had given them each a half-sized bow and quiver of little arrows, something Black Hair had refused to do, saying they were too young.

Then, while the two boys were practicing their marksmanship, shooting at squirrels and blue jays, Francois had entered the cabin. Before she knew what had happened, he had her disrobed and on the sleeping pallet where they madly grappled. In that frenzied atmosphere, they renewed their passion. As they lay depleted, they vowed to remain together forever. That meant leaving Lapwai. Eager for adventure, the boys were delighted to hear the news. They would have gone anywhere with the generous, dark-faced man they barely knew.

Raven Wing quickly learned Francois had no plan. They just traveled. Since Black Hair and the party that went to the rendezvous would return by following the Lolo Trail from the east, they rode west. They went down the Kooskooskie to the Kimooenim. They followed the swift flowing river to where it emptied into the Columbia, and on to the Deschutes. They passed through the lands of the Cayuse, the Walla Walla and Umatilla, until they came to Celilo Falls on the Columbia. Here they camped with the people who fished the tumbling white waters. The skill of those who speared and netted the great salmon as they came leaping over the rocks of the rapids, fascinated Francois and the boys. Raven Wing remained on the bank as they scrambled out to lend a helping hand to the fishermen. She ruefully realized Francois, in spite of his love making and cruelty, was no more than a grown-up boy.

From Celilo Falls they rode along the banks of the Columbia to where the waters picked up speed as the river rushed toward the gorge of the Cascades. At the great Chinook trading center called "The Dalles", they stopped again. Here peoples from the shores of the Pacific came to fish and offer their wares of sea shells and items brought by the great ships with wings. Raven Wing knew the Chinook trading center well. Lone Wolf had often taken the family there when he wanted to trade. Raven Wing lived in constant fear someone might recognize her. During daylight hours she kept to the shadows of the temporary lodge she had erected with the help of her sons.

The long, lonely hours spent in the squalid shelter increased Raven Wing's distress. Her lover was almost the opposite of her steady husband. He loved to wander about the encampment carousing and gambling. Sometimes he stayed away all night. His mood depended upon his fortunes. When he gambled and won, he came to the lodge to caress her with tender hands. When he lost he took her brutally, leaving her bruised and frustrated. He treated the boys in like manner. On the days of successes he returned with presents; on one occasion he gave them each a gift of a pony, not much larger than a small deer. On the bad days he found fault with everything they did, and slapped them viciously when they did not obey his slightest command.

Then came the season for horse racing. Francois overestimated the ability of the colorfully marked Nimpau Appaloosas they had ridden from Lapwai. He lost one, then the other. This disturbed Raven Wing more than the brutal ravaging he gave her body every night after losing. They were far from home and, except for the boys' toy ponies, were without transport.

They were now so poor they stole and scrounged in garbage dumps. As their fortunes declined, Francois' irascible behavior increased. Their love making became a torture for Raven Wing. During one of their last nights in the trading camp, to relieve her bodily pain, she attempted to divert her lover by caressing his misshapen ear. "I always wondered what happened to your poor ear," she whispered.

Francois seized her hand and turned her fingers back until the knuckles cracked. "Never you mind about that." He got up and stomped out. In the morning, he returned. After sleeping a couple of hours, Francois got up and vowed he would win back all he had lost. He gathered up their buffalo robes and buckskins and left. All day long Raven Wing waited. Young Wolf was crying. They had eaten nothing that day but a handful of dried salmon. When Francois appeared, Raven Wing went to meet him, expecting him to have food. Instead of food, he stumbled in smelling of whiskey.

"Your elk skin dress," he demanded, reaching for the only pack Raven Wing had been able to save. When she resisted, he knocked her aside. Buffalo Boy cried out. He reached for the knife at Francois' belt, but the French Canadian thwarted him. He jerked the knife away. For a moment the blade was poised above Buffalo Boy's head. Then out of the dusk a Chinook fisherman appeared. Francois turned on him. One swipe with the knife blade and the fisherman's throat was slit. The boys screamed. Before Raven Wing could pull them away, the dying man's blood spurted out to splatter them from head to foot.

In a daze, Raven Wing found herself helping Francois roll the body down the bank and into the river. Quickly, she bathed the boys and packed their meager possessions. Francois loaded everybody into the murdered Chinook's canoe. Hurriedly, they cast off, the two boys wailing with fright. Their precious ponies were left behind.

View of Columbia River near The Dalles
Sketch by George Gibbs, 1849

XXV

Man did not weave the web of life; he is merely a strand in it.
Whatever he does to the web, he does to himself.

Seattle, Duwamish

While Raven Wing and her sons made their torturous way down the Columbia, Little Ned traveled east. Like Francois, he had no plan. He just wanted to get as far away from the Nimpau tribal lands as quickly as possible. If he remained nearby, he might return and take some terrible action he would live to regret. Whatever happened, he wanted to have his sons think well of their father.

The more Little Ned agonized over his plight, the more he laid the blame for his troubles on Lone Wolf. If only the greedy, domineering Indian leader had left Raven Wing and him alone, his family still would be together. Like a pesky deer fly, Lone Wolf buzzed around and around finding fault. Every time an opportunity to gain prestige or acquire something new presented itself, the Lapwai leader instantly came to him.

The last two trips were the straws that finally broke the camel's back. The trek to meet with Bonneville on the Snake gave Francois the opportunity to captivate the boys with the gifts of knives. The journey to Ham's Fork rendezvous, which had immediately followed, gave Francois the opening he needed to steal in and spirit his family away.

"Aah!" the mountain man groaned so suddenly and loudly a hare jumped out of the brush and darted across the trail. The abrupt appearance of the rabbit made the horse shy. Little Ned had to grab for the saddle horn to keep from falling. Annoyed, he slapped the gelding with the reins. This was all he needed, to be dumped by the trail side and find himself afoot.

Little Ned crossed Lolo Pass and turned south along the familiar Bitterroot River where Buck Stone's trappers had such a good season when they first met Lone Wolf's band. From there the trail took him over the cool heights of Morrida Pass. Below the summit, he stumbled into a brigade of trappers camped near a Shoshone village.

The trappers greeted Little Ned with their usual hilarity and rough banter. They were near the Blackfeet border. Any man good with a gun was welcome. Although the group included such noted mountain men as Jim Bridger, Joe Meek, Kit Carson and Robert "Doc" Newell, Little Ned did not feel comfortable in their midst. The party was too large and too boisterous. He was not in the mood to enjoy horseplay and practical jokes. He longed for studious Buck Stone, Bible quoting No Hair Deacon and the thin, predatory, Hawk Beak. Nevertheless, he had nothing better to do, so he joined Bridger's brigade.

The winter months passed slowly for Little Ned. He could not forget his lost Nimpau family. The trappers sensed his despair and left him alone. The only time his mind was completely absorbed by thoughts other than those of his lost family came on Christmas Day. Blackfeet raiders swept into the camp, stormed the corral and made off with a dozen horses, among them Jim Bridger's favorite racer. Little Ned galloped out with a party led by Kit Carson and Joe Meek to retrieve the animals, but the attempt was in vain. The raiders slipped through a canyon and held off the pursuers with painfully accurate gunfire. When it came time to break camp in the spring, the trappers were short of mounts. To everyone's disgust, they had to ride double and take turns walking all the way to the summer fur fair.

The rendezvous of 1835, was held on Green River. As usual, Little Ned sought out Buck Stone's brigade and settled in with them. For a while the big man's spirits lifted. He made up his mind to forget his troubles, leave the past behind and plan for the future. There was a lot of living left to do.

It was not as easy as he had anticipated as the trappers had heard rumors of Raven Wing's betrayal and were careful to avoid any subject that might touch on Little Ned's life with the

Nimpau. Their efforts were so obvious the former easy feeling of comradeship could not be recaptured. The presence of his former trapping partners kept bringing back painful memories of the days spent with the Lone Wolf clan.

As in the previous summers, a delegation of Nimpau, Flatheads and other Indian tribes were on hand. Also, more men of the cloth appeared. The Reverend Samuel Parker arrived with Fontenelle of the American Fur Company. Accompanying Parker was a medical man, Dr. Marcus Whitman, who agreeably tended to the trappers' injuries and ills. One of those who received medical attention was Jim Bridger. From Bridger's back, Doctor Whitman extracted an arrowhead that the mountain man had carried for years. Trappers and traders gathered to watch, fascinated by the expert way Dr. Whitman wielded a sharpened butcher knife in conducting the operation.

"By gum! Yuh done good," a bearded trapper who walked with a limp exclaimed. "I've got a' arra I'd like ta git shet of, too." Doctor Whitman willingly obliged. He cleaned his tools and proceeded to operate with the same knife that he had used on Jim Bridger.

Little Ned observed the operations, but his mind was on the party of Nimpau. He felt ashamed. He knew how wretched the Lone Wolf clan felt at the way Raven Wing had deserted him. He had been so wrapped up in his own grief he hadn't said a word to comfort them, didn't even say good-bye. He traded some of his pelts for gifts, which included scarlet blankets for Lone Wolf, Granny and Quiet Woman. He sought out Vision Seeker and Running Turtle who greeted him warmly, their eyes bright with pleasure.

For a few moments they stood silently looking at the busy encampment. Finally Little Ned swallowed the lump in his throat so he could speak. He took the gifts from the saddle pack. He handed each Nimpau brother a new Hawken and then the bundle of gifts for the absent family members. He had spent a lot more than he had intended, but during the night a premonition had struck him like a bolt of lightening -- this might be the last time he would have the opportunity to wish his adopted family well.

The brothers were astounded. Running Turtle uttered a gasp of delight. A rifle of his own was something he only could dream about -- to be presented one was beyond belief. Vision Seeker was just as moved. How could his *soyappo* brother be so kind when he had been so painfully hurt by the Lone Wolf clan?

The brothers invited Big Black Hair to their campfire. They smoked and spoke to him of many things, but not one word was mentioned about Raven Wing or her sons. They parted with handshakes. The next morning two paint ponies stood tethered at the head of Black Hair's tent.

"Yer Nimpau relatives came in the night an' left 'em," No Hair Deacon told Little Ned when he awakened. "A pair a' matched pintos like thet should fetch a fortune back east."

"They aren't for sale," Little Ned snapped. The gift touched him. These were Vision Seeker's most precious possessions. He had obtained them in trade with the Cayuse leader, Tiloukaikt. They were swift as the wind and, like all specially bred plateau animals, possessed great stamina. There were no others like them in all of the Nimpau homeland.

Little Ned's trapper friends watched him with quizzical eyes. What did the gifts mean? Had he received word from his wife and sons? Was he going back to them? The big man ignored the inquisitive glances and remained silent.

The next morning he packed up and led the gift horses away. He rode by the Indian village and on toward South Pass. He had made up his mind to get out of the mountains, away from everything that reminded him of his mountain man life. He was not like other mountain men, who took wives and discarded them without regret. For him, taking a wife was a commitment he had to stand by. Even though his wife had run away, she was still his mate. Over the months he had gone over every detail of their marriage. Little disturbing incidents kept coming to mind. Deep inside he began to realize it was largely his fault the marriage fell apart. Right from the start he had handled it badly. If only he had remained with her after the birth of Buffalo Boy everything would have turned out differently. Nothing he did after that could make up for the cruel hurt he had inflicted.

Unbeknownst to Little Ned, Vision Seeker trailed his Boston brother to a hilltop where he watched him and his horses until they disappeared into the summer haze. He wanted to gallop down the trail and beg him to return to Lapwai. He wanted to tell Black Hair the empty cabin he had so painstakingly built had become a haunted place. It was as if the family who occupied it had died, but their spirits still lingered waiting for their physical bodies to reappear.

Lone Wolf had insisted the cabin be torn down and the logs used to repair walls of the long lodge. Running Turtle would not hear of it. "Someday Raven Wing and her mate will return," he insisted. "Everything must remain the same as before."

Running Turtle saw to it the cabin was kept clean and the garden of flowers kept up. He replaced the porch rail Black Hair broke the day he had left. When a chink fell out of the walls Running Turtle carefully replaced it. He rebuilt the fuel shed and filled it with firewood. The log cabin lodge was ready to move into when its former occupants returned.

After watching Black Hair disappear beyond the horizon, a sad thought came to Vision Seeker. He probably had seen his kind *soyappo* brother for the last time. Vision Seeker returned to find Running Turtle repairing a bridle. "Did our brother leave?" he asked.

"Yes, he is gone." Vision Seeker hobbled the horse, sat by the fire and poked the embers with a stick. A flare of smoke rose up to drift south. The smoke hung in the air then suddenly vanished as if whipped away by a blast of wind. Its abrupt disappearance startled Vision Seeker.

"Aiiee!" he uttered.

Running Turtle's eyes had grown round. "It's a sign! Good sign . . . bad sign?"

Vision Seeker remained silent. It was clearly a sign. It had followed the direction Big Black Hair had taken, then disappeared as if cut short by an invisible knife. It had to do with their *soyappo* brother. Did the trail he had taken lead him to his death, his life whiffed away like the puff of smoke? A feeling of dread in the pit of Vision Seeker's stomach tightened. Now he knew for certain, he never would see the big *soyappo* again.

#

Little Ned pressed ahead. He crossed South Pass and steadily kept on the trail that would end eventually in St. Louis. He met many travelers, most of them heading west. Some were old, some young, a few fat but most were lean. He covertly studied each one. What kind of men were these people who were drawn west? He figured some were outlaws looking for an escape from ill-fated deeds. From the way others spoke, they were out for adventure or were curiosity seekers. All of them appeared puzzled that he traveled east. Didn't he know west was where fortunes were to be made?

Several riders cast inquisitive, covetous glances at the matched spotted ponies. "Those are right smart lookin' critters," a man riding a lean, bony roan observed. "Suppose yuh want a bunch of money fer 'em?"

That night Little Ned made camp well away from the trail. After caring for the horses, he cooked a quick meal and rolled up in his bedroll, his Hawken close at hand, loaded and cocked. He did not like the greedy expression on the rider's face who asked about the matched ponies. He had no intention of letting them fall into another's hands. When morning came without incident, he did not bother with breakfast, but hurried on.

In St. Louis Little Ned unloaded his beaver skins at the American Fur Company, boarded his horses at a stable and arranged for passage on a steamer going up river. He had an almost irresistible urge to join his eastern family. He had lost one family. He had no intention of losing the other. It was 1835. The twins, Tildy and Joe, would be 13, more than half grown.

Little Ned was so occupied with thoughts of returning to his former New England home, he barely saw the passing scenery or noticed fellow passengers who curiously eyed the silent big man in weathered buckskins. Little Ned attempted to picture the faces of the twins and envision their way of life. Soon after they were born the grandparents had taken them to their farm in Middlesex County, close to Boston. For a while he had lived there, too, working the rocky soil, but he was no farmer. He could plow a furrow as straight as anyone but it gave him no satisfaction. There were more interesting things to do than wait and watch for the skimpy New England crops to sprout and grow. He tried his hand at deep sea fishing. When that paled, he drove a stagecoach on the Boston-Portland run.

Always he had done things that kept him on the move. He was away when the twins were born. That night haunted him. When his lovely wife needed him most, he was gone. He had failed her. After her death, guilt assailed him. He couldn't stand the sight of his home, or the twins who had killed his wife. For nearly a dozen years he buried himself in the plains and mountains of the far west.

Now that he was among the familiar sights and sounds of his youth, the haunting sadness he thought had passed, returned. The jarring coach trip from Boston to the Jennings' farm brought back memories of courting days and the blissful weeks that followed his first marriage. The feeling of Ann's presence was so strong it was almost as if she rode beside him.

Once, long ago, on the slope that ended at the valley floor, their horse had cast a shoe. They stopped and had a picnic while the smithy came to hammer on a new one. The intersection where a dirt track led into the hills was where Ann and her folks had lived. He wondered what had happened to her parents; were they still alive? At the turn to the Jennings' place, the red barn that had stood there had collapsed. Only a pile of rubble remained.

Little Ned left the coach and strode up the lane toward the white, clapboard house. A rocking chair on the front porch reminded him of his dead grandmother. It was there she sat, rocking and sewing and telling her unending stock of tales. He knocked on the door. The colored leaded glass gave the entryway an exalted appearance, like the entrance to a church. A slim girl with brown hair and blue eyes pulled the door open. The tilt of her chin, and the quizzical expression brought a lump to Ned's throat. She was the picture of her mother. Behind her appeared another face, that of a boy with hair as black and unruly as his own.

"Tildy-Joe," he stammered, his voice choked with emotion. "I'm your father." He folded them in his long, strong arms, overwhelmed with the happiness of finally returning home.

XXVI

There is no success without hardship.
Sophocles

After the harrowing night of murder and larceny at The Dalles Chinook trading center, Raven Wing and Francois continued to paddle down river in the stolen canoe. At Fort Vancouver they stopped. Soon after settling into an abandoned lean-to in the village below the fort, Francois sought employment at Hudson's Bay. He had proven a satisfactory employee before, and had good reason to believe he, again, could find employment with the huge fur trading company.

While they were waiting for trapping brigades to form, Raven Wing discovered she was with child. The coming blessed event neither pleased, nor displeased her. It was her role as a woman to bear children. She accepted this fact as stoically as she did the rising and setting of the sun. This was the way Mother Earth intended things to happen.

Raven Wing's pregnancy pleased Francois. He had proven his manhood again and strengthened his claim on this strong-willed Nimpau woman. For a while he treated her with tenderness. Even so, he began to find a woman, two children and another on the way, burdensome. Brigade captains were reluctant to employ trappers who expected their families to tag along. Francois could not bring himself to leave his woman and his son at the local Indian camp. He had taken a great risk to lure them from Lapwai and did not intend to let them get away. In the back of his mind, there also loomed the threat of Vision Seeker's wrath. If harm came to Raven Wing, this wild brother would do far more than cut off half an ear.

Francois worked at odd jobs around Fort Vancouver and sometimes crossed over the river to labor on projects at the falls of the Willamette where the Fort Vancouver factor, John

McLoughlin, envisioned a future important industrial city. Francois took no interest in his work, but bided his time until something better came along. In his frequent spare hours he took the boys canoeing and fishing. At other times he went into the woods with them to track, snare rabbits or hunt ducks, geese and other game. The boys, especially Young Wolf with whom Francois took pains to give special instructions, were apt pupils. At first Buffalo Boy thought it natural that this man who had replaced his father should give the younger extra attention. Gradually, he realized there was a bond between Young Wolf and Francois that he did not share. He spoke of this to his mother.

"Francois likes Young Wolf better. Have I done something to displease him?"

"Your brain is muddled," Raven Wing scoffed. However, she knew he spoke the truth. To make up for Francois' slights, she found herself giving Buffalo Boy special treatment. This caused Young Wolf to sulk, and brought bitter words from Francois. To avoid conflict, she turned to favor Young Wolf and tried to ignore the bafflement and hurt in Buffalo Boy's eyes.

#

In 1836, while Raven Wing struggled with the pangs of giving birth, an important event took place at the trappers' summer fur fair. The first white women, ever, crossed the prairie to appear at the rough and ready gathering of mountain men.

"The two ladies were gazed upon with wonder and astonishment by the rude savages, they being the first white women ever seen by Indians and the first who ever penetrated into these wild and rocky regions," Osborne Russell, a trapper, wrote in his journal.

At last, the pleas of Rabbit Skin Leggings and No Horns on His Head, who traveled to St. Louis in search of teachers of the Great Spirit Book, had been answered. The two females were part of a missionary group sent to serve among the horse Indians of the Columbia plateau. The party consisted of William Gray, Reverend Henry Spalding and his wife, Eliza. Doctor Marcus

Whitman, who the previous year had gained fame by operating on Jim Bridger, and Whitman's wife, Narcissa, completed the missionary contingent. As usual, when teachers of the Great Spirit Book appeared at the rendezvous, delegations of Indian people were present to welcome them. Hoping to be the first to greet the missionaries, a large body of Nimpau led by Lawyer and Rotten Belly met the missionaries long before they arrived at Green River, site of the 1836 summer fur fair.

One hundred or more trappers/traders, and twice that number of Indian people, waited at the encampment to greet the newcomers. The column rolled up in canvas covered wagons Indian people called "lodges that move on wheels". Women from the Indian encampment crowded around to kiss and shake hands with Narcissa and Eliza. Among these females were the mates of Rotten Belly and Lawyer. Onlookers familiar with eastern society, described the occasion as "one big lawn party".

Vision Seeker observed the meeting from a hilltop where he and Running Turtle kept watch over the herd. This was the type of occasion when raiders took their enemies by surprise and swooped down to steal horses. The brothers had no desire to enter into the festivities. For the Lone Wolf clan, the missionaries with the Great Spirit Book had arrived too late. The disappearance of Raven Wing and her sons had plunged the Lone Wolf family into utter despair. Taking advantage of the situation, Weasel Face had dislodged Lone Wolf from his place as leader of the Lapwai band. Except for answering calls of nature, Lone Wolf seldom stirred from the long lodge. He didn't even inspect or inquire about new foals added to the herd. Quiet Woman and Granny were no help. They crept around the long lodge in a daze, occasionally uttering piercing moans of grief.

Concern over their parents increasingly drew Vision Seeker and Running Turtle together. They had spent hours debating what they should do. They completely took care of the herd and moved into Black Hair's abandoned cabin. Running Turtle continued to tend the garden and flowers with great care.

They had not wanted to leave their parents and make the trek to the trappers' 1836 rendezvous, but Lone Wolf had insisted they might learn word of Raven Wing and the grandsons.

"Perhaps our *soyappo* brother will be here," Running Turtle said hopefully as they had prepared for the journey.

Vision Seeker did not respond. In his heart he knew there was small chance they would see Brother Black Hair. Perhaps it was best for all that they did not meet again. It only would bring back the hurt of the past that never could be healed. However, secretly, Vision Seeker did feel there was a good chance to learn the whereabouts of Francois. His notorious reputation and prowess as trapper and fighter were widely known. Certainly, someone would have seen him. If he could locate Francois there was a good chance it would lead him to Raven Wing. Not until Raven Wing and her two sons returned to Lapwai would life in the Lone Wolf lodge be tolerable again.

Vision Seeker's hopes to gain word of Francois only partially were fulfilled. A roving fisherman did report seeing Francois pass through Celilo Falls and the Chinook trading center at The Dalles. Yes, he had a woman and two boys with him. Where they went from the Chinook encampment, the fisherman did not know.

During their stay at the Green River rendezvous the Nimpau brothers happened upon Buck Stone's band of trappers who gave them a warm welcome. When Vision Seeker asked after Black Hair, the trappers sadly shook their heads.

"Someone said he had stabled his horses in St. Louis and boarded a river boat east. That's the last, and only report we have," Buck Stone said.

"Don't yuh worry. The big geezer'll be back. He likes the life of a mountain man too much ta stay away fer long," No Hair Deacon predicted.

"Yeah!" Tomahawk Head agreed. "T'wouldn't surprise me none to see him sashayin' up the trail any ol' time. How's everything in Lapwai? Granny, Lone Wolf, Quiet Woman, all skookum?"

What the three trappers hoped to learn was what had happened between Little Ned and his Indian mate. Vision Seeker disappointed them. He was friendly enough, but refused to say a word about his family. After a short stay, he swung up on his mount and motioned for Running Turtle to do the same. They nodded their farewells and urged their horses away.

"Yeah! Jest as we thought, they still got problems they don't want to talk about," Hawk Beak observed. "Good thing I didn't offer 'em another drink or they'd fer sure had me hair."

#

The Cayuse and Nimpau found themselves pitted one against another other, competing for the services of the missionaries. Both tribes wanted the prestige of having these teachers of the Great Spirit Book settle in their homeland. Indian leaders sent wives to influence the missionary women. The Cayuse women begged Narcissa and Eliza to live with them. Their lands were good, their horses many, their pastures thick with high grass, their men brave and resourceful. . . . The Cayuse homeland was the best place to set up their lodges.

The Nimpau women, in turn, went to visit Narcissa and Eliza to make similar pleas. They insisted the white women would find the best lodges in their homeland. They were made of logs and earth instead of brush huts or flimsy skins stretched over poles. They lived near the forest where game was plentiful and near streams that carried many salmon. The pleas of both were answered. The missionaries decided the Cayuse and the Nimpau each should have a mission.

The Indian people had suffered too many disappointments to take this announcement at face value and, for a while, it appeared their fears were justified. The missionaries did not go directly from the rendezvous to their prospective mission homes. Distrusting the northern route preferred by the Cayuse and Nimpau, they refused to accompany their new hosts. Instead, the missionary party proceeded to Fort Hall. From Fort Hall they planned to follow the Snake River to Fort Walla Walla, the trail traveled by the brigades of Hudson's Bay. To make certain the missionaries did not change their minds, as Jason Lee's party had done, some 200 Nimpau and Cayuse traipsed along.

Upon arriving at Fort Hall most of the Indian contingent decided they had been gone from their homes too long. It was time to return. They pleaded with the missionaries to accompany them. The missionaries refused but promised they would not change their minds; soon they would come to teach them the ways of the Great Spirit Book. Nevertheless, Rotten Belly, his family and a few others from the Indian group, continued on with the missionaries. They had been disappointed too many times to suffer another defeat. Rotten Belly, especially, vowed not to let them slip through his fingers again.

At Fort Walla Walla the missionaries found they could not acquire the supplies they needed. After again solemnly promising their Indian escort they would return, the missionaries embarked on river boats for Fort Vancouver where they stayed at the home of the fort factor, Dr. John McLoughlin, who ruled the Pacific Northwest for Hudson's Bay. When news of this development came whizzing over the moccasin telegraph to tribes of the plateau, the Indian people's hopes again were dashed.

McLoughlin was a kind and fair-minded person but his allegiance was to the British. He would do everything in his power to prevent the missionaries from settling above the Columbia River. Yet, McLoughlin had more vision than the Indian people thought. The fact American white women had safely crossed the continent made it clear entire American families, in considerable force, soon would cross the plains. They would settle in Oregon Territory, threatening the British hold on the land John McLoughlin ruled. He could fight this movement, or he could help the inevitable come to pass. McLoughlin chose the latter, which earned him the rancor of his superiors and, ultimately, cost him his job. The Cayuse and Nimpau would get their missions, but they also would pay a high price.

XXVII

Teach your children what we have taught our children, that the Earth is our mother. Whatever befalls the Earth befalls the sons of the Earth.

Seattle, Duwamish

Raven Wing, her third son cradled in her arms, watched the flotilla of river boats bearing the missionaries arrive at Fort Vancouver. From the river bank Indian village, she had a good view of the first American white women to cross the continent. Unlike her people who so graciously greeted the missionary group at the rendezvous, she was unmoved. White women - red women. What difference did it make? They were all the same to her. They bred and bore their young in the same painful manner.

When the rumor circulated through the village that the missionaries planned to settle in the uplands, even in her home-land, Raven Wing did experience a touch of envy. She was tired of the constant rain, fog and drizzle of the lower Columbia River. She longed to feel the sun on her back, to see the barren, sun-bleached hills that rose above Lapwai. Also, the wet weather was not good for the children. They sniffed, their noses dripped and they were constantly underfoot when it rained.

Raven Wing hinted to Francois they should return to the dry climate of the inland plateau. He evasively grunted. She knew full well he was afraid to go and did not press him. Even so, a spark of hope began to flicker. If the missionaries settled in the Nimpau tribal lands they would protect her lover. For hadn't No Hair On Head said that the *soyappo's* Great Spirit loved everyone, even sinners?

In early October the missionaries, Whitman, Spalding and Gray, returned to Fort Walla Walla. Narcissa Whitman and Eliza Spalding remained behind in Fort Vancouver. Accompanied by Pierre Pambrun, chief clerk at Fort Walla Walla, the missionary men traveled up the Walla Walla River in search of a likely site to

establish their mission among the Cayuse. Some 25 miles east of
the fort, the missionaries stopped on the banks of a creek that
joined the river. Here, in an expanse of land filled with high
grass, they pounded a stake into the ground. The site was known
to the Cayuse as Waiilatpu, The Place of Rye Grass. For the missionary group it was soon to be known as Whitman's Mission.

Immediately after the missionaries selected the Cayuse
mission site, Spalding and Whitman journeyed east to choose a
mission site among the Nimpau. A group led by the ever present
Rotten Belly came to escort the missionaries to the Nimpau homeland. Rotten Belly was upset that Whitman planned to settle
among the Cayuse. He warned Whitman that, unlike the Nimpau,
the Cayuse were difficult people.

"These people are quarrelsome. They will give you much
trouble," he said. Rotten Belly's warning words would not be
forgotten. A decade later the Cayuse would rise up to destroy the
mission and everything it contained.

Rotten Belly was delighted to have at least one missionary family settle in Nimpau country. Although his band lived a
considerable distance away on the south fork of the Kooskooskie,
when the party entered Lapwai Valley, Rotten Belly waved his
arm expansively. "This is all my country," he bragged. "Whatever you wish, our people will give you. Whatever you want
done, our people will do for you."

The appearance of the missionaries created great excitement. Finally, after all the years of waiting, they had arrived.
Even Lone Wolf, Quiet Woman and Granny came out to see the
procession make its way past the long lodge and up the valley.
Lone Wolf was not impressed. What was all the big fuss about?
Except for the differences in dress and pious manner, the missionaries looked much the same as did mountain men who attended the annual summer fur fair.

The missionaries passed the village and traveled two miles
up Lapwai Creek. There, at a break in the barren hills which rose
up on either side of the valley, they stopped. The site pleased

Spalding. "Here," he said, "I will build my mission."

Rotten Belly agreed it was a fine place. "I will settle here, too, right beside you," he informed the missionary.

There were some who did not view with pleasure the presence of the missionaries. Among them was Thunder Eyes, the *tewat*. He particularly was irked with the flamboyant way Rotten Belly led the missionary party up the valley, generously promising them everything they wanted.

"If he likes these hairy faces so much why doesn't he settle them in his village?" Thunder Eyes queried Vision Seeker. "He gives Lapwai land away like it was his to give."

Vision Seeker did not answer but secretly agreed with Thunder Eyes. He, too, was irked. The land Spalding chose for his mission contained three springs which flowed into Lapwai Creek. It was a place where Lone Wolf's herd liked to come for water and to browse on the rich grass that grew among the willow trees. If this was a forerunner of what was to come, it did not bode well. The missionaries barely had arrived. Yet, already they had laid claim to some of the best land in the valley. What demands would they make next?

Almost as quickly as they appeared in Lapwai, the missionaries departed. Dr. Whitman returned to Waiilatpu to build his mission home among the Cayuse. Reverend Spalding traveled to Fort Vancouver. He went to collect the missionary ladies and escort them up river to the new mission sites. On the return journey Narcissa Whitman stopped at Waiilatpu while Eliza Spalding continued on to Lapwai.

Excitement again stirred Lapwai Valley. The residents, most of them for the first time, gazed upon a white woman. They saw a slender, tallow-faced person of medium height. They quickly discovered her ordinary appearance belied a kind heart and friendly nature. Among the mission group, she was the one bright star. Although her health was not good and the climate did not agree with her, Eliza Spalding would spend almost exactly the next 11 years and one month in the midst of the Nimpau.

Curiosity about the missionary party again brought Lone Wolf out of the long lodge. He took one quick look and returned disappointed. He had seen spotted mares with better looks and shapes than the missionary woman, he informed his mate.

The Spaldings set up what they called a buffalo tent at the mission site and immediately began to erect proper mission buildings. Soon, with the help of their flock, a sizable log structure was erected. As Little Ned had found, building with logs was a difficult task. Though the Indian men regarded the work beneath them, they pitched in. Even Rotten Belly helped fell trees, float them down the Kooskooskie and carry the logs from the river to the mission site, a distance of nearly three miles. The work was not easy. It took a dozen workers to carry one log. When the building was completed it encompassed an area 48 feet by 18 feet; one end was intended for the Spalding family living quarters, the other end was to accommodate the mission school.

Much to Lone Wolf's disgust, Running Turtle, always curious about the ways of the hairy faces, offered his services. He was assigned to the group that carried the logs from the river. He had the honor of lifting the last log into position and received Eliza Spalding's words of praise. When she announced one end of the building would serve as a school, Running Turtle asked to be included in the first class of students. Impressed by his industry and eagerness, she was delighted to write his name in a little black book that she called the class roll.

Running Turtle was only one of many anxious to learn. After school commenced oftentimes entire families or all the occupants of a long lodge would appear for class. People from distant villages came and set up tipis to be near the school. Youngsters and village leaders wanted to receive knowledge from the missionary woman. Some attended merely to view her and hear the pleasant, strange voice. She spoke their language but with a quaint accent. When she came upon a word she did not know in the Nimpau language she would go into little acts trying to put across the meaning of the word she needed. Amused and thrilled at being asked to help, everyone would talk at once. Sometimes the classroom uproar could be heard all over the encampment that had sprung up around the mission site.

Teacher Spalding's explanations especially were enjoyed. She always had a piece of chalk in her hand, drawing pictures to illustrate the lessons. This method of teaching delighted the students. A drawing of an object made it real. When arguments occurred on a subject, those who had observed the illustrations settled matters. Teacher Spalding had drawn a map of it, so it had to be true.

Many of the lessons dealt with the Great Spirit Book. Eliza Spalding told them of the birth of the great holy man called "Jesus" whose birthday they would celebrate during the Season of Deep Snow. She drew an animal with long flapping ears that resembled a *soyappo* pack mule. She called it, "donkey". She made drawings of strange animals called "sheep" and horned animals called "cows". These animals had watched over the birth of baby Jesus in a place like a covered-over horse corral. Everyone readily understood and accepted these teachings. They knew from their own legends Mother Earth first brought forth animals to her surface to prepare the way for the coming of humans.

The lessons caused much talk around evening lodge fires. Running Turtle discovered reports on classroom sessions were ways to arouse Lone Wolf, Granny and Quiet Woman out of their melancholy. When he explained how Jesus died on the cross, his side pierced by a lance, Lone Wolf grimaced.

"Where were the warriors? They should have put a stop to it. No holy man should die this way."

Running Turtle attempted to explain why the man Jesus was forced to die on the cross, but did not understand it himself. He left the long lodge frustrated at his failure to enlighten his parents. He didn't feel any better after telling his troubles to Vision Seeker who merely stared at him as though he did not have good sense.

"Why do you talk about things when you know so little?"

he asked. "Remember, a still tongue makes for a wise head."

In spite of the students' eagerness to learn, school teaching was not smooth sailing for Eliza Spalding. She quickly discovered she, herself, had a lot to learn. Some days the classroom bulged and rang with the chatter of students. Then for days the classroom would be empty and silent, and for good reason. The Nimpau way of life forced the people to follow the seasons. When kouse and other root crops were ready to harvest, the people were off to the warm sides of the mountain slopes to collect them. When the berries ripened they went to pick them. The camas bulb had to be harvested before the first freezes of fall. Then there was the time for hunting and the salmon runs and the never-ending preparation of pemmican, the drying of meat and the curing of skins. The gathering and storing of foodstuffs was a necessity if the people were to survive.

The ebb and flow in the classroom and at religious services impressed upon the missionaries that to teach and save the souls of these people, they first had to "civilize" them. The missionary efforts would make little headway until their flock settled down. This meant the people had to give up their present way of life. Instead of hunting and gathering, they had to cultivate the land, plant crops and harvest them the same as people did in the so-called "civilized lands". The *tewats*, like Thunder Eyes, who deplored such teachings, walked around the village making scathing remarks.

"These people cause trouble," Thunder Eyes said. "They say we cannot live as we do. They lock up our young ones like squirrels cornered in a cave. When they should learn to hunt and fight, they sit in classroom making marks on talking paper. The parents are no better. They sit idle, chirping like grasshoppers watching the *soyappo* woman make pictures on the wall. Who will gather and prepare food for Season of Deep Snow? Missionary man says plow and hoe and dig at Mother Earth like birds pecking for worms. Wagh! What will become of our way of life? It will be lost, covered up by white man's books, hoes and plows."

XXVIII

More things are wrought by prayer than this world dreams of.
Tennyson

Vision Seeker and Running Turtle watched Lone Wolf and Quiet Women grow old before their eyes. The parents' hearts truly were broken. After losing their eldest son, their only daughter and her family and then the leadership of the Lapwai band, they knew this ill-fortune could be due to only one thing. The Great Mysterious no longer looked upon them with favor. A final blow had come with the sudden death of Granny. She was sitting in the dark corner of the lodge. They thought she had fallen asleep. When they called to awaken her, she did not move. In her hands she held a baby moccasin she had been mending. Why she was mending it, no one could understand. It was one Young Wolf long ago had outgrown.

Lone Wolf was overcome with grief. Granny was more than a mother, she was an honored member of the tribe. At the age of four she had been captured by the Cheyenne. After toiling 10 years as a slave, she stole a horse and made a hair-raising escape. Her fortitude and courage had given her a standing equal to that of a battlefield warrior. Great Wolf, a youthful Nimpau leader, had taken her as his mate. Together they had traveled from the western plains to the Pacific. They were present when the first great canoe with wings entered the Columbia River in 1792. They had gone aboard to meet Captain Gray. In 1803 Granny had survived the terrible raid when a band of Shoshone swept down on the Middle Fork of the Kooskooskie and nearly wiped out a late summer fishing party. In the conflict she had lost her mate and three sons. Only by playing dead did she and her youngest son, Lone Wolf, survive.

Two years later she was among those who were in camp when the *soyappo* explorers, Lewis and Clark, had arrived. Hungry and weary from travel, they were so grateful for the hospitality she tendered them, they honored her with a medal, the likeness of President Thomas Jefferson engraved on one side.

Lone Wolf regarded his mother as indestructible. Always she had been around to give advice. He did not take it every time, but never failed to listen. Not until she was gone, did he realize just how much he relied on her wise words.

Eliza Spalding learned of Granny's death from Running Turtle's friends. For the first time ever, her star pupil did not show up for class. Reverend Spalding called on the grieving family to offer condolences. He insisted Granny be given a Christian burial. "Who knows, perhaps God in his mercy will open the golden gates and allow her in," the preacher said. "We will pray for her. It is marvelous what miracles prayer can perform."

Vision Seeker objected to the Christian burial, but Lone Wolf was too grief-stricken to resist. Granny was the first Nimpau villager laid to rest in the mission graveyard. A marker with a cross was placed at the head of her grave. Every time he passed it, Vision Seeker wondered what Granny thought lying there under this strange sign of the white man's god.

Vision Seeker did not have a high opinion of the missionaries. They had failed his people in the past. What would keep them from disappointing them again? He looked upon them as a temporary phenomenon. Like a spring swarm of mosquitoes, they would buzz around for a while and then be gone.

As the Spaldings industriously went about establishing the mission and diligently taught in the classroom, Vision Seeker changed his mind. He began to feel a sense of foreboding. These people were not as simpleminded and anemic as they first appeared. Spalding was a determined, stubborn man with narrow thoughts; once entrenched, he was not likely to give up. Gray, who had come to help in constructing the mission buildings, was easier for Vision Seeker to understand. Unlike Spalding, he did not appear dedicated. Like a slender sapling in a stiff breeze, he wavered back and forth. If trouble were to emerge he had the look of a person who would break and run. Vision Seeker had the uneasy feeling, sooner or later, he would cause trouble.

One day, while in the pasture inspecting the herd, Vision Seeker mentioned his misgivings about the missionaries to a herder named The Hat. The Hat scoffed at his fears. "You must not question what these people say. Do as they ask, have faith and forget the old ways. These hairy faces show us new trails. Our people must follow them and see where they lead."

"Perhaps you are right," Vision Seeker said. "If they destroy the old trails we will have no choice but to go the way they say. I don't like it, though. We are like blind moles burrowing into new earth. Do we find light ahead or do we walk in darkness for the rest of our days?"

As spring approached The Reverend Spalding expanded upon his plan to turn the Nimpau into farmers. He directed the manufacture of picks and hoes and sent orders east for plows. He demonstrated how to break the ground, sow seeds and cultivate plants. Some, who had seen cultivated plots of ground around Fort Vancouver and among the Spokan, readily accepted the new way to garner their livelihood.

Others resisted. Mother Earth was too sacred to rip and tear at her face, they said. For the people of Lapwai Valley there was the troublesome influx of tribesmen from other bands. People from as far away as Wallowa came to set up tipi lodges near the mission site. They tilled and planted ground local people considered rightfully theirs. The White Bird and Rotten Belly people from Kamiah were among the first to set up lodges. Then came people from Asotin and Weippe Prairie. They all wanted plots of ground to cultivate and plant. Before the summer of 1837 had ended, Lapwai villagers gathered in council to plan ways to drive these intruders from the land that had been theirs since the Ancients had arrived.

Gradually, another ugly thorn emerged. The people discovered Missionary Spalding had an unpleasant side. If people did not carry out his wishes, he was impatient. He threatened to have those who disobeyed him whipped. This means of gaining obedience went against Nimpau tradition. Worse, Spalding expected men of the tribe to do the flogging. The public humiliation suffered by victims and their families began to turn people against each other. For almost the first time ever, family fights and quarrels became commonplace. Like chokeberries, the *soyappos'* religion had a tantalizing appearance but a bitter taste.

Spalding ignored the discord and rising resentment. He claimed everything he did was for the glory of God and the good of his flock. The American Board of Missions sent him to save souls and he was not going to let anything stand in his path.

In his sermons Spalding preached on death, the glories of heaven and the terrors of hell. Disobedience was a sin. Those who sinned were condemned to hell. Hell was pictured as a frightening place filled with eternal fire that tortured victims until the end of time. This terrifying prospect kept some followers in line, but not all. People began to grumble and mutter. They wished they never had asked for the Great Spirit Book and its teachers. Thunder Eyes and his fellow *tewats* gloated. Even before Rabbit Skin Leggings and his band of emissaries left for St. Louis to seek the white man's Great Spirit Book, they had warned against it -- the Great Unseen would be offended and take revenge.

While Spalding determinedly carried out his plan to whip his flock into shape, Gray, the third man of the missionary team, became as disgruntled as the disenchanted Nimpau. He decided to leave and return east. Spalding did not attempt to stop him. Instead, he came up with the idea of sending a herd of horses with Gray. He wanted to exchange the horses for cattle which would be driven across the plains the following summer. Spalding reasoned the presence of cattle would be another means to encourage the Nimpau to settle down. The cattle would provide meat and hides. Then there would be no need for tribesmen to travel across the mountains to hunt the buffalo.

Some Nimpau leaders liked the idea. They rounded up a number of horses and placed them in Gray's care. To help drive

the herd east, several of the horse donors and two volunteer herders decided to make the journey. Among them were Vision
Seeker's friend, The Hat, plus Blue Cloak and Ellis.

Before setting out on the trip The Hat came to Vision
Seeker and pleaded with him to go along. Vision Seeker declined. "It is a foolish journey. Mother Earth provides all the
buffalo we need, why should we send for these strange creatures
called 'cattle'?" Although he did not say so, he feared for the
safety of the mission. He had no confidence in Gray. The man
was weak and had little experience in the ways of the west. The
party had to pass through the lands of the Blackfeet, Crow and
Sioux, all warlike tribes. The least misstep could bring disaster.

As so often in the past, Vision Seeker's misgivings were
correct. Gray and his party made it safely to Green River, site of
the 1837 rendezvous; but, against the advice of old timers like
Jim Bridger, Gray refused to wait and travel east under the protection of a fur brigade. In early August, above the forks of the
Platte River at a place called Ash Hollow, a band of Sioux attacked Gray's party. The Nimpau who accompanied Gray were
slain to the last man. Among the dead was Vision Seeker's friend,
The Hat. Gray escaped. It was rumored while his Indian companions fought to save the herd, he had turned tail and fled in the
most cowardly fashion.

Before news of the catastrophe reached Lapwai, two of
the Nimpau horsemen who had left with Gray, returned with their
herds intact. At the rendezvous site Ellis and Blue Cloak had
quarreled with Gray, rounded up their horses and left. When
Spalding heard they had returned, he was furious. He ordered
the two men whipped, 50 lashes each. Ellis quickly mounted up
and took his herd to his Kamiah home. Blue Cloak remained in
Lapwai. He thought Spalding would not carry out the whipping.
Blue Cloak was wrong. Spalding's followers bound and tied him
to a post, but not one of the villagers would step forward and
whip their tribesman. Spalding was forced to carry out the sen-
tence himself.

The abhorrent affair left the people stunned. Friction between those who accepted Spalding's iron rule and those who did
not, increased. Many who had settled near the mission departed
for their own home grounds. Caught up in the turmoil, Running
Turtle came to Vision Seeker and told him the troubles he faced.
He wanted to learn the words and ways of the hairy faces' books
and talking paper, but by doing so he was accused of being a
missionary toad and betrayer of his people.

For once Vision Seeker's mind was barren of advice. The
days were over when one could predict what next season or the
season after would bring. The missionaries' strange ways and
changeable behavior put a stop to that. He remembered the words
of Rabbit Skin Leggings when the people first spoke of making
the trek to St. Louis. "This is serious business," he had said. "If
we ask for this power, we must accept what it brings."

Perhaps what was most disturbing about Missionary
Spalding was his changeable nature. Immediately after execut-
ing a whipping, he could comfort a crying child or tenderly bind
up a wound. After Granny was buried, he came frequently to
visit Lone Wolf and Quiet Woman. He spoke kindly of Granny.
He was praying for her entry into heaven, he said. He was certain
his prayers would be answered. The talks were carried on with
difficulty because, unlike Eliza Spalding, the reverend did not
have fluency in Sahaptin. When Spalding learned of the Lone
Wolf's' grief over their missing daughter and her sons, he promised to pray for their return.

"You should be praying for them, too," he said. "Prayer
is one of the great powers God has provided. 'Ask and ye shall
receive', the Good Book says. He will help you but you must
listen. God speaks to you through the Scriptures. He alone can
answer your prayers." The missionary dropped on his knees. He
bowed his head, closed his eyes, folded his hands and began a
loud and long prayer.

Lone Wolf glanced at Quiet Woman with shock and disbelief. Did these *soyappos* speak to the Supreme Being as though

he were another human? A shiver of apprehension coursed up Lone Wolf's spine. He did not want to listen. From childhood he had been taught, before communing with the Great Mystery one prepared oneself, wiped away earthly thoughts, filled his mind with spiritual things and, unless it was a ceremonial occasion, spoke with the Creator silently and not in the presence of others.

Since a toddler at the knees of Granny, he knew about listening and talking to The Creator. His earliest remembrance was of Granny lifting a finger for quiet. They would sit still for minutes on end, listening to Mother Earth: the gurgle of the brook, the whistle of the wind, the chirp of a sparrow, the howl of a coyote, the squeak of a bat or the rustle of a lizard.

"These are messages from the lips of the Great Unseen," Granny, who was young and beautiful then, would say with her bright smile. "They speak for the Great Mysterious who created us. It is rude not to pay attention to what these messengers say. They tell us what the Great Mystery wants us to know. Respect these little ones. They are Mother Earth's precious creatures like you and me."

"Ah, yes," Lone Wolf thought. Praying for a Nimpau was as natural as breathing. There was no need to speak of it, no need for churches or preachers. To make a temple or shrine to honor the Mysterious or to have a preacher intervene in this holy experience, would be an insult. Prayer was directly between man and Maker. The Supreme Being and man did not need a special place to meet. The Great Mystery was everywhere: omnipresent in the forests; on the grassy plains; in the valleys and on the mountain tops; in the shadows of dawn; in the rays of a sunset and in the film of a cloud. The Great Mystery had all outdoors for a cathedral where the Unseen walked and talked with people each moment of the day.

Missionary Spalding did not try to understand these things. Like a sightless and earless mole that lives in darkness, he heard nothing; he saw nothing. Never once in all the meetings the missionary had with the people, did he ask them or give them an opportunity to speak on tribal customs and their beliefs, nor did he attend their ceremonies. He was not interested. He wanted nothing to do with such things. The Nimpau way of worship was wrong. The path they trod led away from God to a fire-filled hell.

Lone Wolf glanced again at Quiet Woman, the expression of disbelief still on his face. Does this man think we never speak or listen to the One who created us? his look asked. Lone Wolf kept these thoughts to himself. He thanked the missionary for his prayers and walked a short ways with him when he departed. He barely had returned to the long lodge when Running Turtle breathlessly bounded in, shouting at the top of his voice, "Raven Wing is here! Raven Wing has come home!"

Lone Wolf, closely followed by Quiet Woman, ran out the door and up the path toward the log cabin. They met Vision Seeker on the way. "Is it true?" Lone Wolf asked. "Raven Wing and her sons are here?"

"Yes," Vision Seeker answered. "She has a third son."

"Wonderful!" Quiet Woman chortled. "Teacher of the Great Spirit Book speaks with a straight tongue. Prayer is a powerful thing."

RAVEN WING

XXIX

Long before I ever heard of Christ, or saw a white man . . .
I perceived what goodness is. I saw and loved what is really
beautiful. Civilization has not taught me anything better!

Ohiyesa, Dakota

Strangely, the power of the Great Spirit Book did help bring Raven Wing and her sons home. Raven Wing finally convinced Francois the missionaries' presence made Lapwai safe. They would allow no one to harm him. Still Francois dawdled. It took a gambling debt to move him into action. After a drunken spree, the gambler to whom Francois owed the debt, and two of his henchmen, came to collect. A fight ensued. Francois knifed one man and, with Raven Wing's help, sent the other two fleeing. Factor McLoughlin got wind of the fracas. He fired Francois, ordered him away from Fort Vancouver and sent word to every trading post in the Northwest, he never was to be employed by Hudson's Bay again. Chastised, Francois reluctantly agreed to take Raven Wing and her sons home.

Actually, the homecoming had gone extremely well, largely because Lone Wolf and Quiet Woman were so thrilled. Led by her parents, occupants of the long lodge came in a group to welcome Raven Wing. It was a pleasant meeting. Francois avoided it by disappearing into the hills. The villagers, some of whom Raven Wing barely knew, brought gifts of food and useful household items. Afterward, Lone Wolf went to the pasture where he ordered Running Turtle to cut out two identical ponies marked like speckled turkey eggs on their sides and rumps. He brought them back and gave them to Buffalo Boy and Young Wolf. They were old enough now to have their own ponies, he said. Another, less spectacular horse, he gave to Francois. The gifts were pleasing especially to Raven Wing. It meant her father forgave her for deserting her big trapper mate and running away from home.

Lone Wolf's gift giving did not please Vision Seeker. Since Many Horses' death he had kept careful watch over the herd. He knew every colt and mare. He remembered the day each colt had been born and the season in which each mare should be bred. He inspected the herd for sick and lame animals, and was quick to see to their care. He knew the fields where stallions guarded their droves of mares. To keep the stallions from fighting, he kept the droves separated during the estrus of the mares. He safeguarded the animals like the diligent shepherd did his sheep.

When Lone Wolf appeared, Vision Seeker was on the hillside counting and inspecting the animals of the herd. Without saying a word to him, Lone Wolf ordered Running Turtle to catch the three gift horses and lead them away. Vision Seeker prized the speckled ponies. They had replaced the two matched ponies given to Black Hair. He had special plans for one of them. It was swift of foot. With training it would make a racer, perhaps the swiftest one in the valley. He did not begrudge the boys and Raven Wing the gifts, but to see the man he loathed in control of these special ponies was more than he could stomach. If Francois did not treat the horses, Raven Wing and her sons well, Vision Seeker vowed to run the French Canadian trapper out of Lapwai for good.

It soon became clear to Raven Wing, Lapwai was not the pleasant place she remembered. The influx of outsiders caused resentment and discontent. The villagers quarreled and wrangled over inconsequential matters. Teachings of the missionaries were also an upsetting influence. Some people believed them and some did not. The aftermath of the whipping of Blue Cloak hung over Lapwai Valley like a dark cloud. It was cruel. It was not right. Bitter complaints were voiced on every side.

However, almost everyone spoke well of Eliza Spalding. She always was pleasant and spoke their language. When she grew large with child, village women clucked with sympathy. She did not complain and worked in the classroom until the day the child was born.

"It's a baby girl," Running Turtle, who kept close watch

on his teacher, reported to Quiet Woman. "She takes the same name as her mother, Eliza."

Women from all parts of the valley came to view and hold the new baby. When Eliza Spalding returned to the classroom, they would steal in to take the child from the cradle. They would cuddle her, change her and lull her to sleep singing favorite lullabies. Quiet Woman and Raven Wing were among those who came to see and hold little Eliza. Mrs. Spalding, in her usual kind way, spoke to them. She knew Quiet Woman through the avid student, Running Turtle, but Raven Wing was a newcomer. Upon learning Raven Wing had school-age sons, she invited them to attend school.

Raven Wing hesitated, wondering what her man, Francois, would say. He had little use for the missionaries. He called them "Protestant Troublemakers". Raven Wing knew he did not feel comfortable in Lapwai, but could not come up with a reason for his fear. She continued to insist he was safe. The missionaries and the power of the Great Spirit Book would protect him.

These thoughts ran through Raven Wing's mind as she weighed Eliza Spalding's invitation for the boys to attend the mission school. Perhaps, with the boys under the lady missionary's protection, Francois would be reassured no harm would come to him. At least, it would be one more argument against traipsing off again. With that pleasing thought, Raven Wing accepted the invitation.

"Yes, it is good for the boys to have an education," she said, surprising Eliza Spalding by speaking in Boston accented English learned from her mate, the big Boston trapper.

Reverend Spalding also became aware of the newcomers' arrival. For some time he had been interested in the log cabin. The location at which Spalding initially established his mission, did not please him. He wanted to rebuild the mission on the flat acreage that bordered Lapwai Creek, near where it entered the Kooskooskie. Spalding planned to make the mission larger and more self-sustaining. His plans included a gristmill and a sawmill. To power the mills, he needed a greater supply of running water than the creek provided at the present mission site. That log cabin, Spalding decided, would make an excellent head-quarters to oversee the building of the new mission.

At the time the idea came to the missionary, only Vision Seeker and Running Turtle occupied Black Hair's cabin. Before Reverend Spalding got around to ask for the use of the cabin, Raven Wing and her family had moved in. This presented Spalding with an awkward situation. It was far more difficult to ask a family to move, than it was two single men. He pondered over the problem and began to ask questions. Who were these people; where did they come from? If they were members of the Lapwai Valley band, why did he not know about them?

Gradually, the story of how Raven Wing had deserted her husband and taken up with the French Canadian emerged. Spalding was appalled. Had he been praying for the return of a sinner, an adulteress? He was furious with Lone Wolf. "Why did the hatchet-faced Indian and his non-communicative wife allow me to carry on?" Spalding sputtered in his rage. Had he beseeched the Lord to return a woman who was no better than a harlot? The missionary was fit to be tied. He stomped around the sitting room, kicking aside the furniture. His wife, Eliza, skittered out of the house, taking refuge in the classroom.

The presence of Raven Wing and Francois living in obvi-ous sin, kept the missionary awake all night. Why did he struggle to save the souls of these people -- that is if they had souls? They acted no better than animals. On that Sabbath, as he arose to slap the Holy Book on the wooden case that served as a lectern, people could tell they were in for a scolding. Reverend Spalding started calmly enough with the Proverb, "Can a man take fire to his bo-som, and his clothes not be burned?" His head swiveled around taking measure of the congregation, his small eyes glittered like those of a coiled snake. The crowd stirred uneasily.

"Wearing a black robe, he had the look of a carrion crow," Running Turtle, the only member of the Lone Wolf clan to attend the service, later reported to Vision Seeker.

It did not take long for Spalding to get to the heart of the matter. He named the couple living in sin and, as if present in person, ordered them to cease their adulterous ways. Raven Wing and the mountain man called Black Hair officially still were married, he declared. She and the man from Hudson's Bay were breaking the Seventh Commandment. "In Biblical times the penalty for this was death by stoning!" Spalding's thunderous voice sent shivers shooting up the backs of those who understood the words.

Before the service ended, Running Turtle slipped away to report to Vision Seeker what the reverend had said. "Hmm!" Vision Seeker grunted. "This is not good. People may take the man seriously. Raven Wing could be in danger."

"Aiiee!" Running Turtle groaned. Now that his sister had returned and his parents were happy, he wanted nothing to disturb the family's new found tranquillity. "What can we do? We cannot allow Raven Wing to leave again."

For a long while Vision Seeker and his brother sat in silence. Each thought of ways to free their sister from her swarthy lover. He was the one who Spalding could not tolerate. "Maybe it's time someone cut off the rest of his ear," Vision Seeker finally said.

Running Turtle gave Vision Seeker a startled glance, then quickly looked away. The vicious glint in his brother's eyes suddenly made his mouth feel dry. For a second he could not believe this was the soft-spoken brother who communed with spirits and could see what tomorrow would bring. Running Turtle's mind flashed back to the blood drenched robe in the abandoned tipi that later had burned to the ground. Flies had coated the spot where a bit of flesh was held fast by the brownish stained buffalo hair. For days the fetid odor had clung to his nostrils. The source and cause of the blood and rotting flesh now was crystal clear. It was the missing part of Francois' ear. His brother was responsible! Although the day was warm, Running Turtle shivered.

Reverend Spalding's tirade against the sinful couple sent a groundswell sweeping through the village. Many of the villagers remembered Black Hair with affection. He had kept himself apart and did strange things, but always had been kind. He had taken their children under his wing and taught them in the ways of talking paper. He had been a good mate for Raven Wing and fathered two sons. No one could remember any harm he had done. The next evening after Spalding's condemnation, a group of young men marched on the lodge of Raven Wing and her lover. They circled the cabin and shouted what they understood of the reverend's vitriolic sermon.

The hubbub outside created turmoil inside. Francois seized his rifle. "You told me this place was safe. I never should have believed you," he snarled at Raven Wing. He cocked the rifle and sat with it across his knees and placed his pistol and knives by his side. Raven Wing picked up the baby and shooed the two older sons into the back room. The baby whimpered. Buffalo Boy and Young Wolf sat with their hearts in their mouths. They remembered the terrible times when Francois went crazy mad, slapping them and beating their mother. The night Francois murdered the Chinook fisherman was etched forever in their minds.

"Come and get me!" Francois shouted to the Indian youth who surrounded the cabin. "I'll show you the pathway to your missionary's heaven and hell." To give emphasis to the words, he thrust the rifle barrel through the window and sent a bullet zinging over his tormentors' heads.

Raven Wing attempted to reason with Francois, but he would not listen. He cursed and stormed; if anybody was killed it would be her fault. Gradually Spalding's youthful followers grew tired of shouting and departed, but not before hurling rocks and war lances at the cabin. Several of the missiles thudded on the roof, another crashed against the door.

Late in the night camp dogs created another uproar. A lone rider thundered out of the village and up the Lolo Trail. In the morning the news reached the long lodge; Raven Wing's French Canadian man was gone. Quiet Woman quickly wrapped around her head the bright colored shawl Big Black Hair had given her and motioned with her lips and chin to Lone Wolf.

"We must go to Daughter. She needs comfort. Let us take her into the long lodge . . . have her live with us. She must not leave Lapwai again."

The couple walked in silence up the sloping trail to the log cabin lodge. Vision Seeker and Running Turtle already were there, lounging on the porch that overlooked the garden. Raven Wing, holding the baby, sat between them. Buffalo Boy and Young Wolf were on their knees playing with buffalo dice. No one appeared in the least upset. When Quiet Woman invited Raven Wing to move into the long lodge, she refused.

"No, it is best we stay. Black Hair will expect us to be here."

Vision Seeker gave his sister a look of surprise. Did she have a change of heart? Did she want her husband back? And how could she be so certain that he would return? Did the Unseen send her a special message? The last meeting with his Boston brother still was clear in his mind. The signs he witnessed afterward, were even more vividly remembered. Of course he could have misunderstood them. It would not be the first time premonitions had betrayed him. He gave Running Turtle a nudge with his moccasined foot -- the signal to keep quiet.

"How wise of you to wait in the cabin," Vision Seeker quietly said to his sister. She needed all the encouragement the family could give her.

"Oh-hah," Running Turtle stuttered in agreement. He glanced down at the front garden in full bloom. A soft breeze ruffled the flowers. Waves of color spread from one end of the garden to the other. He was reminded of the hours he had spent watching each plant grow. They emerge from Mother Earth spindly and ugly, now look at them, he thought, each one a miracle. His *soyappo* brother was so wise to surround his lodge with beauty.

"It will be a day of happiness when Black Hair returns," Running Turtle blurted with such sincerity and heartfelt emotion Buffalo Boy and Young Wolf stopped play to stare. Raven Wing and her parents studied the youth as though a new human species suddenly had dropped out of Father Sky.

Running Turtle shifted uncomfortably. "I understand wise words of the missionary woman. 'When the whole family is together, the soul is in place'."

> *This we all know. All things are connected*
> *like the blood which unites one family.*
>
> Seattle, Duwamish

The exciting saga of Raven Wing and the Lone Wolf clan continues in *The Last Rendezvous*, Volume III of the Lone Wolf clan historical series. Ask your book seller or contact:

MAD BEAR PRESS
6636 Mossman Place NE
Albuquerque, NM 87110
Telephone-Fax 505-881-4093

AUTHORS' NOTE

This story is historically true. The rendezvous', also called summer fur fairs, took place each year. The Battles of Bear Lake and Pierre's Hole happened. Rabbit Skin Leggings, No Horns on His Head, Black Eagle and Man of the Morning journeyed to St. Louis in search of the Great Spirit Book; not one returned to his homeland. Nez Perce Blue Cloak, Ellis, Flint Necklace, Kutenai Pelly, Spokan Gary, The Hat, Thunder Eyes, Lawyer, Rotten Belly and Tiloukaikt of the Cayuse all lived, and had a hand in making this history.

Likewise, Jim Bridger, Doc Newell, Antoine Godin, Joe Meek, Jedediah Smith, Lucian Fountenelle, Doctor "White Eagle" John McLoughlin, Nathaniel Wyeth, Captain Bonneville, Bill and Milton Sublette played key roles in the fur trade.

Christian missionaries Jason Lee, William Gray, Spaldings and Whitmans came west in the 1830's, intent on converting the horse Indians of the plateau country. Their efforts made an impact which still effects the way these people live.

The Lone Wolf clan, Weasel Face, Buck Stone's brigade and Francois are fictional, but exemplify the Indian people and the first mountain men they encountered.

The Northwest tribesmen's unquenchable desire to possess the secrets of the Great Spirit Book is true. Thousands of Indian people came to rendezvous', hoping to entice missionaries to live among them and teach them the Bible's mysteries. For years white men ignored their entreaties. When missionaries did arrive their hard-nosed, inflexible approach to life dismayed the natives. The Indian people felt betrayed, a feeling that exists among many to this day.

- an historical series in the style of Storyteller depicting the role American Indians played in the "Making of the West."

Lone Wolf Clan Book Sequence

The Lone Wolf Clan
An awesome vision launches the Lone Wolf Clan on a journey that changes their lives forever.

Raven Wing
A tale of love and spiritual seeking embroiled in a clash of cultures.

The Last Rendezvous
A tale of high adventure and tragedy in the final days when mountain men reigned supreme.

Cayuse Country
A flood of emigrants cross the "Big Open" threatening to overwhelm the Cayuse homeland.

Land Without A Country
It was a great land coveted by many but held by none. Who would have the courage to claim it as theirs?

Death On The Umatilla
Whitman Mission murderers are at large; a volunteer army attempts to bring them to justice.

A Difficult Passage
Whitman Mission murderers remain at large; a Regiment of Mounted Riflemen is ordered to bring them in.

Cry Of The Coyote
The antelope are gone; the buffalo wallows are empty. Only the cry of the coyote can be heard.